Jo Thomas worked for many years as a reporter and producer, including time at Radio 4's *Woman's Hour* and Radio 2's Steve Wright show.

Jo's debut novel, *The Oyster Catcher*, was a runaway bestseller and won both the RNA Joan Hessayon Award and the Festival of Romance Best eBook Award. Her recent book *Escape to the French Farmhouse* was a #1 bestselling ebook. In every one of her novels Jo loves to explore new countries and discover the food produced there, both of which she thoroughly enjoys researching. Jo lives in Pembrokeshire with her husband and three children, where cooking and gathering around the kitchen table are a hugely important and fun part of their family life.

Visit Jo's website: jothomasauthor.com
or follow her on:

🐦 Jo_Thomas01
f JoThomasAuthor
📷 JoThomasAuthor

Also by Jo Thomas

THE OYSTER CATCHER
THE OLIVE BRANCH
LATE SUMMER IN THE VINEYARD
THE HONEY FARM ON THE HILL
SUNSET OVER THE CHERRY ORCHARD
A WINTER BENEATH THE STARS
MY LEMON GROVE SUMMER
COMING HOME TO WINTER ISLAND
ESCAPE TO THE FRENCH FARMHOUSE
FINDING LOVE AT THE CHRISTMAS MARKET
CHASING THE ITALIAN DREAM
CELEBRATIONS AT THE CHÂTEAU
RETREAT TO THE SPANISH SUN
KEEPING A CHRISTMAS PROMISE

eBook short stories:
THE CHESTNUT TREE
THE RED SKY AT NIGHT
NOTES FROM THE NORTHERN LIGHTS

Summer at the Ice Cream Café

Jo Thomas

PENGUIN BOOKS

TRANSWORLD PUBLISHERS
Penguin Random House, One Embassy Gardens,
8 Viaduct Gardens, London SW11 7BW
www.penguin.co.uk

Transworld is part of the Penguin Random House group of companies
whose addresses can be found at global.penguinrandomhouse.com

First published in Great Britain in 2023 by Penguin Books
an imprint of Transworld Publishers

A CIP catalogue record for this book
is available from the British Library.

ISBN
9780552178686

Typeset in 11/14pt ITC Giovanni Std by Jouve (UK), Milton Keynes.
Printed and bound in Great Britain by Clays Ltd, Elcograf S.p.A.

The authorized representative in the EEA is Penguin Random House
Ireland, Morrison Chambers, 32 Nassau Street, Dublin D02 YH68.

Penguin Random House is committed to a sustainable future
for our business, our readers and our planet. This book is made
from Forest Stewardship Council® certified paper.

To all the foster carers out there and brilliant social workers who help make families happen, especially Auntie Janice.

1

'Phfffff! Books!' says the removal man, with a puff, a grunt, and a girding of his loins. 'Where do you want these, love?' He's lifting the heavy crate.

'Oh, anywhere!' I say. I haven't planned this at all. I certainly hadn't planned to move on the hottest day of the year so far at the end of June. But that is the great thing about leaping through a window of opportunity. Nothing is planned! And, right now, that feels wonderful! Except the books. I'll read them all now, I promise myself.

The removal-truck doors are wide open on the track beside the house. The whole world can see my belongings. It's like walking in and introducing yourself at a party completely naked! They've seen everything about you before you've even had a chance to say, 'Hello, nice to meet you.'

There's the smart gold-and-red-striped three-piece suite I bought when I could finally afford to walk into the showroom, turn down the monthly-repayment scheme and offer to settle up with cash. That was a day, I think. That's when I knew life was on the up.

Then there's the exercise bike I bought during lock-down, hoping to relieve some tension in the house and thinking it was time I got my body into shape: Josh had stopped looking at me, and once I started dating, I decided it would help. It didn't. The huge bouncy ball I sat on to keep myself moving at my office desk – it took up the spare room – makes a bid for escape out of the van. It rolls down the ramp, along the track and bounces across the main road, coming to a standstill by a group of locals beside a muddy trac-tor. Lexie, the removal woman, marches across the road in her steel-toe-capped boots, leopard-print leg-gings and short-sleeved polo shirt, company name on the breast, to retrieve it. Much to my relief I didn't have to. I'll introduce myself to the onlookers when I'm ready.

Lexie's dad is pulling out more boxes of hardback books, mostly on cookery, which I buy but never have time to read.

And there it is, centre stage, right in the middle of the removal van: the huge, battered pine kitchen table that had belonged to my grandparents. I refused to get rid of it after they died. This was where family life had taken place while I was growing up, round that table. Josh and I had bought our flat because it had a big enough kitchen to take the table. Just. The removal company were cursing me, I'm sure, getting the table into the flat and, by the sound of it, getting it out again. In this house, there is plenty of room for it in the kitchen.

I turn and stare at the house. I can't believe it's mine. I've always loved it, wondering what it would be like to live in it, to look right out to sea from the back garden. I'm sad for the people who had to sell it. It had been in their family for years and inheritance tax had made it impossible for the next generation to stay on. But at least they know it's gone to someone who loves it. I can't wait to get everything in and shut the door. But for now I'm still on full display, as if the travelling circus has arrived in town.

I hear another tractor pull up outside and stop. The chug-chug-chug of the engine cuts out.

'*Shwmae*, Dewi!'

'*Shwmae*, Lloyd!'

And the small gathering – two tractor drivers, Carys, an older woman I recognize straight away with two fidgeting Jack Russells, the window-cleaner, with his brush on a pole, and the postman, handing out mail to the group – loiters on the other side of the road, watching the removal van with interest. I'm standing just out of sight, under the shade of a larch tree hanging over the gateway.

'It's a bad business, all this,' Dewi Roberts says, climbing down from the cab of the tractor. He's barely changed, and neither has Carys. I smile, watching them from the shade of the tree.

The others shake their heads.

'Must have gone for a fortune!'

'All that money and gone on tax!'

They shake their heads again.

'You'd think the old man would have thought of it, passed it on before he died.'

'So sad. That family's been there for generations. Now all the money's gone.'

'It went on sale on the Friday, gone by the Monday morning. I heard buyers from London were calling and bidding on it, cash buyers. Buying it unseen!'

'Madness!'

I cringe a little.

'They're in pretty quick. Done and dusted within weeks.'

'Definitely a cash buyer.'

'Who'd buy a house they hadn't even seen?'

'And for how much?'

'I heard it went over the asking price. Ordinary folk didn't get a look in.'

'They should have sold to locals.'

'It's hard when rich families from London are offering you cash.'

'Without even coming to view it.'

'It's hard to turn it down. Money's money!'

'*Ie*, it is.'

'Second-home owners, are they?' Lloyd Owen, the other tractor driver, asks, watching my kitchen chairs and, in particular, the big old pine carver with the familiar worn cushion tied to its seat and a bag of bedding being removed from the van. 'Looks like posh stuff.'

'Could be a holiday-rental property.'

'Not with an old pine chair and table like that,' says Carys. 'Looks like it's come from a second-hand shop.'

I don't know whether to feel affronted or giggle.

The speculation continues. I'm finding it half cringe-worthy and half funny. But at the same time, I can't help but chuckle about the 'table like that' finally coming home to Swn y Môr.

'Are you the new owner?' Dewi calls to the removal man across the road, over the cars with roof boxes, camper-vans and caravans heading along the coast.

He shakes his head.

'Only I wanted a word about renting some land,' Dewi continues. 'I have a proposition,' he says, walking across the road, nearly stepping out in front of a group of bikers, who manage to swerve and miss him.

I bet he does. He probably reckons the new owner knows nothing about how things work around here. Then I take a deep breath, glance back at the house – *my* house – and step out of the shadows of the larch.

'In that case, you're looking for me. I'm the new

owner,' I say, coming to stand in front of the open doors at the end of the van. 'And, no, it's not a second home or a holiday rental.'

The group are silenced and puzzled.

'Don't tell me you're going to knock it down and put up gerts, or whatever those tent things are called!' says Carys, with a scowl.

'Yurts, Carys, they're called yurts,' says Lloyd.

'Well, whatever. Bloody ugly things!'

'They'll take off from that headland in a brisk wind!' says the postie, who I recognize as Thomas Pritchard from school. 'We get a lot of wind here. Hot air, y'see. From the Gulf Stream.'

'Hot air is right,' mutters Carys.

'It's not like—' Lloyd starts.

'It's okay. I know what it's like,' I say, holding up a hand. 'But I'm not putting up yurts.' It's not a bad idea. But I'm not here to build a new business, far from it. I have other plans. I have everything I need, if I'm careful, enough to live on, and that's all I want right now. I'm not planning any more businesses. I've had quite enough of that.

'Well, what are you going to do with it?' says Lloyd, looking confused.

I take a deep breath. 'I'm going to live in it,' I say, and watch their faces. Their expressions change from surprise, to curiosity, to raised eyebrows.

'With your family?' asks Carys.

'Just me,' I confirm, excitement growing.

'What? You bought this on your own?' says Carys, incredulously.

I sigh. Next they'll be asking how much I earn each year and to see my bank statements. 'Yes, I bought it. On my own,' I say firmly, finishing the conversation.

'In that case, could I have a word about renting your land? I'll give you a good price,' says Dewi.

'I'm sure,' I say, and laugh, which feels good. 'Like you offer all the newcomers around here. Don't think I don't know your tricks.'

The two farmers look at each other, then back at me. And suddenly I feel my past and present collide.

'Do I know you?' asks Lloyd, narrowing his eyes. The past twenty years haven't been kind to him. I remind myself that Lloyd Owen has always looked like an old man. I don't remember him not wearing wellingtons and a battered old fluorescent coat with string tumbling from the pockets.

I decide to put them out of their misery. 'I'm Beca, Beca Valentino, from Valentino's Gelateria, and, yes, I'm back to live here,' I say. 'Yes, I'm on my own and, no, I'm not doing yurts. Now, if you have all the information you need, I'm going to get on. Oh, and if you're thinking of making me an offer to rent my land, double it. I know the price of land rental around here.' I pick up a side table. They have all I'm prepared to tell them, for now.

'Well, *jiw, jiw*, if it isn't little Beca Valentino,' I hear, as I walk away.

'Thought she was in America.'

'I thought she died.'

'Where's she got that kind of money from, then?'

'Not from her family.'

'What she's doing back here, buying this place?'

I can still hear them as I'm walking up the driveway and the path towards the house. I look at the porch with its stained-glass window lit brightly in the warm sunshine and hear the seagulls calling overhead. I take in the long leaded windows on either side of the front door and the two smaller ones at roof level, equally distanced between the chimney stacks. And beyond the house, the green grass of the Pembrokeshire headland, overlooking sparkling blue sea, separating this west Wales coastline from Ireland, dotted with sailing boats enjoying the sea breeze. This place. It isn't love at first sight, because I've loved this house all my life. I didn't need to come and view it. It's exactly where I'm meant to be right now.

'It's a lot of rooms for just one person,' I hear someone call after me.

And I can't resist: I turn back to the group from beneath the neglected arbour with a rampant rambling rose over it. 'I have plans, Dewi Roberts, big plans,' I call back to the gossiping farmers, as I walk the last bit of the path, a thorn from the overgrown rose snagging at my top. Pruning it will be one of my first jobs. And despite the aches of packing and moving, the weeks of keeping the cleaning business going with absent staff, doing shifts myself so I could hand over the business to Maria, there's a swing in my stride and a spring in my step. In no time at all everyone will know who's bought Tŷ Mawr. Word of mouth. It's the one thing I couldn't stand when I left this place. But right now, if they want to gossip, let them. I breathe in the salty sea air. I'm back, I have plans, and this time they don't involve business.

2

I wave the truck off, then head inside and shut the door. I unwrap a mug and fill it with water from the kitchen tap, taking time to look out of the window at the field, full of grazing black and white cows, with calves, and the still sparkling sea beyond that. I'm here in the kitchen, in this house, Tŷ Mawr. I'm sipping the water – even that tastes like home, soft and refreshing, not chalky and hard – when I hear a car pulling up outside on the drive. I turn and see the boxes everywhere. I want to explore the house, unpack my belongings and put them in their places.

I can't believe I'm here. Bad things happen in threes, so they say, but so do good. Getting the offer from Maria, my top team leader, on Tidy!, my cleaning business, was certainly a good thing, once I'd had time to consider it. At first I thought, Oh no! She wants to leave. What will I do if I don't accept her offer and lose her? Then I thought, what will happen if I accept? Some careful financial-planning advice from one of our clients meant Maria could buy the business from me and secure her family's future, making it a family business of her own. And I can move on. A new beginning. No more difficult clients. No more staff shortages or late payments. I'm moving out of big business. I'm going for a quieter life. My business days are behind me. I want the simpler things in life. Just like I had growing up.

Making the first phone call to social services and being accepted, eventually, as a foster carer had been the second good thing.

And then this. It was like a sign. As a child I passed this house every day on the bus going to school and back again. In the evenings and weekends I would look up at it from the quiet sandy cove away from the tourists where we swam and gathered around the barbecue in the setting summer sun. And then it was on the market. I knew it wouldn't hang around. Properties in Sŵn y Môr don't these days. They come onto the market and are gone within days. There'd been so much interest in the house that it had gone straight to auction. Highest bidder by the end of the day. That's three good things.

I'm like a child wanting to open my presents on

Christmas morning, but that will have to wait. I have a herd of cows to get to know first.

'Well, well, if it isn't little Beca Valentino,' says the old man, as he struggles stiffly out of his faded red four-by-four, leaning heavily on his stick. 'This is my grandson.' He points the stick at the young man getting out on the other side and looking up at the house, like someone who knows he's punching above his weight.

'You won't have met him. Born after you left the area, I expect.'

I smile at him, but he's clearly unhappy about my presence on the front doorstep where, no doubt, he thinks *he* should be standing.

'I couldn't believe it when they told me who'd bought it,' says the old man, still leaning heavily on the stick with gnarled, arthritic hands. He starts walking towards me on bandy legs. He's wearing a flat cap and dark blue overalls, despite the heat.

'I'm sorry for . . .' I have no idea what to say. For your loss? 'I'm sorry it turned out this way for you,' I manage to say. 'And I'm sorry about your father too,' I add, looking at the tired old man.

'Well, it's not what we'd hoped for. Dad loved this place. Ninety-nine was a good age. Dare say I shan't be far behind him without the farm to keep me busy.'

I feel slightly awkward, as if I'm taking the family home. The young man glares.

'But maybe it's time I took things easier. We've managed to buy the bungalow and stay in the area. Who'd've thought a bungalow could cost as much as that, eh? And I've got the garden to plant up. It's not big, but I'll make it work. Beans, tomatoes,' he says thoughtfully, and manages a smile.

I nod. The grandson is still glowering and gazing up at the house as if he's imagining all the possibilities.

'Tsk, tsk. But I have to say, I'm grateful to you,' he says, with a slight shake in his voice. 'I'm glad it was someone local. Glad it's not going to be a second home or holiday let . . .'

'It's not, is it?' The grandson flips his stare accusingly to me.

I shake my head. 'It's not. First and foremost, it's going to be my home,' I reassure them.

'You've done well for yourself while you've been away, Beca Valentino. Your grandparents and parents would be proud.'

'Thank you.' This time it's me with the crack in my voice and I wish my grandparents were there. I wish my mum and dad were still alive to see this. I wish I hadn't stayed away so long.

'Right. Let me introduce you to the girls.' I go to follow him and then he stops. '*Diolch*,' he says in Welsh, thank you, 'for taking on the girls. It would have broken my heart to sell them. It's good to know they'll be staying here, on the headland where they belong.'

'It's fine,' I say, having no idea if it will be or not. It's been a long time since I've looked after a herd of cows. Not since Dad was a herdsman and I went to work with him: I did relief milking at weekends and holidays, then cleaned caravans. Round here, it was what we did: we all had two or more jobs. And this may be a hobby herd now, but it was the one stipulation when I was buying the house. The cows came too. And that's exactly what I want from my life. A simpler way of life, tending cows, being outdoors, and having evenings to myself, early nights, maybe even catching up on *Strictly*. Doing all the things I never had time to do when I ran the cleaning business. This is exactly where I want to be. Away from London, a quieter life. And, of course, there's my dream of sharing it with children. Fostering. I've been to the meetings, joined the support groups, finally been approved. It's this life I want to share with children in my care.

'I've always wanted to farm,' I say – lie. It's the last thing I wanted to do when I left this place. But after years of building the business, working with difficult clients, and never being off duty, I'm going back to where I started, with Dad in the milking parlour. Let's hope the cows don't answer back, make unreasonable requests or not turn up for work. The smile on the old man's face and the softening of his grandson's make me feel better. I'm going to be a dairy farmer. Fresh milk with morning tea. It may not make me a fortune, but I'm in a house I love, in a place I want to be. I don't need to be a millionaire. I just want to be happy. Just me. Starting out on my own. But first I have to remember how to milk a cow.

As I step into the parlour, it's like no time has passed. I would say it's like riding a bike.

'This is Blodwyn. She'll look after you. She'll lead the other girls in when it's milking time. And this is Dorothy. Watch out for her, she can be a bit grouchy. And Rosina, give her a wide berth or she'll wee all over you when you pass by,' he says, as we walk down the six-berth milking parlour. The cows are already in here, ready for their full udders to be relieved.

He touches each on the hindquarters while his grandson gets to work washing udders and attaching the milking apparatus. I watch him, then join in.

'And this one is Arianwen. She has the star shape on her tail . . .' I'm trying to remember all their names.

'But mostly they answer to *i'r merched*.' He smiles, as do I, relaxing.

'The girls.' I nod, understanding. It's been a long time since I've spoken any Welsh. Not since school. There really wasn't a need for it once I left here. But it feels good to hear it again. I work side by side with the old man's grandson, seeing the girls in and out of the milking parlour onto the green pasture, the headland overlooking the sea, the orange ball of the sun sinking in the sky behind them. A small fishing boat is coming

15

in from a day's excursion, leaving a trail of white water in its wake that disappears as if it was never there.

'And, remember, the truck will come every afternoon to pick up two milkings' worth.'

'I will.'

'So that's it,' he says, standing in the doorway of the milking parlour, the setting sun behind him silhouetting his short, stout, slightly crumpled outline. A long way from the man who grew up on this farm, worked it, built it up and now is winding it down, retiring from it.

He's taking in the milking parlour, remembering his time there and saying goodbye. 'I'll wait outside,' I say, wanting to give him time.

I open the gate to the field and walk across to the headland. I pull my arms around me. It might be hot and sunny, but out here the wind is flicking across the grass and it feels so good on my face. I lift it to the breeze and drink it in. Then, I look down at the cove below and the waves, rolling back and forth on the shore. I'm where I belong. I breathe deeply. It's like the last twenty years never happened. I'm back in Sŵn y Môr, and no time has passed at all.

Suddenly I hear footsteps behind me. I turn. It's the grandson.

'I'm just giving him a minute with his cows,' he says, beside me, staring at the view.

For a moment neither of us says anything. We just

watch the seagulls glide overhead in the sky filled with soft, white clouds.

'Like I say, I'm sorry things had to be this way for you,' I say, taking hold of the situation.

'None of us wanted it, but with my great-grandfather gone, tax and inheritance tax . . .'

'I'm going to keep the herd going.'

'I hope so,' he says. 'I hope you're not one of those move-out-of-the-city-for-a-taste-of-the-good-life types, thinking they can go back to where they started out. You left for a reason.'

I feel like I've walked into a gorse bush as I remember exactly why I left. Your business is never your own in a small town like this. And then I remember exactly why I came back.

'Whatever you may have heard,' I say evenly, 'I went away. Made good money. Enough to look after my family when they were still alive and let them live in the town where they grew up. Now I have enough to buy this place. And I'm back with good reason.' I shut down the conversation. I feel as prickly as that gorse bush. I hated gossip then, and still hate it now. I'm not going to let it in. I'm older, wiser and don't have room for it in my life.

'I doubt I'll ever be able to afford to buy a house in the town I grew up in,' he says, 'but at least I can get out of here now.'

In a way, then, this is an escape for him, however

much of a show he may be putting on. He's not tied to the farm any more. He may be scared of leaving, but this was the excuse he needed. He was pushed out, or so he thinks, but maybe it was the push he needed.

'You have your whole life ahead of you. Go and see the world if you want to. Or stay if you don't. But it's no one's fault. We all have to work our way up in the world. Find out what's important to you. Pick your mountain to climb,' I say. 'Just make sure it's the right one. You don't want to get to the top, and realize it was wrong!' He's like I was, angry and young, thinking there was more to life than this. 'If you want to go, go. But if you want to stay, there's no shame in that. Make your own path.'

He nods slowly, as if I've just said something he's never heard before. He lifts his head, looks across the headland.

'There's a whole world out there,' I say. 'But there's one here too. Whatever you decide to do.'

As he turns to me, his face softens. 'There is something I've wanted to do,' he says.

'Well, maybe now is your time.' I smile.

'Maybe it is.' He smiles back. And then, to my surprise, he says, 'Thank you.' As if in some way I had just given him the permission he was looking for to stop feeling angry about the sale of the farm, about life, and to find his own path. I wasn't expecting that, I thought.

My experience of young people is, well, me. I felt trapped here, so I left, but I was angry when the *gelateria* was sold. I made my own path, but I think it was the wrong one. Now I plan to put that right.

'I've always wanted to see New Zealand, the farms there. Maybe I'll go. Maybe I'll come back one day.'

'Just make sure if you go that it's for the right reasons. Not because you couldn't see what you had here, or because you felt angry and blamed others. You still have this.' I gesture to the beach. 'It belongs to everybody.'

'You've got kids, right?' he asks. 'Away at school? Left home even? Now you're moving back?'

I swallow.

'No . . . no kids,' I say. It's always the same. People assume.

He raises a blond eyebrow. 'Shame.' He turns down the corners of his mouth. 'You're good at this shit.'

I laugh. 'Thank you.'

Not a parent . . . That time's passed me by. Or has it? I'd been married to the business. No time for anything else. Covid threw a dark cloak over so many aspects of life. Work became harder as restaurants closed and people stayed at home. Employees who tested positive couldn't turn up to work. Everything in my body was aching after months of having to cover for staff shortages, getting up at the crack of dawn to clean offices and restaurants before the staff got in. But now, being here, he's making me feel I'm doing the right thing with my new plan and my spirits soar again. So, this is it. A new beginning. Just me. No more mourning my marriage. No more trying to get back to dating, definitely not. Dating after my marriage fizzled out became nigh on impossible, as my final years of fertility started slipping away. Dating, I realized, had become about the car you drive and your last holiday destination. Compatibility is about questionnaires and ticking boxes. It was time for a change. It was time to come home.

We walk back towards the milking parlour, savouring the setting sun on our backs, the sweet smell of grass and salt in the air, like all the ingredients of a simple but fabulous dish you'd remember for ever.

As the two men drive away I turn to the house. It's mine. As are the cows, I remember, with trepidation. My home.

3

My stomach rumbles. I can't remember when I last ate anything. When I went to bed I fell into a deep sleep as soon as my head hit the pillow. This morning I've managed to complete my first milking. And now, I think, as I wipe my hands and look at the washed-down parlour and the cows contentedly grazing outside, there's only one thing that will reassure me I really am home. I want *gelato*! Probably not everyone's idea of breakfast, but this is a special day. I've been dreaming of it ever since I agreed on the house. Not any old ice cream but from Valentino's, my grand-parents' shop, just up from the harbour and the beach. They sold it years ago and it made them enough to buy the bungalow they retired to, where Dad lived after them. But they'd sold the café with the guarantee that it would stay the same, so Valentino's would always be at the heart of the town. That's how things work around here. We like to make sure the person moving in keeps a bit of the life that was, just like the old man and his cows.

I'm dreaming of rum and raisin, mint choc chip, my favourites, to celebrate my new life in Swn y Môr.

After I've showered, dressed and slipped on my flip-flops, I walk across the field where the cows are grazing to the gate at the far side, then onto the narrow coast path and down the wooden steps, where long grasses stroke my ankles, to the cove. I pass the old boathouse – still standing, *just* – with its weather-beaten, blue-painted doors, then cross to the other side of the cove and the coast path. It's by far the best route into town – much quicker than going along the main road by car.

I feel like a teenager all over again, with a whole new lease on life, the warm, grainy sand shifting under my soles and between my toes, the sun on my face, like it's feeding my soul, while the sound of the waves soothes away my stress. I'm home, back in Pembrokeshire, as far west as you can go in Wales, and I couldn't be happier.

I walk along the coast path and up the hill towards the town with a smile as bright as the sun.

I stop and stare. Something doesn't feel right.

It's market day in the town. The road is closed to traffic. Beside the pond and the benches around it, the stalls with green and white awnings are starting to pack up for the day. They sell everything from honey to vegetables straight from the ground, locally produced gin, dressed crabs, Welsh cakes, bread and even hand-made woollen blankets and throws. But, although it's busy and bustling, that's not what I'm staring at. There, where Valentino's has always been, with its red and white awning, takeaway service hatch at the front, with rows of ice creams behind the glass and the high counter is . . . Wildes. With a trendy grey and white sign and a front door that's now also grey with a chrome handle, instead of the big brass one I loved to pull back with a ding of the bell. For a moment I won-der if it's been so long since I've been back that I'm looking at the wrong shop. I haven't been here since Nonno died, nearly three years ago now. Seems like yesterday.

I look up and down the small high street. It's busy, like a butterfly emerging from the cocoon of the last two years, more beautiful and brighter than before. But . . . I stare at the building. No, that's definitely Val-entino's. Only it's called Wildes. I walk slowly through the market stalls, like I'm twelve years old, finishing school and hopping off the bus to pop in on my grand-parents for an ice cream or, on cold winter days, hot chocolate with extra cream and marshmallows. All my friends envied me, getting free Valentino's *gelato* when-ever I liked. I liked to treat my best friend too – I can still hear Griff's voice calling me as I walk towards the shop. We'd sit on the high stools at the polished bar while Nonna fussed over us, especially in summer, when we were crispy from dried sand and salt water and brown as berries, as she would say, from the sun. We'd sit outside sipping Coke floats from tall glasses with long straws, or eating knickerbocker glories, topped with sticky glacé cherries.

Now I stop and stare at the shop front, oblivious to the crowds moving around me, the holidaymakers meeting old friends and buying local produce to take back to their rented cottages, caravans and tents. Some children come out of the door. There's no bell ringing, but they're carrying ice creams. Not as big as I remember and, judging by the looks on their faces, and their father's, as he double-checks his receipt, it's not the treat they were expecting.

I look at the façade. I can't help hoping things have stayed the same inside. I step tentatively towards the double-fronted building, the door in the middle. I always loved its symmetry: it was just a stone house in the middle of the town until my grandparents turned it into one of the best-known ice-cream and coffee shops in the area.

I pull back the unfamiliar chrome handle, hoping to be transported back to the Valentino's I used to know, but inside, I barely recognize the place. I'm searching for any features that might remind me of what it used to be. The high stools at the polished bar, the Valentino's sign with Italian and Welsh flags, Dean Martin playing in the background. It still smells of coffee, but there's no hissing or calling over the noise of the machine, the clatter of cups into saucers. Now, there's gentle modern jazz. Inside, it's grey and chrome. All of the red-covered stools and banquettes are gone, with the *gelato*, the dessert menus on the tables and the pots of paper napkins.

There used to be big pictures on the wall of ice-cream sundaes topped with fudge and chocolate sauce, banana splits and, of course, knickerbocker glories that went on for ever, plus a little cottage made of ice cream – a favourite for birthday parties – treasure chests, a sailing boat and a clown with dolly mixtures for his features and red syrup for a smile . . . It's all tumbling into my head, as clear as if the pictures were right there in front of me. It was a joy to see children stare, eyes widening.

Now, in place of the pictures, there is a big board listing panini and suggestions for filled baguettes. There's a wall of wine bottles, and glasses hanging over the bar where ice-cream cones used to stand. There are families eating salads, quiche and soup of the day.

'Can I help you?' says a voice from behind the counter.

I freeze. It can't be. I turn slowly. It is! I feel sick.

'Eddie?'

We say nothing for a second or two.

'Do I know you?' he says, and it feels like a punch in the guts.

'I . . .' I have no idea what to say. It's all so different. 'This is Valentino's,' I state, looking around again, trying to get my bearings.

'Was!' He beams. A smile I remember only too well. 'It's Wildes now. My place. Ed Wildes.'

This all feels so weird. A face I know behind the counter in my family's shop, which I barely recognize.

'Has it been sold?' I manage. It's like my childhood has been swept away and put out with the rubbish. The Llewellyns, who bought Valentino's from my grandparents, had run it for years, keeping it just the same, as they'd promised Nonno and Nonna. Just like it was when I was last here.

'Yes, to me!'

That smile, again. He wipes a wine glass with a tea towel and puts it on the shelf, among the fake trailing ivy.

'I thought . . . There was an agreement to keep the place as Valentino's,' I say.

He gives a little frown, but still with a smile.

'There was, for the last owners, but that finished when they sold it on to me,' he says, as he rings up a bill and a family of four heads off with a promise to call again before the end of their holiday. 'You seem to know a lot about this place.'

'I'm . . .' I take a deep breath. 'I'm Beca? Beca Valentino. Remember, Eddie?' I'm rattled. 'My grandparents owned this place.'

'Of course! Beca! I knew I recognized you!' he says, moving around the counter. 'Sorry. Gosh, a lot of time has passed since we . . . since I used to come here to my grandparents' holiday home. Haven't been called Eddie in years! It's Ed now.'

I nod.

'What are you doing back here? Holiday?' he says, but I'm not really taking it in. I'm still too shocked to see how much the place has changed and the fact that he's here.

'I hope you like what I've done with the place.' He holds out a hand proudly.

'It's very . . . modern,' is all I can say. My grandparents' taste might not have been everyone's, but at least it was fun.

'So, holiday, is it?' he asks again.

I tear my eyes away from the panini menu. 'No, I've moved here,' I say flatly.

'Ah, so it's you who's bought Big House, Tŷ Mawr?' He mispronounces it but I don't correct him.

I nod.

'I'd heard a familiar face had moved in.'

'One thing hasn't changed, then. Word gets around fast here,' I mutter.

'Oh, yes,' he says, moving back around the counter to serve ice creams from the upright freezer at the far end. Clearly I wasn't quiet enough.

I move towards him and peer over.

'Would you like one?' he says.

'Um, actually, yes. I came to get a pot to take away. Sort of a celebration of me moving in.'

'Well, what's it to be?' he says.

'Mint choc chip.' I smile at the thought of it. 'Always.'

'Mint choc chip it is,' he says, and takes a pot from the freezer. 'Go for another too?' His hand is hovering over the other flavours and I can't help smiling. I'm hoping my freezer will be up and running by the time I get back.

'Rum and raisin.' I go for Nonno's favourite.

'I hope you enjoy both.'

The door opens with more customers. I know this place is only busy because of the holidaymakers who come back year after year. That's what makes Swn y Môr the thriving little town it is.

'It's good to see you again, Beca,' he says.

'Thank you,' I say, keen to get out. I'm feeling all sorts of things I didn't expect to experience when I came into town.

'And Tŷ Mawr . . .' He brings me back to the here and now.

This time I correct him gently. He never could get his tongue around the Welsh language or place-names.

'You looking to rent it out?' he enquires. 'Holidays? Bought it as an investment?'

'I have plans,' I say, reluctant to share more, not yet.

He puts his hands together. 'Actually,' he says suddenly, as if something has just occurred to him. 'I have some things that might be of interest to you – well, belong to you,' he says. 'When we were clearing this place out for the renovation we found some bits and pieces left in the attic. I think they must be your grandparents'. I remember them.'

'Yes,' I agree.

'Why don't you pop in during the week and I'll give you the boxes?' He smiles again. The smile I remember from all those years ago. It's a nice smile. A very attractive one, actually.

'Sure,' I say, and dig in my wallet to pay for the *gelato*.

'No, no. On me,' he says. 'A welcome gift. Come back and see us again soon. We do lunch, and there's a great wine list. We're going to try out sushi soon.'

'Thank you.' I smile tightly, not sure how I feel about wine lists and sushi. I'm about to ask if the fish will be local. But instead I turn towards the door. I've had enough change for one day. I'm grateful for the *gelato* I'm holding in my arms, cold against my T-shirt. It's making me feel connected to this place. Just for a moment I have the feeling that comes with leaving Valentino's clutching *gelato*. I just wish my family was still here to share it with me.

'See you in the week,' he calls, wiping down the shiny chrome work surface.

'Yes,' I say, hoping I won't have to see him when I

pick up the boxes or, indeed, any time soon. I step out-side and remind myself to breathe, as I stand on the small terrace, under the new grey awning, with tri-angular patio heaters for evenings and winter days, bay trees by the door.

I hurry away from the shop into the crowds as the stallholders continue to pack up for the day.

Again, I hear my old friend Griff's voice. But this time I really *can* hear it. I look around and there he is.

He's surrounded by crates of whole and dressed crabs, in a sun-bleached blue linen jacket, a loose white T-shirt under it and, despite the sunshine, a small woollen hat, his curly hair tumbling out of the front. Around the walls of his stall are paintings of lob-sters, crabs and the harbour. His paintings. Suddenly it's like when we were teenagers, like I've just got back from cleaning caravans and he's just come in from the fishing boats with his dad.

'Griff!' I say, a pot of ice cream in each hand. He peers at me and I can feel his uncertainty. Don't tell me he doesn't recognize me. 'It's me, Beca!'

'Yes,' he says. Suddenly neither of us knows what to say. I feel myself blush. I swallow and do what I really want to do, forgetting everything about the last time I saw him. I throw open my arms. He steps towards me tentatively and then I go to hug him hard but end up clutching him awkwardly, with my pots of ice cream in each hand. I don't let go. He doesn't hug me back, like I'm expecting, just lets me hug him.

Finally I let him go, stand back and gaze at him. He's older, a touch of grey around his temples, fuller in the face, but still Griff. He's staring at me, as if he's thinking the same thing. Do I look the same? Am I still the same Beca?

'So it's true, then?' he says tentatively.

I can see something's playing on his mind. Is it that I allowed us to lose touch, that I haven't been back to see him, or was it the way we left things all those years ago? Is he cross with me because I went? Surely not, after all this time.

'It's true.' I try to read his mind, worried he's not happy to see me. 'I'm back.'

'And you bought Tŷ Mawr. On your own. Cash buyer from London. Over the asking price.' He raises an eyebrow. 'You've done well for yourself.' His smile softens and spreads slowly.

I shake my head. 'Like I say, that's one thing that doesn't change around here. The gossip!' I roll my eyes.

'Well, things have been a little more difficult on that front since Enid from Tide's Reach died.'

'She died? How sad.'

He nods, serious now.

'But we still have our sources.' His smile returns. 'Carys from the fishermen's cottages for one.'

'She must be the only one not to have sold up,' I say, looking around, taking in the changes.

'The neighbours complain about her hanging her washing outside the front door, where she sits on her chair and watches the world go by. And the dogs barking – that's another complaint! But she takes it all in her stride.'

'She was there with Lloyd Owen and Dewi Roberts, watching me move in.'

He still seems distant with me, as if there's something on his mind.

'See, we still have our ways of news travelling. Even if some of our best sources are no longer with us. Your grandfather used to know everything going on around here.'

I turn back to the shop, a wave of melancholy washing over me. 'I can't believe it's changed!' I say, feeling childish. But this is Griff. I can say it to Griff if not to anyone else. Or I used to be able to anyway. But maybe that's changed too.

'Things do change,' he says.

'I know. I'm being ridiculous. Of course things change.' I hold the *gelato* to me. 'You don't, though.' I drag my attention away from Wildes. That'll take some getting used to. *Wildes*, I say in my head, looking at Griff, who seems happy and content in his own skin, like he always did.

'*You* did!' He laughs. 'Look at you in your posh clothes!' He waves a hand at me.

I look down at what I'm wearing. Flip-flops, three-quarter-length trousers, a T-shirt. Hardly posh. But they weren't cheap. I could afford them when I had the business. Now I have to be much more careful with money.

'It's good to see you, Beca,' he says, warming a little. 'You should have visited more.'

I blush again. Maybe I've left it too long to come back, hoping to fit in where I left off. 'I know, but I had work.' He's right, though. I should have visited more. It just became hard with the business. And the longer I was away from this place, the harder it seemed to come back. 'But I've moved on. All that has changed now.'

'I told you, things do!' he says, glancing back at Wildes.

'What about you? Still fishing?' I ask.

He shrugs. 'It's hard,' he says, sadness behind the blue eyes.

'But you're still painting.' I look at the pictures. 'I'm glad.'

'Thanks to you, persuading me all those years ago,' he says, blue eyes sparkling now. 'I wouldn't have thought of going to college if it hadn't been for you. You made me realize everything I wanted and loved was right here.'

'Let's catch up,' I say. 'Meet for a drink. If the pub is still where it used to be . . .'

He doesn't respond.

'Griff.' The woman walking towards us is from the Welsh blanket stall.

'Nia!' I recognize her straight away. She's a few years younger than us.

'Beca! I heard you were back!'

'News travels fast in Sŵn y Môr!' I say, the words grating on me already.

'What did I hear you say? A drink?'

'I was just trying to convince Griff to meet me for a drink and a catch-up, and to tell me what else has changed around here.'

'Oh, lots has changed,' she says, gazing at Griff.

'Oh! Are you two . . .?' I'm surprised.

They smile and shake their heads.

'Happily co-parenting, I think is the expression,' Griff says.

'Co-parenting?'

'Nineteen years ago now!' Griff laughs. 'I told you, Beca . . . Everything changes!'

I'm caught off guard. 'Gosh. Yes. I remember Dad telling me.'

'You were never here long enough when you visited to find out for yourself,' says Griff, and I detect a hint of telling-off in his voice. 'In and out before news got around that you were visiting. And that's going some, to beat the gossip in Sŵn y Môr.'

'I know. I just . . . To start with, here was the last place I wanted to be. Then, as the business grew, it was just flying visits and later to see Nonno at the nursing home.'

I look at the two of them. 'What happened?' I ask.

'We were better parents when we weren't living together,' Nia says, with a smile.

'That's brilliant!' I say, and falter. 'Not the splitting-up part, I mean . . . Congratulations, both of you! See?' I say, digging myself out of the hole. 'There's so much to catch up on. Twenty years' worth!'

Griff laughs – the laugh I remember so well – as I try to negotiate the situation, wondering how something so big could have passed me by. His initial crossness with me seems to be evaporating. He's right: I should have visited more, stayed longer. Stayed in touch. Maybe it was because I was too caught up in my new life to pay any attention to the one I'd left behind. And, to be honest, things were just awkward after I left, with Ed and with Griff.

'Are you still in the cottage?' I ask, gesturing to the harbour.

Griff nods. 'Yes, though it's rented to holidaymakers for the summer. I've moved to the chalet in the garden. Come and find us.'

'Us?'

So there's someone in Griff's life. Of course there must be!

Suddenly a little blond dog appears from under the table, with curly hair like it's been permed.

'Me and Cariad!' He scoops her up and hugs her.

She's clearly affectionate. 'What kind of dog is she?'

'A cockapoo,' he says, with humour in his voice, watching another pair pass with their owners.

'Seems like you're no one around here without one,' I say.

'She was a rescue. A lockdown purchase by all accounts. Left behind by holidaymakers. Looks like they were camping, she went on a wander, and when she got back, they'd packed up and gone.'

'What kind of people would do that?'

I reach forward and stroke her curly fringe, which looks a lot like Griff's. The thought makes me smile.

'We'd better start clearing up,' says Nia to Griff.

'Yes, of course, and I'd better get this *gelato* back before it melts,' I say quickly.

'*Hwyl*,' says Griff.

'Bye, *hwyl*.' It's good to be slipping into Welsh again. I start to walk down the hill to the harbour, then turn back and wave.

Valentino's has changed. Has everything changed? Eddie, now Ed. The Eddie who turned my life upside down is standing in Valentino's because he owns the place. My family's *gelateria*! Not a trace of the past left there. He barely even remembered me. But I remember him. He changed everything. Does the Beca I left behind still belong here? Or am I trying to slip back into something I left behind twenty years ago? Is this still the place I expected to come home to? Something scratches at the back of my mind. Have I done the right thing in pouring every penny I had into a house I dreamed of as a child? Have I made a whopping mistake moving away from everything I've known for the last twenty years? Suddenly I feel like a stranger in my own home.

4

I take a scoop of the melting ice cream, pull back my arm and launch it into the air with the little wooden spoon. It lands on the grass, just a short distance from the bench I'm sitting on, looking out over the harbour and the smartly painted cottages along it, towards the coast path.

Seagulls squawk and flap, swooping in like a platoon of paratroopers for the spoonful of ice cream melting into the dry, parched grass.

Its powdery, artificial flavour is leaving a bad taste in my mouth. I scoop out another lump of the mess and fling it, this time narrowly missing a huge hovering gull that attempts to catch it mid-flight.

I try again, putting all my frustration behind it, and this time it hits the seagull, which dives on it and gulps it greedily. Suddenly there's a bark and a shout and a little blond dog comes galloping towards the bird, which reluctantly flies off. I can almost see it vowing to return, while the dog licks up the last of the ice cream.

'Are you supposed to be throwing ice cream at seagulls?' I hear a man's voice and freeze. 'Cariad!' he calls to the dog – she practically falls over her legs in her hurry to get back to her owner, but is also keen to mop up the rest of the sticky sweet stuff.

I breathe a sigh of relief at seeing Griff ambling towards me, a loose lead hanging by his side and a smile on his lips.

'I didn't mean to throw it at them. I . . . they were just . . .'

'Are you okay?' He drops the smile and frowns, coming to stand beside me.

'I'm fine. Just . . .'

He seems to drop the guard he's been holding up since I saw him in the market.

'Is it your *nonno*? Are you thinking about him?' He slides onto the bench beside me, just as he would always have done.

'No, yes, it's just . . . everything.' I sigh. 'Sorry I couldn't invite everyone to the funeral, what with the Covid restrictions. I was just wondering what I was thinking of really, coming back. Because you're right, everything changes. Nothing stays the same. I don't know why I thought it would.'

'Well, you've only been back five minutes and you're already wishing you weren't here. We've clearly made a great impression.'

And there's the Griff I used to know.

'And that's why you're throwing frozen hand grenades at our local wildlife, is it? You're thinking you'd much rather be in the city, working flat out, than sitting here looking at that,' he says, jerking his thumb towards the setting sun, people still out on paddleboards, dogs barking, boats coming into harbour after a day on the water.

I try not to laugh at his stern take on me feeding the seagulls.

'Well, something's got you all wound up,' he says. 'I can see that.'

I look down at the pot of melted mess in one hand, the wooden spoon in the other. I can't bear the feel of the flat wooden spoon on my tongue: it reminds me of those sticks doctors use to see if your tonsils are swollen when they tell you to say, 'Ah.' There must be something better. A good waffle wafer or better-quality wooden spoon!

He nudges me with his elbow.

'It's nothing, really,' I say, feeling silly. Cariad bounds over and rests her head in my lap.

'It's her way of saying hello,' Griff tells me.

I ruffle her head.

'So, come on, are you going to tell me what's wrong?

You've only just got here and by the sound of it you've had enough.'

I let out a long sigh. 'It's just this.' I hold up the pot. 'Why didn't Nonno tell me the place had changed hands?'

'Maybe he didn't want to upset you. What you didn't know couldn't hurt you. Sometimes people try to protect the ones they love by saying nothing. Maybe he thought you wouldn't find out. He probably wasn't expecting you to move back.'

'I know, but something about it all, after lockdown and everything . . . And work was different. I wanted to be here. Now I'm back and it's all changed and I'm just surprised. It's like my whole childhood has been rubbed out of a photograph.'

'It's just a shop. You still have the memories,' he says, ever wise.

'It's not only that the shop's different . . . You're right, things have to change. But *this*!'

'Ah,' says Griff, understanding. 'The ice cream.'

'It started melting so I thought I'd sit here and enjoy it, celebrate being back.'

'And it's not the same,' he says gently.

'It's nothing like Valentino's. It's tasteless! I can't believe he serves that. People come back year after year and expect Valentino's *gelato*. This is just sugar and artificial flavouring.'

It's Griff's turn to sigh. 'Nothing stays the same.

41

People here have seen more and more visitors coming in and they want to make a profit.'

'But surely not by serving up rubbish. And it would have to be Eddie! Ed Wildes! Of all people!' I even find his name hard to say. It sets my teeth on edge, like fingernails scraping down a blackboard.

Griff looks at me sideways. 'Maybe you should tell him.'

I think for a moment. 'Maybe I will! This town's popularity with tourists was built on that *gelateria*. People came from miles around, through word of mouth, to try the new flavours and the sundaes and buy *gelato* to take home, wrapped in newspaper and freezer bags.'

'Yup. And they bought fish from the harbourside, but that's nearly gone too,' he says, gazing out at the pleasure boats bobbing on the water.

'Because of the likes of him. Ed Wildes. Coming in, buying up the big houses.'

Griff raises an eyebrow and I know he's thinking, Right back at you!

'I'm not some second-home owner coming in, Griff. I'm a local. I'm going to live here.'

'Yes, I know, I'm sorry. Just, well, it's been hard watching so many houses go to people who don't even come down and view them, just buy them at auction from their offices in London.'

'Like I did, you mean. I'm not sure I'm ever going to feel like a local again.'

'You left, Bex. It's just going to take time for people to remember you were once a local.'

It's good to hear Griff call me Bex, like he used to. He and my family were the only ones who did.

'I remember when we used to catch mackerel by the bucket load, tie them along a bamboo pole to carry over our shoulders and sell them to the campers.'

'In those days the campsite was just a field, with one loo and a shower. Not like it is today.'

We look at the smart caravans, the clubhouse and boats, mostly RIBs, parked up on trailers there.

'I remember the year we put the prices up, by ten pence a fish, and everyone was outraged,' he says.

'But they still bought them!'

'And we'd spend the money on cider and sausages and light a fire down at the cove.'

'Ah, undercooked sausages and cheap cider, those were the days!'

Griff laughs and so do I. The earlier strangeness seems to dissipate with the laughter.

'Good to have you back, Beca,' he says, patting my shoulder. And I relax. 'I mean it. I was cross with you for not staying in touch, but I've never been able to stay cross with you for long.'

'Yeah. You're right. It's just ice cream. I mean, look at this.' I point to the afternoon sun over the sea and coastline. 'Good to be back, Griff. I think!'

'I'd better be getting home. Only came to give the dog a leg stretch. Come on, Cariad.'

'Griff?'

He stops and turns back to me.

'Oh, nothing.'

'Go on. You've started, you might as well finish.'

I breathe in and take a run at it. 'I was just thinking, maybe if I hadn't left, maybe things would be different, maybe I might have got my life sorted by now,' I say, facing the familiar harbour view, surprising myself, as if I was still twenty, with sliding doors right in front of me. 'Maybe I shouldn't have left at all.'

Griff presses his lips together. 'You always wanted more than this place could give you.'

'Not now. Everything I want is right here.' I wish my family were still with me, but everywhere I look, there are memories. They're here.

'Everything apart from good *gelato*.' He laughs.

'You're right.'

And then he says, 'I'm glad,' and loops the lead around Cariad's neck. 'Maybe you just need to get involved, meet some people.'

'Maybe.' I still feel like a stranger in town.

'Now, no more throwing ice cream at the seagulls. We have rules about that sort of thing around here.'

'Promise!' I smile.

'And don't stay out late.' He chortles just as if we were teenagers all over again. 'It really is good to have you back, Beca.' And, like he always did, he makes me smile.

'Yeah, good to be back.' I watch him go, then turn back to the bay and listen to the waves rolling in and out on the sandy shore.

There's a little while before I have to milk the cows again but something niggles as I throw the ice-cream pot into the bin and see the remains of other half-eaten ice creams. Half-eaten ice cream: that speaks volumes. No wonder the seagulls hang out here. I look at the narrow coast path, in front of the expensive cottages with the view over the harbour. Griff was born in one of those cottages. Of course they're all for holiday-makers now. And no matter how much I love retracing my steps, I can't help feeling part of me and the town has been rubbed out now Valentino's *gelato* has gone. But does that matter? I'm here for a new beginning, aren't I? Not for the old life I was so desperate to leave behind.

5

Maybe Griff's right. He usually is, I think, as I stand to go back to the farm. My farm, I remind myself. I decide to take the road, to see if it's all the same there or if that has changed too.

I walk up past the yacht club at the heart of the harbour, past the pub where I can smell beer and cleaning fluids. I hear deep, gravelly voices and snatches of Welsh. I pass the row of what were once fishermen's cottages, now all with little signs in the window, giving their holiday rental details. And there, in the middle of the row, one stands out like a sore thumb. It's Carys Thomas's house. Clearly not a holiday cottage, it's festooned with wet washing, hanging from a makeshift line across the front. There's a stepladder propped against the wall, a sad scarecrow, dead plants in pots along the path, and a single seat for when the sun hits it in the mornings. Just past that, the white and sage-green sash cottage is the town hall. Not much has changed there, I think. In fact, it could do with touching up.

There's music coming from inside, a thump, thump, thump with occasional shouts of encouragement. Curiosity gets the better of me and I inch towards the open door. In my day it was used for town gatherings, the annual Christmas party and voting in elections. Now it's full of women in Lycra, dancing to a heavy beat in front of an instructor. I look at the notice on the door: 'Zumba with Suzie'.

That must be Suzie. She's in her sixties, stick-thin and clearly very supple, waving her arms and urging the group on. I'm transfixed. They seem to be having a great time.

'Maybe you need to get involved. Meet some people,' Griff had said. Is this what he means?

'Okay!' The music stops. People clap and bend to clasp their knees. 'Let's take a break. Drink your water!' says Suzie, in a clear, polished accent. I don't recognize anyone in the group.

'Hey, come in!' Suzie waves at me.

'Oh, no, it's fine. I'm just watching!'

'Come in, join us! Just arrived, have you?'

'Well, not quite,' I say.

'Traffic can be dreadful leaving town, can't it?'

I think by 'town' she means London.

'You new to the area? Bought yourself a piece of Paradise to escape to?' She beams and her face seems to stay in that position.

'Sort of.' I'm not quite sure how to introduce myself.

'We've been holidaying here for years and love it. Come and meet everyone,' she says. 'Most of us have been coming for as long as we can remember. Ladies, meet . . . What's your name?'

'Beca,' I say.

'Rebecca,' she says.

'No, Beca,' I repeat. 'It's Welsh.'

'Oh, I see.' She's surprised. 'Well, you'll have lots in common with the locals then.'

'Do I know you?' one of the Lycra-clad women asks.

'I don't think so,' I say, backing off.

'Do you know the Faulkes-Hamiltons?'

I shake my head.

'They've had a terrible time of it,' says another, hair perfectly in place with what must be a whole can of hairspray. I wonder what that must do to the environment.

The women stand together, looking at me and smiling, but without warmth.

'Join in,' says Suzie. 'We're going to do a quick bit before we finish and then we'll be going for drinks at the yacht club if you fancy.'

'Oh, no, I don't think—'

'Oh, do join us!' says another.

'Yes, it'll be fun.'

I remember Griff's words about joining in, put down my bag and go to the back of the class. The music starts again.

'Yes, the Faulkes-Hamiltons,' the first lady carries on to her friend. 'Had a terrible time of it. Nearly lost their son to a terribly unsuitable type. Said he was in love.'

'Oh, no!'

'They had to stage an intervention. Shipped him off to the States for "work experience" with a family friend.'

'And what happened?'

'Thankfully he saw sense and found a far more suitable match. They told the girl he'd fallen in love out there.'

'Nearly happened to Ed Wildes from what I remember,' says another.

'From Wildes?'

'Yes. Got involved with a local girl. From what I remember his parents ended up practically buying him off. They sent him to uni in a new car and bought a house for him there.'

'And did it work?'

'Money always does. He was engaged to someone far more suitable by the end of the first year.'

I feel like I'm standing in a wind tunnel, and my eyes blur. I turn to find my way out, but am shuffled back towards the group and told, 'Pump it!' Anything to block out the words that are swimming around my head right now. I kick off my flip-flops. My blood is pumping as furiously as the music and all I can see is red.

'Never again,' I say aloud, as I open the front door and enter the stained-glass porch of Tŷ Mawr. 'Never again!' I confirm, pushing open the door, throwing my bag down in the hall and heading straight for the kitchen. I turn on the tap, grab a glass and fill it with water. I drink some, then splash the rest over my hot, sweating face. I go back to my bag and grapple for the ibuprofen gel for my knee, which is throbbing.

A quick bit, she said! And charged me a tenner for the privilege. I tried to make a swift exit at the end but was bombarded with requests to join WhatsApp groups for town gardening, bell-ringing at the church, tea-and-cake mornings once a month and the yacht-club committee. All accompanied by the same questions. Had I made my money and retired early? What was my husband's and my line of business? Where had we moved from? Had we got children and which school were they boarding at? Dinner-party invitations seemed to fizzle out with the realization that I had no partner, and the only thing they wanted to know was where to find good cleaners. There was surprise that I'd given up my property in London to live here full time. Also, would I be tidying up the front garden at Tŷ Mawr? 'It's got terribly overgrown in recent years, which doesn't quite fit with the town's image.' And there were offers of sour-dough starter, plus cuttings and seedlings – no doubt to match the other front gardens on the roadside.

I snappily declined the invitation to a glass of rosé or a G-and-T at the yacht club, pushing my way out to calls of 'See you next week,' and a whispered 'I'm sure I know her from somewhere.' I marched home with thoughts of 'over my dead body', furious that I had even dipped my toe into that water. Furious at what I'd heard. Furious with Griff for telling me I needed to get involved. That isn't why I moved back: that bit of my life is over. I've left it behind. Ed Wildes is in the past. I didn't come back to be part of a community that knows more about me than I do, or to feel I need to be part of the bake-and-chat group to fit in. I bet Carys Thomas isn't invited to it. I bet she wouldn't want to be. I came here for a reason. I just wish I wasn't feeling so unsure about it. I wonder what Nonna would have made of it, and start to laugh, as she would have done. This place was always fuelled by gossip and it looks like that hasn't changed. I decide to open a bottle of wine later. Maybe I'll have a glass, after I've done the cows.

No, this place hasn't changed a bit. Maybe I just for-got why I wanted to leave in the first place, I think, as I limp to the cowshed, feeling anywhere but at home.

6

I don't sleep that night, even though I'm exhausted. I lie awake, hearing those words about Ed Wildes and his unsuitable girlfriend . . . who was me. My stomach knots with nerves for the following day, which I've been building up to for months: it's my meeting with the social worker.

I'm grateful when dawn comes, relieving me of my night of torment, and I can head for the milking parlour, with the soothing sound of the cows waiting for me. After milking, aching and exhausted, I'm still not ready to face the day. I need to settle my nerves, work out exactly what to say when the social worker arrives, about why I'm here and why I want to make my plan for this place work.

Instead of heading back to the farmhouse, I go to the gate at the end of the field that leads to the coast path and gulp the sea air. I ache even more than I did after the Zumba. The thump, thump, thump of the music is still going through my head, as is the talk of sourdough and the lack of good cleaners. But there is no way I'm going to start another business here. I've had enough of clients and cleaning.

I head out of the gate to the steps. I need to shake this irritation. If only my knee didn't make me wince every time I negotiate a step. I hold my face to the sun and the seagulls.

I hear it before I see it: gales of laughter and shrieks of joy as I move on down towards the cove.

'Come on, Tilda, get on with it!'

'I'm coming – don't rush me!'

'Whoooah!'

'Wooohoo!'

I can hear splashes as the women walk across the sand and pebble beach into the lapping water. Some wear swimming caps, others swimming gloves, and all are in costumes of different colours and shapes.

I walk slowly along the grass-edged path, over the stones, smelling the salt and seaweed in the air, the early-morning mist rolling in from the sea. I find myself smiling at the group, one by one dropping their shoulders under the water and bobbing in the waves, with shrieks and laughter.

I reach the bottom of the steps and stand in front of the old boathouse there, at the top of the slipway.

'Geronimo!' shouts a woman, as she leaps from the large rock we used to jump off as kids and crashes in, creating a splash and waves.

There are shouts and more laughter in the undulating water. It's carefree, joyous and infectious.

I watch them and smile. The sun is starting to rise, but there's an early-morning nip in the air.

'You joining us?' one calls, and waves.

'It's lovely once you're in!' yells another, treading water in the swimming-hole. Only locals knew about it when I was young. It's a deep hole where you can swim, before the estuary feeds out to the open sea.

'They're lying! It's freezing!' calls a third. She's wearing a butterfly cap and swimming breaststroke in fast circles.

'Oh, stop it, Mair! It's doing you the world of good.'

'Kill or cure, that's what they say. It may just kill me,' she pants back.

Others are floating on their backs, like starfish, toes poking out of the water. Some are properly swimming, others simply dipping their shoulders in and out, just enjoying the cold water. They're all smiling, including Mair, whose frantic circles are slowing down.

'Hey, Beca, isn't it?' A large woman signals to me, her bingo wings wobbling. It takes me a moment to recognize her without her clothes on. 'I looked after your grandfather at Sea View, the nursing home,' she reminds me. I realize it's her uniform that's missing.

'Oh, yes, of course!' Nonno had survived the longest. Nonna had died first, in her sleep, then Dad, from a sudden heart attack in the milking parlour, and Nonno had clung to life, dying in the nursing home just before the first Covid lockdown. I walk towards the water's edge where the woman is standing in a brightly coloured swimsuit covered with puffins.

'He was a lovely man,' she says, putting her hair up into a bun.

'Thank you.' I feel a lump in my throat, and wish I'd been here more often, that my visits hadn't been fleeting. I wish I'd taken the time to breathe this air and understand what I was missing . . . just being here. But after he'd gone, this was the last place I wanted to be. Until now. I swallow. I wish he was here.

'You're very brave!' I change tack, indicating the water.

'Brave or stupid!' She laughs. 'No, we love it! We're the Sŵn y Môr Mermaids. We meet most days when we can. Really takes the stress out of the day. Are you on holiday?'

'Living here. Just moved in.' I point up to Tŷ Mawr.

'Well, in that case, you should definitely join us!' She beams. 'It's my switch-off at the end of a night shift,' she says. 'Or it peps me up before I go in.'

'Good for mind and body,' says another.

'You just have to take the plunge!' someone shouts. 'Makes you feel like a kid again.'

I glance at their bags and towelling dressing-gowns.

'It's cold at first, but then, well, it makes you feel alive. You just have to get over the horrid bit first.' Nonno's carer smiles warmly.

Maybe I'm doing the right thing, after all. I'm not going to let the gossips, or Ed Wildes, chase me out of town again. And now I have a house to sort out – quickly!

'Maybe another day.' I grin and wave, then turn for home, soaking up the early-morning sun and the memories that are rushing back at me, of hanging around the old boathouse, lighting fires on the beach. I remember my plan, and why I wanted to have this meeting with the social worker this morning. I hurry back up the coast path, listening to the banter from the swimmers, and head through the gate into the field where the cows are grazing, the calves contentedly following their mothers' lead.

I can still hear the swimmers.

You just have to take the plunge! I think about their words. The hardest part is taking the first step.

That's what I'm doing. I have my first meeting with the social worker today. I have a chance to do something I thought I wouldn't be able to do. Now, it's about to become reality. And if it goes well, I may join in with the swimming.

7

'So, this is the kitchen.' I'm more nervous than I've ever been at any business meeting, showing my anxiously anticipated guest around later that morning, looking at the piles of boxes that I still need to unpack. The meeting had been arranged weeks ago, when I got my moving date. But I wish I'd taken more time to get things organized. Despite the boxes, though, my eyes are drawn to the view beyond and they seem to disappear. The early-morning mist has rolled off the sea and across the pasture where the cows are and is giving way to sunshine. It's glorious.

We stand together, enjoying it. I feel so lucky to be here and that's something I need to share. But I'm as nervous as a kitten, way out of my comfort zone, despite the training I've done and the support groups I've joined.

I turn away from the window and the view that I can't get enough of and put a pot of tea on the pine table, with a jug of milk from the cows I milked at dawn. That makes me smile. I don't have to wait for a delivery because I forgot to put in my order on time, or dash to the small, overpriced corner shop in the city centre. I put two mugs on the table, where many mugs have been placed in the past to soothe life's worries and celebrate achievements. I notice the burn from my first attempt at lasagne and another from Christmas one year when Nonna's floral centrepiece caught fire. We doused it with a jug of water, wrapped it in the Christmas tablecloth and deposited it outside the back door.

I put my hand on the table and feel my family with me.

Am I mad? I wonder.

Maybe, says Griff's voice. *But better that than boring!*

Do what makes you happy, I hear Nonno say, and smile to myself.

The business didn't make me happy, although I was good at it. One of the best around. Neither did Josh. Looking back, we would never have worked out, even if we'd moved here together. He'd said as much when he finally announced we were over. 'I love you, care for you, but I'm not in love with you. Haven't been for a couple of years.'

The words still sting. Just like the words from the

women at the Zumba group yesterday, as if I've been slapped in the face and can still feel a tingle there. I was over Ed, way over him, when I married Josh. We enjoyed city life together, friends and socializing. But then came lockdown and we had to spend all our time together.

He had suggested trying for a family, moving to the countryside. It took me a while but I came to like the idea, really liked it. A family of our own. A move to the countryside. When I discovered I was pregnant I believed life would change for the better.

Until that dark, miserable, rainy evening. As the cramps increased, more frequent and stronger, I knew I was losing my baby. I had the miscarriage alone in the hospital, surrounded by other women holding their newborns to their chests. I had never felt so alone, or that life could be so unfair. The young mums made it look easy, and I realized I'd left it too late. My time had gone.

Later, when I was at home, Josh wanted to talk. I thought he might suggest IVF or even adoption. I was open to ideas. What I wasn't expecting was for him to tell me how relieved he felt, that it was for the best. He'd been trying to make the relationship work, to fall back in love with me. That was why he'd suggested the baby, he said. It was over, and so was my life as I knew it. I needed to make a change. I needed to come home. Throwing myself back into the business wasn't the answer. I needed to do something that meant more than spreadsheets, rotas, complaining clients and staff shortages, no matter how big my income from it. It was meaningless. I had to draw a line under that part of my life: the business and the knowledge that I wasn't going to have a child with Josh. I'd left it too late. The doctor had confirmed it. My chances of getting pregnant had been slim and even more so as time went on. And no amount of business success would plug the hole in my heart.

This is my new chapter. I was so lucky to grow up here, with the sea and the sand. And to sit at this table, in a family-sized kitchen. It's back where it belongs. Just like I'd hoped to feel when I arrived. I've been lucky in business. Now it's time to give something back. Let others have the same start as me.

'So what made you want to foster?' says Maureen. 'Call me Mo.'

'Oh, um . . .' My thoughts are back to the here and now, with Mo sitting beside me, smiling, and the sun streaming through the kitchen windows – which, frankly, could do with a good clean. That's something I may be able to fix.

'Don't worry, I'm not here to start the process with you all over again. You've been passed by the panel. I'm just here to see what sort of accommodation you have and what sort of children you're happy to take.'

Great. I can relax a little.

'Well, I've got a good life, done well for myself because of the start my parents gave me. I wish I'd realized it earlier. It's time to give something back,' I say, as the pieces fit together in my head and come out of my mouth as I'd hoped they would.

'And what age were you thinking of? Babies? Most people want babies and there aren't many around. Children usually come into our care a little later in life, when it's been proved they can't live with their birth families.'

'Not babies. Um, I don't have much experience in that department.'

'It's okay, you can say what you're thinking,' she says kindly, and I relax a little more. Smoothing my fingers over the scrubbed-pine table gives me the strength to be open and honest about my thoughts. This isn't just a dream I've had for a while. It's tangible. I didn't feel I could share it with anyone. Josh would have laughed and told me I was mad. But right now, it feels entirely possible and I'm not mad. This is going to be my new job. I remember when I first thought of it. We were on holiday and had made friends with a couple and their children. In that moment I thought how lovely it would be to be cooking tea, not dinner, like we did every night even when I was dead on my feet. It was always 'What's for dinner?' I wanted to cook tea and enjoy the pleasure it would bring to young faces. I wanted to cook fish fingers, and Nonna's spaghetti with *ragù*, and watch as bowls were emptied. I wanted to hear shrieks at jumping in and out of the waves, see children building sandcastles and eating ice cream on the rocks. When, first, Nonna died, then my father and then finally Nonno, the dream wouldn't go away. Maybe I was trying to hang on to something I'd lost. My home, my childhood. But perhaps giving it to other children would be a good way to remember it and be grateful for all I'd had. I think back to when I was running in and out of the sea and building sandcastles. The sandcastle competition at the end of the summer was always one of the highlights of my year.

'Well, I suppose I was thinking four or five years old. At school but young enough to enjoy what I can offer. The beach, sandcastles, crabbing, the cows. Maybe a bit older, six or seven, but not too much. There's nothing for teenagers here, really, and I'd hate for them to be bored. I remember how keen I was to leave when I was a teenager.' I give a little laugh, but it comes out sadder than I expected.

'Most of us want to fly the nest at some point,' says Mo.

I didn't so much fly the nest as flee, with no map or plan. Again, my heart twists as I think of how my family must have worried and hoped I'd come back sooner rather than later. Sadly, it was later . . . too late. I wish they were here.

'So key stage one or two?'

I look at her blankly.

'Years one and two, maybe three. Five to seven or eight,' she says kindly.

'Yes. Sorry, I didn't know.'

'It's okay. It's a steep learning curve. All parenting is, although when you're giving birth you have nine months to get used to the idea. Still comes as a shock, though. And why fostering, not adoption?'

'Well . . . I may be dreadful at it.' My laugh is a little higher-pitched than I was expecting, nerves gripping my stomach. I need to dip my toe in the water. See if this is for me and vice versa. 'I could do respite. Short stays. And that's where you need people, isn't it? I've seen the television adverts.'

'Well, we're grateful. A lot of our children need long-term fostering and can't be adopted. But we also need respite care, as you say, for parents or fosterers. It's about what's right for you, and the child. You're just the sort of person we need on board.'

'And it really doesn't matter that I'm single?'

Mo shakes her head. 'Far from it! What you have to offer here is perfect.'

'Well, obviously I want to get the house decorated first.' I make a mental note to contact decorators as soon as I can. Maybe ask around for some names.

'What you have here is just perfect,' she repeats, smiling. 'They'll be very lucky to stay with you.'

'And the cows? That's okay?' The nerves are making me ask the questions, making me doubt myself.

'People grow up on farms. I'm sure it'll be a great opportunity for some children to experience life in the country as long as you take all the safety precautions. This could be the perfect place for children to have some time out, away from everyday life, a break from their usual care arrangements. And the fact that you have been passed by the panel, are first-aid qualified and have your experience in schools is all good.'

'Well, I ran the cleaning firm that serviced the schools. But, yes, I did like being there and getting involved. I used to volunteer to hear the children read and that led to helping out with their Christmas shows.'

'You're just the sort of person we're desperate for!' says Mo, with a wide smile.

'Right,' I say. I'm nervous and excited all at the same time.

'All we need now is for you to decide when you want to start. You get yourself unpacked and settled in, then let's get the ball rolling,' she says.

She puts her card on the table.

After Josh left, I'd thrown myself into dating, hoping to find Mr Right, start a family, change my life. I didn't need Mr Right to do that. I know that now. I'm doing this on my own. I pick up the card. 'Okay. I'll be in touch when I'm ready here. Once I've found a decorator.'

I walk her to the front door and open it.

'And . . .' my nerves are rushing to the surface again '. . . you're sure I'll be able to do it?'

'You'll be fine. Like I say,' she regards the rambling rose that needs cutting back, the overgrown front garden, the sea beyond the house, the cows in the field, 'any child who comes here is very lucky indeed.' She bids me goodbye and gets into her little yellow Panda, driving away with a cheery toot.

I hug myself. I was the lucky one, I think. And it's time someone else had that chance. I took the plunge! I'm going to be a foster carer. I remember sitting at that table and having spaghetti for tea. There will be spaghetti for tea again! I feel like I could cry. I may not be a mum – that time may have passed me by – but perhaps I can make a difference to a child's life like my parents and grandparents did for me. The idea makes me much happier than my business could ever have done.

8

'You're going to do what?' Griff raises an eyebrow.

I hesitate. Finally I'm saying it out loud and I just hope I'm not going to get the reaction I'm dreading: *You're mad! Whatever for?*

'I'm going to foster,' I repeat. 'Give kids a chance to have a taste of the sort of childhood I had. We had. I'm going to be a foster carer. I might be useless at it but I'm down to start soon.'

'And that's why you wanted this house?'

I nod, watching his face carefully.

'Not some high-end B-and-B, glampsite or wedding venue, like people are talking about?' The corners of his mouth are twitching.

I shake my head.

Griff goes to tie up to the jetty the boat he's stepping off. Without thinking, I step forward and hold out my hand for the rope, like I always did. It's heavier than I remember or maybe I'm not as fit as I was. It's been over twenty years, after all. He looks at me and I have no idea what's going through his mind.

He's climbed off the boat with Cariad beside him and is standing in front of me. 'You're something else, Beca Valentino!'

'What?' Doubts floods in, and the seagulls seem to squawk louder overhead, as if they're laughing at me. The clanking of sails on boats bobbing in the harbour seem to applaud the laughter at the fool, setting herself up for a fall.

'Only you!' He puts his hands on his hips. His chest is broad, as are his shoulders, but he's not the young man I said goodbye to all those years ago. A lot has changed since then, for both of us. He has flecks of grey in the stubble on his face.

'Only me what?' I say, ruffled and defensive.

But then a smile spreads across his sun-kissed face to his eyes, where the wrinkles at the corners make them smile too.

'Only you could come back here, buy one of the best houses in the town, with amazing views, and not want to turn it into somewhere for tourists, some sort of holiday business.'

'Tourists have plenty of places to stay,' I say, snappier than I'd intended.

'I seem to remember your family were tourists once.

When your grandparents arrived in this country, they decided they didn't want to live in a city and moved here instead.'

'Yes. And they've been a part of this town ever since. I should have come back long before now.'

'But then you wouldn't have been able to afford Tŷ Mawr. It's your hard work that's paid for it. Your business made it happen.'

'How do you know?'

'Word gets around.' He's teasing, knowing how much I hated gossip. But nothing stays secret for long around here.

'So, do you think I'm mad?'

'Better than being boring!' he says, just as I'd thought he would. I remember him saying it when I decided to leave. He didn't want me to go but he knew I would anyway.

'So, I need some help.' I bring my thoughts back to the here and now and push away the memories of my knee-jerk decision to leave. 'I really need a decorator.'

'Well, there's Arwel, if you can get hold of him. But he won't work with Derw, the electrician. They fell out a long time ago. You could try Michal, from Poland. But he's really booked up. Lots of renovations and work going on just before the school summer holidays start. You'll be lucky to get hold of anyone before the autumn now.'

I let out a long sigh, then breathe in the restorative salty sea air. Big lungfuls of it.

'But I can send you numbers. Give me yours,' Griff says, in his laid-back way. He gets out his phone and taps in the numbers as I speak.

'There, done,' he says. 'I'll send you some contacts.'

'Thanks,' I say. 'Nice boat. Yours?' It's a smart blue and white RIB, with passenger seats in white leather and chrome railings.

He glances at it fondly. 'No.' He gives a little laugh. 'I wish. Just doing maintenance on it. There's more money in looking after boats for other people, these days, than there is in taking out the fishing boat. That, and renting out the cottage over the holidays.'

'I know you said fishing's hard, but you haven't stopped, have you?'

'I still fish, mostly lobster pots, crab and mackerel, of course. I won't stop. I can't.' He laughs again, carefree and happy, and I envy that about him. Always have. He lets things wash over him and not bother him. I wish I could do the same. 'It's in my blood. A bit like this place.'

'It never leaves you,' I say. 'I used to dream of it when I couldn't sleep.'

'I'm glad,' he says softly, and we're back to where we were before I left.

'I'd better go,' he says. 'I'm meeting Nia for lunch. She wants to talk about college options.'

I frown and he chuckles. 'For our daughter! Not us! We're not teenagers any more. She'll tell me off for being late.'

'Oh, yes, of course.' Nonno told me about the baby, but Griff being a father is still weird. A whole part of his life I never saw. 'Still got the same timekeeping issues, then?' I jolt myself back into the here and now.

'You walking up to town?' He tips his head in that direction, away from the harbour.

I nod. 'I'm going to Valentino's.'

'Wildes?'

I try to shrug nonchalantly, as we fall into step with each other, Cariad at Griff's heels. 'It's going to take me a while to call it that,' I say, teeth gritted, as we walk along the harbour. We walk past the beach and up the hill to the town, passing the holidaymakers coming in the other direction, loaded with chairs, footballs, body boards and cool bags for the day.

'He's got that place too now,' Griff points to the big hotel, with people sitting outside enjoying the sun and views over the bay, 'with a few business partners.'

'What? Who?'

'Ed Wildes. He's got the Harbour Hotel as well as the ice-cream shop and a few holiday homes too. He's buying up anything and everything. Looks like he and his partners have deep pockets.'

'What's he doing back here?' I ask crossly.

'Came from London. Worked in the City from what

I gather, then set up a wine company that collapsed. Divorced and moved into his grandparents' second home on the harbour.' He flaps a hand towards a three-storey house looking out over the beach. It's one of the best on the coast path and must be worth a fortune, despite its shabby state. 'He started working with investors to buy the hotel and then Valentino's. Don't tell me you've never been tempted to look him up on Facebook?'

'Never!' I say, and wish I meant it. Of course I'd looked him up on Facebook, but it told me little of what he was up to. Anyway, I'd given up that habit a while ago. Ed Wildes is well in my past. I look at the pub. 'Don't tell me he's got the pub too!'

'No – that one's still in the hands of Dai Half Pint.'

'Because he never filled the glass all the way up!'

'And because he's only five foot and a fag paper.'

We laugh, gloriously easy in each other's company. I can't remember the last time I've just enjoyed talking, chatting and laughing, feeling like me. Not Beca the businesswoman or Beca, Josh's wife, stepping on eggshells so as not to start another niggly argument. I relish the glow of the laughter, so glad yesterday's initial awkwardness has disappeared. I'm not sure I could have coped if Griff hadn't been happy to see me back.

'He chooses when he opens, who he serves, and he's refused several offers on the place apparently. Says he doesn't need the money. He's not selling to incomers. The only way he'll leave that place is in a box.'

'It's been years since I was there.'

'Nothing's changed. Literally nothing,' Griff says. Then, 'Okay, I'd better go. I'll send on those decorators' details. I'm warning you, trying to get one to turn up is almost impossible at the moment but I'll see what I can do.'

'Thank you.'

'And you're going ahead with this, are you? Fostering?'

'I am.' I'm confident now of my decision. 'I've been passed by their panel. Now I just have to get the house ready.'

'You always did go for what you want.' He pauses, and I wonder if he's going to say something else. But he doesn't. 'Right, I'd better get going. Nia will be tamping – I mean, furious.'

'I haven't forgotten what tamping means.' I giggle. 'I'd better go too. I'm picking up some bits and pieces from Ed Wildes that were left in the attic of the *gelateria*.'

'Now play nice!' Griff raises his eyebrows in warning.

'I will!' I reply, like the teenager I left behind.

He peels off down the lane to the small estate, a mix of social housing, local residents and lock-up-and-leave second homes, bikes and scooters on front doorsteps, dogs barking, children playing in the sun, their parents watching. That, I think, could be me soon.

'Oh, hi,' says Ed.

My stomach tightens as I walk through the door, still missing the sound of the brass bell over it.

'You took the bell down.' I bristle.

'It drove me mad!' He gives a light laugh. I remember it well. At least that hasn't changed about him. But lots has. His blond hair is blonder than I remember it, and thinner. His teeth are very white. He's still an attractive man, if you like that look. Which I don't. Far from it, I tell myself. He's charming, always was, but I feel a pang. I loved that bell. It was like the sound of children's laughter to me. What could be nicer than that?

Again I look around, searching for some memory of the old place, a sense of Valentino's. But he has stripped every part of the past from it. A bit like he did with our relationship. If that was what it was. He just acted like it had never happened and moved on. Stripped it from his memory and inked it out.

'Do people still remember this as Valentino's?' I ask, glaring at him. 'Do they remember it as it was?'

'All the time,' he says, and the vice-like grip around my throat, pressing on my windpipe, eases just a little. 'This place meant a lot to people, you know that.

People who holiday here come back year after year. That's what makes it such a good place to be in business. And this place is a good business. They expect it to be here.'

'But you didn't think to keep it as it was?' I narrow my eyes at him.

He cocks his head and smiles. Once again, a charming smile. 'You're a businesswoman now, from what I hear, Beca. A successful one. You know what it's like. You have to move with the times.'

Slowly I nod, remembering the ways in which my business had had to adapt over the past couple of years to keep going. I'd offered higher levels of cleaning and service to keep customers feeling safe despite Covid, using different products. But I still want to tell him I think he's made a mistake, not keeping Valentino's as it was. Updating it, maybe, but this . . . As for the ice cream! I open my mouth to express my disappointment, disgust even.

'Hopefully, people still see this as their go-to coffee shop and lunchtime spot,' he continues. 'They seem to love it.'

I'm cross because of the changes, the awful *gelato*, but his smile disarms me. It makes me remember the Eddie I used to know, the young man I loved . . .

He holds my eyes for a second or two. 'I've got that box for you in the office. I'll just fetch it.'

'Of course,' I say, ripping my gaze from his and

slamming the door on the memory. But he's left me on the back foot, with a warm flush in my cheeks. I give myself a little shake and stretch my neck. I'm never going back there, I tell myself. I must be tired after the move and the meeting with Mo. I deal with people every day, difficult ones at times, and I certainly don't get flustered or blindsided by a smart smile. And I don't intend to be now.

He's disappeared, and it takes all my self-control not to follow him to the back room I knew so well. It was part of my domain, my grandparents' shop. I want to see if that's all changed too or if it's stayed the same. I crane my neck but can't see anything. Where the thick curtain used to be there is now a grey door with frosted glass, shutting out the public. It's much quieter here than life was in the city. There's Carys sitting in the corner with her two Jack Russells. The dogs are on the chairs and she's feeding them the bread that came with her soup. I'm surprised Eddie—Ed, I correct myself. It helps if I think of him as someone else, Ed, not Eddie. I'm surprised he lets the dogs on the chairs . . .

'Changed, hasn't it?' Carys says, not looking at me but at the dogs.

I can't see anyone else she might be talking to. But there's a lull in customers so it must be me. Carys never talked to me. She never really talked *to* anyone, only *about* them, from what I remember and from my recent moving day.

'Yes,' I say, trying to sound positive. There's a pause as she feeds more of the bread, dipped into the soup, to the dogs. More than she's eating by the look of it.

'It was far better in your grandparents' day,' she says, still not looking at me but at her bowl and plate. 'None of this fancy sweet-potato stuff,' she adds, and I hide the smile that pulls at the corners of my mouth.

'You could get a big cup of frothy coffee, a sandwich and an ice cream, and feel like you wouldn't eat again for a week.' Carys seems to be on a roll. 'I remember you,' she turns to stare at me now, 'sitting at the counter with young Griff. Never apart, you two. Your nonna loved having you both here. You always felt like you were joining the family when you came in.' This is not the Carys I remember, the one who terrorized us as youngsters, shouting at us to move from outside her house if we were loitering there or to get off the pavement if she was walking along it.

Tears prick my eyes, hot ones, reminding me that the past hasn't been inked out completely.

'Shame you left!' she says suddenly, sharply. But Carys was never one to mince her words. She never married, never moved away – spoke lots of different languages from what I heard but was always sharp-tongued and scary when I was a kid.

I know I shouldn't but I can't help myself so I do it anyway. I double-check over my shoulder. Ed is still out of the room. 'What do you think of the *gelato* now?' I say, as offhand as I can manage.

'Expensive!' Carys says, with a frown, making my eyebrows shoot up. She's so direct, but I have no idea why I should be surprised: she's the Carys I remember.

'She doesn't mean to be so sour,' Nonna would say. 'She's had a sad life.' But it didn't make us any more forgiving of her sharpness.

'Don't touch the stuff nowadays,' she says, with a downward turn to her mouth, wrinkles gathering where laughter lines should be. 'It used to be a treat. Now, well, it's not like it used to be. I only come in for a change of scenery and because the dogs like the bread. And because he doesn't charge me.'

'Doesn't charge you?' My eyebrows shoot up again. Well, maybe I've got him wrong. Looks like Ed Wildes isn't in it just for the money. I'm very surprised. Looking after the older ones in the community? Perhaps he's not quite the hard-headed businessman I took him for. The man who inked out the past for his own benefit. It's clearly not all about profit if he's letting Carys eat here for free. But the *gelato*, or ice cream: he said it was cheaper. Why would you change that if it's not all about profit? I'm confused.

I look at the ice creams in the freezer. They're all different colours. Bold, garish and artificial. I wonder where they come from.

I lean as far around the counter as I can, trying to get a look at any packaging.

'Here we go!' Ed says, and I nearly pitch forward as his voice makes me jump. He's holding a cardboard box.

'Oh, I was just . . .' I straighten myself and clear my throat. 'I just wanted to get a closer look at your ice creams. They're so bright.'

His smile widens. 'They look great, don't they?'

'They look like they've been dyed.'

'Here,' he says again, handing me the box. 'Like I said, I thought you might like whatever's in there. Family stuff, you know. Photos, things like that.'

'Thank you,' I say stiffly, and take it. He could have thrown it out, and I should be more grateful. But it's hard. I never expected Valentino's not to be here and the last person I expected to be in the place is him. The young man who made me leave. My head says maybe I shouldn't be quite so hard on Ed Wildes: I should give him a chance. My heart says never.

'I know your family were local, and known. There are photographs that were on the walls here. I didn't want to just ditch them. I was going to try to get them to you somehow, so this is perfect.'

'Thank you again.'

He opens the door without the bell to show me out. 'How are things going at Tŷ Mawr? How are your plans?'

'Good,' I reply, from behind the box. 'Once I can get a decorator.'

'Ah, not easy! I had to bring in people from back home.'

'Home?'

'You know . . .'

'From London?' I say, aghast.

He shrugs. 'It was the only way.'

It can't be the only way, I think. We never brought people from London to paint and decorate.

'So, ready to share your plans?' he asks.

'My plans?'

'For Tŷ Mawr? It's a big place. Plenty of room for events.'

Ah, he wants to know if he's got competition.

'Not yet.' And if I was, he'd be the last person I'd share anything with.

'Well, when you are, perhaps we could have a catch-up, a drink . . . or ice cream! For old times' sake!' He beams.

I look at the freezer section. I'm not eating that again.

'Share some knowledge,' he says. 'We businesses have to stick together.'

'Right,' I say, wondering how he could help with the farm and the children I plan to bring to it. But he clearly thinks I'm going down the B-and-B or wedding-venue route. And, for now, that's fine. Let him think that. I don't need to share my plans with anyone, especially not Ed Wildes . . . or not until I've got used to the idea.

'Well, thanks for this,' I say, stepping out onto the high street.

'No problem. And let's catch up for that drink soon, Beca!' I get the impression he's already found out I'm single. 'As long as it's not in that awful pub!'

Maybe his heart is in the right place: he's given me this box and Carys her free meals. But he doesn't have a place in my heart any more, that's for sure. 'Us newcomers have to stick together!' he says, and I roll my eyes as I step outside.

'Well, *jiw, jiw*, I heard you were back. That's a sight for sore eyes, a Valentino stepping out of Valentino's,' says a voice.

'Erm, it's Wildes now, remember?' corrects Ed.

'It'll always be Valentino's to the locals,' says Rob the Bank. That was where he worked until it closed. We were at school together. I smile, letting the sun soothe the tension from my face. I glance back at Ed, the Eddie I'd imagined might come looking for me in London and never did. Clearly I didn't feature as much in his thoughts as he did in mine. Until I married. The what-ifs. What if he came looking for me? What if he was the one? What if . . . And now here he is, and I feel no burning desire to kiss him or tell him I love him. I don't feel as if I've found my soulmate. That Eddie Wildes was in my head. This one is going thin on top.

It's just the smile that remains and, even then, the teeth are definitely not the same as they used to be. Eddie Wildes, my first love, is gone. This is just a man I used to know. The past is where he should be, I tell myself firmly. This is my new beginning and I don't plan to set foot in Wildes again. Ever!

I wander home along the coast path, where families are on the beach at the first cove, near the harbour, small encampments of folding chairs, umbrellas and windbreaks. Children play with balls, which dogs steal, with occasional sandwiches from open cool boxes to shouts of 'Oi!' I head up the sandy steps to the gate of Tŷ Mawr, just in time for afternoon milking. The cows, with their calves, are already lining up, waiting for me, in the afternoon sun. It feels good to have a purpose, to be needed, even if only by cows.

9

Milking done, I'm shattered and practically ready for bed, although it's still early. Everything aches, especially my knee. I rub it, then straighten to stretch out my back. I'm not the young woman I thought I still was. I'd forgotten how strenuous this work is. But it's more than twenty years since I was helping Dad in the yard. And it's been at least ten since I've done any daily cleaning in the business – until recently, when staff shortages meant I had to pull on the rubber gloves again. I knew then that it was time so I sold up and came back here.

The sun is only just starting to lower and there's still a lot of warmth in it. The seagulls are making their voices heard. I'll make a cup of tea and take it outside to drink it overlooking the sea.

I make my tea with care, remembering that nothing

in Nonna's kitchen ever felt rushed. Out of the window I can see the swifts swooping and circling over the field of cows, looking like they're happy to be back. I wonder if they wish they could stay when autumn comes, if anywhere ever feels like home. It seems they're perpetual travellers, never putting down roots. Perhaps that's me. Have I never really put down roots? When I was here I was desperate to leave. When I was away I was desperate to come back. What about now? Is this it? Or just the honeymoon period? Something is niggling at me and I can't work out what it is. I'd expected to feel as much at home as if I'd slid on a pair of old slippers. Is it because Nonno isn't here? None of this is home without my family and maybe never will be. Tears prickle my eyes. Have I made the biggest mistake of my life by coming back? I've made other mistakes, like marrying Josh, and leaving here. But maybe coming back is the biggest. Maybe there was nothing for me to come back to.

I look at the box from Ed Wildes that I've left on the kitchen table. Ed Wildes. The bit of my past I was hoping to have left behind. Maybe that's it. When you can't think where to move forward to, you go back. Maybe we're the same. I think about him telling me, 'Us newcomers have to stick together.' Is that what he thinks I am? But I was brought up here. You left, though, another voice says, and I recall Carys's words in the café. Am I a local? A newcomer? Or someone who lost themselves along the way? I should feel like I belong here, but with everything changing, Valentino's gone, maybe my place as a local has disappeared too.

I peer into the box to see what treasures are in it. It may be a load of junk Ed Wildes has offloaded onto me. Ed Wildes, I think again, and wish I didn't. I don't want to think about him. I stopped thinking about him a long time ago and I certainly don't want to start again. The same smile. Damn you, Ed Wildes! I bang my mug onto the table, tea slopping up the sides. I'm not going to be made to feel like a stranger in my own town by Ed Wildes. I turn back to the box, dip my hand in and pull out a handful of papers.

There's an instruction manual for a vacuum cleaner, a gas bill and an old paper napkin with the Valentino's logo on it. I run my thumb over it. Not much. I put my hand in again, as if it's the lucky dip at the summer regatta. A big tub, full of fresh sawdust – I can almost smell it. The regatta always took place at the beach, at the end of the summer. There would be hot dogs sizzling on a barbecue, and a cockles-and-whelks stall. The pub would have a beer tent and the queue for *gelato* would snake down to the beach. Bunting flapped in the wind, and I'd hear bands playing on the grassy patch where I sat the other day, throwing ice cream at seagulls. I wonder if the regatta will happen again this year, or if it's something else that's disappeared.

I can smell my grandparents' house in the box. And

I can almost smell those long summer days on the beach, when I'd hoped they'd never end. But they did. I wish they hadn't. Although I've had a great career, made money, I wonder what life would have been like if I hadn't left. Would I have taken over Valentino's and kept the name at the heart of the town? If I'd stayed maybe I'd have kept out Ed Wildes and his cheap ice cream. Gah! Ed Wildes again! I thrust my hand into the box with renewed purpose and pull out an old wooden spoon, with a Valentino's menu. I sit down on one of the pine chairs at the table, feeling like I'm back in the café, wishing I could hear Nonno singing along to his favourite Dean Martin songs on the record player.

I dig into the box again and this time pull out photographs, black-and-white, of my grandparents outside Valentino's, presumably when it first opened and they moved into the flat upstairs. I browse through them, images of my grandparents, my parents, me as a baby with Mum, and there at the heart of it, Nonno's *gelato* cart, which he wheeled down to the beach on regatta days. There he would sell the ice cream he and Nonna had been making all their lives to the recipe they'd brought with them from Sicily.

There are more papers in the box, receipts, old envelopes, some with jottings on them in Nonna's handwriting. Shopping lists, notes to Nonno. There's a couple of clothes pegs, too, and I suspect Ed has just put in anything that was lying around in the attic when he was clearing it out. That's him, get rid of anything he doesn't want, ink it out. I take a deep breath to calm my irritation at how he treated me when he no longer wanted me in his life. I think of the gossips at the Zumba class. Then I look at the photographs of the regatta again. I hold them to my chest, wishing my grandparents and parents were still here, sitting round the table, warm and salty after a sea swim.

My phone rings, bringing me back to the here and now.

'Hi, Beca, it's Maureen, Mo, from social services.'

'Oh, hi!' I say, surprised to hear from her again so soon.

'I'm just wondering if you'd given any thought to our meeting yesterday.'

'Oh, yes. Really keen.' I need to get on and find a decorator. I'll check to see if Griff has messaged me some numbers when I hang up after Mo and I have spoken. 'Once I've got the house sorted I'll get back to you. Just want to get it all, well, you know, perfect.'

'That would be great,' she says, and hesitates. 'Any idea when that might be?'

'As soon as I find a decorator I'll let you know. I just want them to feel at home here. A lick of paint will brighten everything up.'

'It would be brilliant if you wanted to go ahead soon.'

'Great!' Butterflies rise, and flutter in my stomach. This could be about to happen. I could soon be serving fish fingers for tea!

I finish the call and gaze out of the kitchen window at the beautiful view with the cows in the field under the setting sun. My tiredness evaporates, replaced by excitement. I feel like I'm twitching all over. I check my phone for numbers from Griff. Nothing. And there's nothing I can do until I get a decorator. My fingers drum on the work surface. I'm loath to unpack any more of the boxes until the walls have been done but I must do *something*! What, though? I look around. I could tackle the front garden, cut it back. But I quite like its unruliness, its individuality making it stand out in a town full of neatly manicured front gardens. A little act of rebellion.

I could spring-clean the milking parlour. But it was spotless when I took it over. Clearly better cared-for than the house. I drum my fingers on the side again. I find some decorators online and send them each a text message, but get no replies. I wonder about starting the painting myself, but that could take for ever. Besides, I want it to be done properly. I want it to be perfect, just like I imagine it. Frustration bubbles inside me.

I grab my basket, throw a few things into it, fling open the back door and head for the steps at the edge of the field down to the cove. I can hear laughter before I see anyone.

When I get to the bottom step, I stop. Am I really going to do this? It's been twenty years since I stripped off and dived in. In those days, nothing seemed to stop me. But today it looks like it could be cold, despite the warm setting sun. There are stones underfoot. What if I need a wee? I could just turn around and go back . . .

'Hi,' says a woman on the shore, tucked into a small nook, pulling off her towelling dressing-gown to reveal a bright flower-patterned bikini. Just above the waistband of her bikini bottoms is a bag. I try not to stare. 'You joining us?' she says.

'I'm not sure. It's been years!'

She bends over and checks the bag. 'You'll love it once you're in,' she says. 'We all thought we were mad when we started. I'd just had this fitted.' But that's not what grabs my attention: rather, it's her smile.

'There was a time I didn't think I'd be able to do this again,' she says, 'so now I take every chance I can. This is the best medicine for rehabilitation and pain relief.'

Another woman comes up, her face lined with the map of her life. 'This makes you feel like a child again,' she says.

Maybe it's exactly what I need, a bit of rehabilitation and relief. A bit of laughter! I take the final step down onto the shingle and sand.

The women already in the water turn to me.

'Don't worry, no one's looking or judging here,' says the woman in the bikini. 'Just do it!'

'Oh, I'm not worried about . . .' I give a little cough.

Is that what I've been worrying about all these years, being judged? Worrying what people will think of me, that I'm not good enough? Wanting to show the world I could succeed, to give them something worthwhile to talk about? I've spent so long thinking I had to be the best. The best daughter, worrying about letting them down. The best in business, because I wanted to prove I could be. But everything doesn't have to be perfect, does it? That's what I loved about growing up here. We didn't care that we didn't have the new trainers, the latest fashions. A lot of the second-homers did. We didn't. It's what separated us. I think we sometimes envied them their money and labels, life on the move. Summers here. Winters in the snow. We made do. We worked, had one or more part-time jobs . . . and the beach. Most of the time it was enough. Until I felt I had something to prove to Eddie Wildes and his friends. I let pride get the better of me. Not any more. It's time to stop worrying.

I throw off my towelling dressing-gown, ignoring the fact that my boobs are bulging out of my top and my belly is on show. Instead I enjoy the sea breeze on my skin and the sun on my face.

'Do it!' says a woman in a bikini, standing in the shallows. 'Here, we celebrate our imperfections!'

It's not about being perfect: it's about the imperfections. It's about being here. That's what's important. I think about my mum when she was a couple of years older than the age I am now. I take a big breath, swallow the anxiety and crash into the water up to my knees, creating a swell. It's cold and I stop for a moment, then keep going, till the sea is up to my thighs. It may be summer, but the water's still cold.

'Just do it!' calls the woman in the bikini.

'Feel the fear!' yells another.

'And do it anyway!' they shout together, rallying me and laughing.

And then, with one big breath, I drop my shoulders under the water. The cold makes me gasp and I'm desperate to run out again. But I stay, moving my arms and legs quickly, holding my breath. I'm swimming to the cheers of the other women, feeling like I did when I was a teenager.

'Welcome to the Sŵn y Môr Mermaids,' one calls, and the others cheer.

I did it! I took the plunge and I'm swimming again. It feels fantastic. I'm here. And I'm going to live for today. Because I feel so alive! And, right now, I could take on anything life throws at me.

10

I wave goodbye to Leah, Tilda, Mair and the others, now pulling on towelling dressing-gowns and pouring tea from flasks, their joking and gales of laughter making me smile. I've been added to the WhatsApp group – one I want to join! – and they promise to let me know when they're swimming next.

I head up the slipway, towards the old boathouse in front of me, which is tired and in need of tidying up. Then I stride up the worn rocky path to the weathered wooden steps, with long grasses growing at either side and down to the rocks on the beach.

'See you soon!' they call after me and I wave, as I power up towards my gate.

'Yes!' My skin is tingling. Any aches and pains from the move and years of housemaid's knee have disappeared.

As I lift the latch on the gate and push it open to a groan, I make a mental note to oil it, adding it to my growing to-do list, then look out over the grazing cows. This place really is perfect. I can't get over how happy I feel right now, just to be here. Or how cross I am that I've left it so long . . . or that I left at all. I push down those dark thoughts. The humiliation I felt when Ed Wildes turned up with Portia. The way he looked at me as if I was practically a stranger, not someone he'd spent each summer with and had made plans with to go travelling. The rashness of my decision to leave, the speed with which I decided to go, desperate to get away from the gossip about 'Ed', no longer 'Eddie', his new girlfriend and their, yes, their engagement. Announced at the yacht club as I cleared glasses, washed them and fought back the angry tears as he caught my eye but never said sorry. I was desperate to find a new life in the anonymity of London. But I should have stayed. This place is amazing.

Suddenly my phone rings. Just a short time ago it rang all day long with customers making demands on my stretched staff, and staff who were unable to work. Now, it barely rings and the sound makes me jump.

'Hi, Beca, it's me again, Mo. I'm really sorry to bother you, but . . .' She sighs.

I'm looking over the headland and the sea beyond, watching the pattern of ripples on the water, feeling the grass under my bare feet, my skin tingling.

'The truth is, we're desperate.' I hear her swallow. 'I have an emergency. One of my carers needs to go for an operation. She can't look after the children in her care. I need to find somewhere for them to stay, just for a short time, maybe a few days,' she speeds up, 'a weekend, like a visit.' She's falling over her words. 'I wondered if you'd dip your toe in the water, see how you get on. Of course I understand if . . . and I know it's short notice, and you wanted to decorate first, and are still training . . . but I just thought maybe you could take the plunge.' She's gabbling, and I can't help but think of the water just now, how it felt when I dived in. My skin is still tingling.

'Okay,' I say quickly. 'I'll do it.'

There is silence at the other end.

'Mo?' I hold it away from my ear to check the signal. But the signal's great. 'Mo? You still there?' I say.

'Pardon?' she says.

'I said, are you still there?'

'Yes, still here! Did you say . . .'

'I said I'll do it. A short-term placement? Like a visit? For the weekend? To see how I get on?'

'Yes,' she says, sounding shocked. 'Exactly!'

'Then I'll do it.' I'm feeling confident.

'You will?'

'Yes. I mean, like you say, the place doesn't have to be perfect, does it?' I'm imagining a small child here for the weekend, running in the field, saying hello to

93

the cows, paddling down at the cove and making sand-castles, just like I did when I was little.

'No,' she says. 'Doesn't have to be perfect at all.'

'And it'll give me a taste of what I'm in for.'

'Yes,' she says, and I wait for more details.

There's a pause. Then she says, 'So, you'll have the boys, then?'

'Wait – the boys?'

'Yes, there's two. They need somewhere to stay until we can get them settled somewhere long-term. Or they may go back to where they are, but we're waiting to see how the carer's operation goes. In the meantime, we'll look for somewhere new for them.'

I pause, then think back to the swimming, taking the plunge. This is what I set out to do, isn't it?

'We'll give you all the support you need,' she says, exactly as I'd hoped she would. 'There are more train-ing days, if you want them, a network of carers and a magazine—'

'Yes, yes, I'll do it,' I repeat, butterflies in my stomach again, my confidence shifting and slipping, like sand beneath my feet. But I wouldn't back out now. This is what I've been planning for. It's why I bought the house. I just didn't expect two of them at once. But maybe they'll be brothers. Or friends. They can make sandcas-tles together. Twice the fun, I tell myself. I can do this!

'Okay, great!' says Mo. 'We'll be over first thing in the morning.'

'Tomorrow? As in tomorrow morning?' I'm taken aback.

'Yes. As I say, I wouldn't ask if it wasn't an unusual situation, an emergency, what with one of our more experienced carers needing to go into hospital. I'd have them myself but I just don't have room.'

'No, it's fine. I do. Yes, yes!' I say. 'I'll be ready!'

'Great! Oh, and Beca?'

'Yes?'

'Just don't expect too much. I mean, these boys have moved around a lot. Your place is wonderful, just as it is, but don't worry if they don't enthuse about it, at least not at first. We just need you to keep them safe for the weekend. That's your job.'

'I know, I know,' I say, remembering what it was like to be that age. Actually, what age?

'Right, I'll get them sorted then. Thanks!'

'Oh, erm, what are their names?' I ask quickly, stopping her hanging up.

'Blake and Joe.'

'Blake and Joe,' I repeat. 'Okay. And how old—'

'I'll fill you in on all the details when I see you.'

'Fine,' I say, but she's already hung up.

I look at the house. Best I get this place into shape. I walk back, swinging my flip-flops, towel and basket over my shoulder. The swim and the prospect of two young visitors coming to stay for the weekend galvanize me: I pick up my pace and find myself almost jogging to the back door until my knee twinges, reminding me that one swim doesn't cure everything.

I start upstairs, making beds. I find the bags of packed linen. None of it says young boys to me. I wish I'd had time to go and buy some Thomas the Tank Engine covers. But we're a long way from a big supermarket. And maybe they don't like Thomas the Tank Engine. In the first spare bedroom I look around at the faded pink rose wallpaper that must have been there since the sixties and the high-cotton-count duvet cover I've put on the double bed. I push open the windows and take time to breathe in the salty sea air. Hopefully they'll be more interested in the outdoors, in the cows and swimming.

I add a vase of hydrangeas I've picked to the top of the chest of drawers with a tray that contains a water bottle and a glass, as I would for adult guests.

The second bedroom is a faded blue, with a single bed against one wall. It's a day bed I had in my office – I gravitated towards it when Josh and I were in lockdown and I needed to work twice as hard as usual to organize rotas for cleaning the businesses I'd looked after for so many years. Meanwhile Josh would lie in bed eating Pringles and binge-watching Netflix. I really didn't like Pringle crumbs in the bed.

I've only got double duvets and white covers, nothing fun, but they're good quality and they'll have to do. The duvet hangs over the sides of the single bed and touches the floor and, once again, I wish there was something I could do to make it all seem less . . . grown-up. I add some cushions and a blanket, then decide against the water bottle, the glass and the flowers.

I don't have anything to add to the rooms to make them more child-friendly, no pictures. A second later I remember the pictures of sundaes, banana splits and the ice-cream house among the photographs I had from the café. Laminated photographs that used to hang on the walls of Valentino's. I run downstairs, pull them out of the box on the kitchen table and then, with nothing else to use, I grab the Sellotape and run back upstairs, ripping off pieces with my teeth as I go. The wallpaper is going to come off anyway, so I may as well use the Sellotape and brighten things up.

I stand back to look at my handiwork. A montage of ice-cream pictures. It's not quite what I'd hoped for to greet my first placements, but it's better than fading wallpaper.

Then I start to work my way down the house, sweeping the wooden stairs, and rearranging furniture in the living room, to the right as you come in through the front door along the terracotta- and black-tiled hallway.

I push the settee in front of the fire and set up the television in the corner. Finally, I make it to the kitchen. I bake a batch of muffins for their arrival as the sun sets on the day. Tomorrow there will be children here, just like I've dreamed.

Exhausted, I leave the rest of the kitchen for the morning. I have to be up early anyway for milking. I check the cows, then stumble upstairs to bed, the house smelling of furniture polish and muffins. Now all I have to do is work out what I'm going to cook for tea . . .

The next morning, the sky is pink, purple and orange, like a watercolour painting, when I go to greet the cows in the milking parlour. I take a moment to admire the sea, some boats already out on the water. Mo was right. No one is criticizing the paintwork inside the house with that view to gawp at. Having milked the cows, checked them over and told them my news, I go back to the house. I grab a cup of tea and put a jug of fresh milk into the fridge.

I pick up the box Ed Wildes gave me with the photographs and move it to the floor next to the others I still have to unpack. I'll go through the rest when I have more time.

And then I do the thing I've been dreaming of: I go into town and buy what I need for tea. There's only one thing that will make them feel welcome, Nonna's spaghetti bolognese, or *tagliatelle al ragù*, as she would tell me and Griff, but to us, it was spaghetti bolognese and we loved it. And that is exactly what I'm going to make tonight.

With the *ragù* bubbling, and after a final check of the rooms, I hear a car pull up on the drive. My heart leaps. This is it! Calm down, I tell myself. It's just a couple of children staying for the weekend. It'll be fun!

11

The two lads stand in front of me, one with a blank expression, the other as if he's stepped out of the Tardis and has no idea where he is. In fact, they probably *don't* have any idea where they are.

'This is Blake and this is Joe,' says Mo. She looks at her notes. 'Blake Davies and Joe Michaels.' So, not brothers.

Blake is wearing black jeans and a hoodie, a dark fringe just visible, with his head tilted down. He's carrying a saggy black bin bag, tied with a knot at the top. My heart tears a little. That can't be his belongings. Mo is smiling, but appears a little strained. Joe has dark red hair and is carrying a cheap but cheerful Spider-Man rucksack, bursting at the seams.

Suddenly I'm tongue tied, as if I'm the one who's stepped out of the Tardis into completely unknown territory. These were not the young children I was expecting. Joe looks to be ten or eleven and Blake maybe fifteen, a teenager for sure.

Then I remind myself that I'm not the child: I'm the one who's supposed to be in control, looking after them for the weekend. Big or small, they're still children, in care. And in need of care.

'Hi.' I raise a hand. They don't respond. 'Hope you like spaghetti bolognese, because I've made it for tea.'

Joe pushes his glasses back up his short nose. 'I think I do. Is that the wiggly worms? Does it come in a tin?'

'No.' I relax just a little and smile. 'I made it. And I suppose the spaghetti is a bit like worms.'

'Oh, I'm not sure I could eat worms,' he says seriously.

'They're not really worms,' I backtrack. 'It's just pasta.' It's already a minefield and the worries come rushing back to meet me head-on.

He nods, big and slow.

'And is this your house? Is it a farm? Have you got a dog?' He doesn't wait for the answers. He clutches the straps of his rucksack and marches inside, as if it's the most natural thing in the world to turn up at a stranger's home and not know how long you'll be there. 'I'm not sure I've stayed on a farm before. Have I, Mo?'

'No, Joe, you haven't.'

'Will I have to eat the animals?'

'No,' I say, smiling. 'We produce milk here, from the cows. Perhaps you'd like to help me later.'

'Oh, yes, I'm sure I could milk the cows for you.'

'Well, let's start by helping, shall we?' I'm wondering how to deal with his enthusiasm.

'Which way to my room? Am I sharing? I like sharing. Well, not with Adam at my last house, the one before the one I was living in just now. He was mean. He used to fart all the time too.' Joe screws up his face, putting his hand over his mouth. Then he stops and pokes his head into the living room where I've added blankets and cushions to the chairs, the big television and more cushions along the windowsill.

'Is this for the visitors?' he asks.

'Um, well, if we had any. But it's for you to watch television,' I say.

'Wow!' he says, and Mo was right: I didn't need to wait to get this place picture-perfect. It looks like it was just that all along.

'Am I up here?' he asks, setting off up the stairs.

'Yes – I'll show you,' I say, with no chance to ask Mo any questions. We're on a roll, and there's no turning back. And it's just for the weekend, I remind myself.

I hear Mo encourage Blake to go upstairs behind me.

'Go on, Blake, take your bag up.'

I hear a harrumph and heavy footsteps on the stairs.

'Can I have this one?' Joe goes into the single room, with the view over the fields and the cows from the window in the eaves.

'Of course. Blake, you're in here.' I point to the bigger room next door.

He steps in and stares at the faded rose wallpaper in thinly veiled disgust. He peers out of the window towards the road. 'And that's the town over there, yeah?' He points to the left.

'Yes.' I try to smile.

'And the station?' He's craning his neck.

'About five miles away.' I'm wary now and I'm not sure why.

He lets out a loud sigh and turns back to the room.

'I was expecting someone younger,' I say, pointing at the laminated pictures of ice creams on the wall. I'd been so proud of them earlier, and now feel like an idiot.

'How long we here for?' he demands, looking thunderously over me to Mo at the top of the stairs. 'Longer than the last place?'

'Just till I can sort something else, Blake. The weekend, all being well. It's really good of Beca to have you. She's helping us out. You're her first placements.'

'Great,' he says.

I can see he's unimpressed and desperate to leave, scanning the road. To be honest, I think, a weekend will be quite long enough for both of us.

'They'd only been at the new place for a couple of weeks before this situation came up,' Mo says to me.

'Well, make yourselves at home. I've got muffins when you're ready,' I say, sounding like a children's TV presenter, jollying them along.

Joe is singing to himself.

Mo nods to me to join her downstairs in the hall. 'Well, that seems to have gone well,' she says, much to my surprise.

She's holding her car keys, ready to leave. 'I have another client to get to,' she says, checking the time on her phone. I can hear messages pinging through, like a game of Space Invaders.

'You're leaving? Already?' I'm out of my depth. And not in a good way, like when I was swimming.

'You'll be fine. I can see they're settling in.'

'Is there anything I should know?' I say quickly, glancing upstairs.

'Well, Joe has some learning difficulties, non-specific, but he can look after himself. In fact, he quite likes it. He has a slight stutter, usually made worse when he's anxious. It's something to look out for. He can suffer from anxiety. But generally he's very content when he knows what's happening, if you explain things to him and he's kept in a routine. But you should keep an eye on him. And he loves to take things apart. He likes . . .' she searches for the word '. . . help-ing,' she finishes. 'Joe sees himself as a hero in the making. Possibly due,' she lowers her voice, 'to his early life. It was his form of escape. Superheroes.'

I'm trying to remember everything she's said.

'And Blake?'

'Blake is withdrawn. He's had a very tough upbringing. No childhood at all, really. He was forced into being an adult way too early and now sees very little reason why he should have to be a child. Oh, and his language can be a bit . . . ripe.'

'I see.'

'He's been known to take off in the past, but he's not considered a flight risk any more. He seems to have accepted that he has to stay in the system until his eighteenth birthday. He'll probably just keep himself to himself.'

'Right.' I nod. 'And you'll be back on Monday to pick them up?'

'Yes. If there are any problems I'll let you know. And if *you* have any problems, just call me,' she says. 'I'm off to the Lake District for a couple of nights, so if I don't have a signal, leave a message. I'll get right back to you. And there's an emergency number.' She hands me a piece of paper, presumably delighted at the thought of a couple of nights away now that her charges are in safe hands for the weekend. I wish I felt I was that safe pair of hands. I'm terrified.

'I'm off, lads!' she calls up the stairs. 'Enjoy yourselves!' She smiles at me.

If anyone deserves a couple of nights away it's the likes of Mo. What a hard job. A weekend is the least I can do. 'We'll try. Although, I have to say, they're not the age I was expecting.' I think of the colouring pencils and books I'd bought and the sandcastles I'd planned we'd make with my new buckets and spades, and wonder what on earth we're going to do until Monday.

'I know, and thank you. You're doing us a big favour. Next time, I promise, they'll be younger. Much younger,' she says, peering up the stairwell. When neither boy appears, she shrugs and opens the door. 'Of course, you'll be paid the going rate for teenagers.'

Pay. I hadn't even thought about the money. I step forward to say I'm not in it for that, but she's already gone.

I see the yellow Panda bump along the uneven drive at speed. Now it's just me and my two charges. Suddenly I feel weighed down by responsibility. But, I tell myself, even if I won't be able to change their lives, I can try to give them a really nice weekend. I take a deep breath and go back upstairs.

In the smaller room, Joe is busy putting his pyjamas under his pillow. His underpants are neatly stacked in an open drawer and he's lined up a collection of what looks like fast-food free-gift figurines on the windowsill. He's still singing and is obviously in his own world. Blake has dumped his sagging bin bag in the middle of the floor of his room and is lying on the bed, shoes on, clutching his phone.

'What's the Wi-Fi password?' he asks gruffly.

I take a deep breath. 'I'll find it for you,' I say. 'But maybe we should have some guidelines about phone use, just to ensure we make the most of your time here this weekend.'

He doesn't respond and, after a pause, I find the Wi-Fi code and hand it to him. He doesn't thank me. I remind myself that there's no pressure to make a difference to their lives in one weekend. I just have to make it a nice one.

I make sandwiches and put out some crisps before calling up to them to come down for lunch. Blake appears but takes his plate upstairs. Joe sits at the table, eats with gusto and asks if he can milk the cows. I smile. 'Let's go and meet them and I'll show you how I milk them,' I tell him.

'And do you drink the milk?' he asks, as we walk to the milking parlour.

'Yes!' I tell him, smiling at his enthusiasm again. Maybe it isn't going to be quite such a bad weekend. Although I wish I knew what Blake is up to in his room, but that's not my place. Keeping him safe and fed until I can hand him back on Monday is all I have to do. If I can find a way to put a smile on his face, that would be a bonus.

*

'Tea time!' I call, after milking and having cleaned the parlour. I wish I could have gone for a swim with the Mermaids and told them about my visitors.

Joe arrives in the kitchen and slides onto a seat. Blake stands and stares sullenly at the food as I put the bowls of pasta, tangles of spaghetti with rich red sauce and a sprinkling of cheese on the top, on the table.

'I'll take this to the TV.' He goes to grab one.

'No,' I say gently. 'Let's eat here together. Get to know each other.'

He sighs. 'Is that a rule?'

'Erm, maybe more of a suggestion.'

'Well, is it or isn't it?' he asks.

I'm put on the spot. I don't want to be draconian, but he seems to want to know the boundaries. 'Yes, that's . . .' I swallow. 'It's a house rule,' I say, hating how that sounds. He sighs and sits down.

I attempt conversation but Blake says nothing. It's only Joe who wants to talk and in the end I have to tell him he can take time to eat too.

'Not hungry?' I say to Blake. He's moving the food around his plate, not eating.

He shakes his head and pushes back his chair. 'Got any pizza?'

'No, sorry.'

'They always do pizza on our first night.'

I say nothing, feeling uncomfortable.

'Okay if I watch TV or have you got rules about that too?'

I cringe. Great first impression. It's supposed to be a fun weekend. 'No, go ahead! Take a muffin!' I say, feeling every bit of his contempt.

As Blake gets up, Joe looks at the pencils and colouring pads I'd picked up at the shops. 'Are they for us?'

'Yes, sorry.'

'You were expecting younger kids, I know. People always are. That's why no one ever wants us.'

'Oh, no!' I say. 'Of course I do. I'm delighted you're here.'

'They all say that too,' he says, lining up the pencils. He opens a book and begins to colour.

'But you're happy to take the pay cheque,' says Blake, picking up a couple of muffins and leaving the room.

Once again, my heart twists and I wonder if I've really got what it takes to do this. You need broad shoulders, possibly broader than mine.

Having given them towels, shown them where to hang them in the bathroom and told them it was bedtime, I go back downstairs and pour myself a large glass of wine. Just one, I tell myself, in case anything happens in the night and I need to be alert. I sit on the window seat in the kitchen and stare outside. I know Mo said to be prepared for them to be underwhelmed, but I wanted Blake to show some kind of reaction. To enjoy being here.

I take a big sip of the spicy, punchy red wine and think back to when I realized I wanted to do this, to have children in my life. A few years ago I was going on holiday with Josh. After a day on the beach, we'd made friends with a family in an apartment opposite. They invited us for tea. The children were freshly showered, with wet hair, sitting in their pyjamas on the veranda. The mum was cooking spaghetti bolognese. It brought it all back to me, the comfort I felt from Nonna's. And the ice cream afterwards, of course.

Then there were fish fingers for tea. It was after the miscarriage, when Josh had left, taking with him all my dreams of starting a family together. One evening I was tired from work and just picked up what I could in the local Spar. The shelves were practically bare, because of a delivery issue. All I could see was a packet of frozen fish fingers. If they were good enough for Nigella . . . I grabbed them. And, oh, wow, did they taste good! I couldn't remember the last time I'd had fish fingers. At that moment I just knew: it wasn't about getting pregnant or giving birth, I just wanted to cook fish fingers for the little ones I was caring for. It was then I knew I was going to foster one day. And that day is here, but not in quite the way I was expecting.

*

That night I don't sleep. I'm not sure anyone does. I can hear Joe talking to his figurines and Blake moving around. I've already failed on the phone ban. Maybe I should have been firm. I'm really not sure what to do. I'm on the back foot and floundering.

And what did Mo mean when she said he wasn't a flight risk 'any more'?

I have an overwhelming feeling of sadness and loss for both of these boys, who have no sense of home or family, and for me: maybe it was all a pipe dream. It's too late for all of us. They'll never get their childhood back. I can't make a difference. I feel so sad I curl up into a ball and let tears roll down my face into my pillow, tears for the family I never had, the one I've lost in my grandparents and parents, and my helplessness with the children I wanted to welcome into my home.

12

Light streams in between the bedroom curtains I'd hung in a hurry that don't quite meet. I'm up early as usual, just before six, for milking, my knee stiff, as it always is in the mornings. As I walk down the lane towards the parlour, the early-morning mist rolls up from the sea, tumbling over and over, travelling at speed across the green fields. Cobwebs sparkle with heavy dew, like diamonds scattered across the hedge-row. I breathe in the cool salt-seasoned air, trying to shake off my exhaustion after a night of very little sleep.

Neither of the boys is up, thank goodness. The longer they sleep, the longer I have to work out what to do with them for the next couple of days. Two more nights, and then they'll move on to somewhere more suitable. A big town or city. Somewhere with bowling, cinemas, shopping centres, things young people like to do. I think back to when I was young here, desperate to see what the world had to offer . . .

I pick up a cloth in the milking parlour and throw it down again, frustrated. This place isn't what those kids need. What was I thinking of? I don't know what rose-tinted glasses I was wearing when I came up with the idea. I put on my overalls and wellingtons, and as the cows line up next to each other, I wash their heavy udders, then attach them to the milker.

A little later I'm clearing up while they move back out onto the pasture to graze. The mist has all but cleared, the sun is coming up, and small boats are leaving the harbour, sailing boats and small RIBs out for a day's fun. I'm hosing down the floor when I hear a car pull up on the drive. I turn off the tap and step out into the beautiful clear sunny morning. The smell is wonderful, fresh, clean, and somehow full of promise for the day ahead. It's going to be a hot one. I brush my forehead with the back of my hand and shake the front of my overalls to fan myself, squinting into the sunny morning towards the vehicle that's just been parked. There, stepping out of the truck on the driveway, is Griff and my spirits skip as I wave.

'Hi!' I smile. Griff is here, and I'm not sure I could have stayed if he hadn't been happy to see me back.

'Just like old times!' He grins at me in my overalls and wellies.

'Except I was twenty years younger and my knees didn't ache!'

'And you'd probably been out partying all night and hadn't slept!'

'True!' We laugh gently.

'I'm just about to make some tea. Fancy a cuppa?' I say, drying off my hands.

'Sure, if I'm not interrupting. I just got in from doing the lobster pots. Thought I'd come over with the name of a decorator.' He hands me a piece of paper. 'Knew you'd be up.'

'You could have texted me,' I say.

'I know.'

'Ah, you prefer the old-fashioned way.' I study the familiar handwriting.

'Well, that, and I wanted to see how you were getting on. Have a look at the place. Seems you've settled in.'

'Yes, and I have guests.'

'Guests? Oh, look, I'll leave you to it.'

'No, no, not that sort of guest,' I say, although I'm not sure what sort of guest I mean. 'Actually, you'd be doing me a favour. Come in, and if they're up, you can say hello. I have no idea what to talk to them about.'

He raises his eyebrows.

'Two boys, emergency foster care,' I say succinctly, as we walk towards the house. I've passed on all the information I have about them by the time we reach the back door. I push it open. Joe is sitting in the kitchen in his pyjamas, taking the toaster apart with a knife.

'Hi, Joe!' I look at him and the toaster.

'Fixed it!' he says.

'Oh . . . great!' I say.

'It wasn't working,' Joe says.

'Well . . . maybe it just needed turning on at the plug on the wall,' I say, but Joe is still inspecting it.

'So, Joe, how did you sleep?'

'Not very well, thank you,' he says, staring curiously at Griff. His dark red hair is standing on end, which suggests he slept.

'This is my friend Griff,' I say.

'Hi, Griff. I'm Joe. I'm ten and three-quarters. And I want to be a superhero when I grow up.' He's clearly used to being introduced to lots of people. I'm not sure if he's joking about superheroes.

Griff smiles. 'Sounds great. What are you doing there? Can I help?' He sits down at the table and Joe hands him the toaster. Griff starts to show him how to put it back together. And suddenly I could cry. I have no idea why. It's probably tiredness, stress, feeling way out of my depth. I take a deep breath and put the kettle on the range. Then, thinking the toaster may not be usable for a while, I slice some bread, put it in the grilling rack and onto the range hotplate. This is all I need to do this weekend. Just make sure they're well fed and safe. I breathe in the smell of the browning, caramelizing toast and pull it from the hotplate, out of the toasting rack and onto a plate. The smell wraps itself around me, like a hug. I fetch butter and jam from the fridge and put them on the table in front of Joe and Griff, with a small pile of plates and knives.

'Would you like tea, Joe, or something else? Milk, maybe?'

'Milk? From the cows?' His eyes light up.

'Yes.' I smile and nod.

'*Yessss!*'

I pour him some milk, tea for Griff, and put on more toast. Maybe it won't be so difficult after all.

Soon there's a tower of toast on the table. Maybe more than we need, but it makes me happy. Griff and Joe are chatting about fixing things, Griff saying he fixes problems with boats, and Joe telling him he's never been in one, when a dark shadow falls over the sunny breakfast table.

'Blake. Morning!' I put on a big smile.

He doesn't smile back.

As he sits down heavily, the chair clatters and scrapes on the tiled floor, making my nerves jangle. 'This is my friend Griff,' I say, standing to make more toast and tea. Still Blake doesn't respond. He's got his phone out and is staring at it.

'Hi, Blake,' says Griff, casually, without attempting to catch his eye.

Blake gives a brief nod.

I breathe in the smell of toasting bread again. It reminds me of mornings with Nonna.

Blake finally looks up from his phone and down at the toast I put before him, with mistrust. 'Haven't you got, like, any ordinary bread? Shop stuff?'

'Just this, I'm afraid,' I say, cross with myself for apologizing about the lovely handmade loaf I bought from the bakery in town instead of supermarket sliced.

He doesn't say anything, then slathers on butter and jam and eats it anyway.

Griff smiles at me. 'I'd better get going,' he says, standing.

'Really? Can't you stay a bit longer?' I look at Blake on his phone and Joe standing the toaster upright.

'There, all done!' he announces, then stands and plugs it in. There's a bang and the electrics go out.

'You'll be fine!' says Griff. 'Need me to do the fuse box before I go?'

I shake my head. 'I can do it.'

'You can,' he says.

He's talking about more than the fuse box. He's smiling at me. 'You're doing great. I'm proud of you,' he says, kisses my cheek lightly and lets himself out of the back door.

And what he said means everything. I feel my spirits lift off the floor, like a roller-coaster ride climbing slowly upwards again.

'Okay, let me sort out the fuse box,' I say.

'I can do that!' says Joe.

'No, Joe, it's fine. You can hold the stepladder for me. That's a really important job.' He nods happily in agreement.

'Who fancies a walk afterwards?' There's no response. 'To the beach?' I continue to throw out ideas. 'Up into town?'

'Got any good shops?' Blake asks.

'There's a café!' I say, almost desperately. 'We could get a . . . panini?' Isn't that what Ed Wildes had said he was serving now?

'Do they do sandwiches?' asks Joe, suddenly worried. 'I like cheese sandwiches.'

'I'm sure we can ask for that, Joe,' I reassure him, hoping that Ed will be accommodating, and by the same token, I can't believe I'm voluntarily going to Wildes. The very place I swore to myself I wouldn't set foot in again.

'*Yesssss!*' says Joe, with a little fist pump into his side. 'And ice cream? I love ice cream!'

'Okay, let's go to your café,' says Blake. 'Not like there's anything else to do here.'

'It's not my . . .' I stop myself. It's just one trip up to the town and a sandwich. It's something to do with the boys.

I can do this, I repeat to myself, not sure whether I'm reassuring myself about entertaining the boys or setting foot in Ed's place again.

'Will your friend Griff be there?' Joe asks.

'No,' I say. I can do this without Griff, I think. I can. I can do this on my own. This is what I planned. Just me. On my own. It's just a panini . . . and a cheese sandwich . . . and ice cream . . . and Ed, who asked me to go for a drink the last time I saw him. I chew my lip. If I'm going to live here, I'll have to face him at some point, drink or no drink. I need to do this. And I really want to make the fostering work. But what if I can't? What if it isn't over with Ed? What if I can't get through this weekend with the boys? What if I can't stop thinking what-if?

13

As I finish repairing the fuse box, Joe goes to get dressed and Blake arrives back downstairs. He's changed into the same clothes he arrived in, the black jeans and hoodie, and has pulled up the hood. I wonder if he has any other clothes with him. Later I'll suggest washing them for him. Or maybe he'd prefer to wash them himself. I'll show him the washing machine. I shut my eyes. It's like walking on eggshells, not knowing what to say in case I come out with the wrong thing. But, first, it would be good just to manage a conversation with him.

'This way,' I say, walking out of the back door and down the track, past the cows and the milking parlour. I explain that they get milked twice a day and about the truck that turns up to take away the milk to the cooperative. Neither boy says very much.

We head out of the gate, onto the coast path, and once again I'm transfixed by the sparkling sea below us and wonder if they are too. We trot down the sandy steps to the cove where I swam, which is empty now. People generally stop at the cove next door, one over from the harbour and the busy beach there.

We pass the old boathouse, its painted blue doors peeling and weeds growing up all around it. We walk across the shingle and the sand. Oystercatchers are dipping their long orange beaks into rock pools. I listen to the waves lapping on the shore. I breathe in the air, feeling it fill me with courage, just like the water did yesterday. I turn to the boys. Blake shoves his hands into his pockets and hunches over. 'Couldn't we have driven?'

'I can drive!' says Joe, raising a hand.

'This is much quicker,' I say cheerily. 'Parking is a nightmare in town, especially with caravans and camper-vans everywhere now it's summer. Besides, I wanted to show you the beach.' We walk along the narrow grassy path, up the hill on the other side of the cove.

Blake harrumphs. 'Is it much further?' he says, as I stop at the top and look back towards the field of cows. My cows.

'Is it a long way down?' Joe says, and moves to the edge.

'Yes!' I jump forward and grab his arm. I just have to

keep them safe for the weekend. Just the weekend! 'Come on, not much further. Just around the next cove and then we'll be at the harbour. We'll have built up an appetite.' I'm sounding like the bouncy children's presenter again.

'Here we are,' I say, outside Wildes, with a stab of sadness that I'm not taking them to Valentino's. Neither boy seems impressed.

'What do people *do* around here?' Blake says.

The small high street is busy with dog-walkers, and children with shrimping nets and buckets making for the beach.

'Lots of water sports,' I say. 'Sailing, kayaking, paddle-boarding. And then there's crabbing. We have crabbing competitions.'

'Crabbing competitions?' Joe screws up his face.

'To see who can catch the most crabs.' I remember climbing over the rocks with Griff. We knew the best places to find them and the best bait to catch them.

'Oh, I could do that!' says Joe.

'Why would you bother?' says Blake.

'Well . . .' he has me stumped for a moment '. . . for fun,' I say.

'What do you do with them when you've caught them?'

'Put them back into the water,' I reply.

'Phfff. Pointless,' he says, and walks towards the café's door.

I steel myself to follow, knowing Ed will be inside.

'I'd like a cheese sandwich, please,' says Joe, decisively, sitting at the shiny table, the menu in his hands but upside down. Blake is slouched back in his chair, his phone in one hand, the menu in the other. The phone irritates me even though I know I should let it go. But he should put it down to eat the meal I'm going to buy him. It's elementary manners. Surely I can teach him this one basic courtesy.

'Sorry, no cheese sandwiches,' Ed says, holding his iPad in his hand and looking between Joe and Blake. 'I've got goat's-cheese quiche, or bacon and Brie panini?'

Joe's face falls.

'Yeah, I'll have the panini thingy,' says Blake, not looking up from his phone.

'Erm, is there anything else you'd like, Joe?' I scan the menu, trying to find something to suggest.

Blake sighs heavily, clearly unhappy the indecision is going to hold up his lunch. He slouches further into his chair, bringing the phone to his face.

'Just have the panini, man,' he says. 'It's like a cheese sandwich with bacon.'

'Do you have ketchup?' asks Joe.

'We can do ketchup,' says Ed, smiling.

'In that case, I would like the panini with ketchup,' Joe says, having given it serious consideration. He puts down the menu.

'Fine, two panini. And for you, Beca?' I look at the menu, trying not to catch his eye. 'I didn't know you had family staying.'

I snap my head up. 'Erm . . .' I have no idea what to say. 'Joe and Blake *aren't* family. They're just with me for the weekend,' I say, and wonder if I could have worded that better. 'So we're out for a treat!'

'And ice cream,' Joe joins in. 'Do you have ice cream? I love ice cream.'

'We do,' says Ed.

'I'd like two scoops, please, of chocolate.'

'Noted,' says Ed, and looks back at me.

Carys is in the corner, with her dogs, a bowl of soup and bread that she's feeding to them, just like last time.

'I'll have the soup, please,' I say, pushing all thoughts of chocolate fudge sundaes, banana splits and glacé cherries from my mind as I gaze at the familiar yet unfamiliar walls – anywhere but at Ed. I don't want those stirring sensations in my stomach again.

We wait for our food in an uncomfortable silence. Blake is on his phone. Joe is taking apart the salt and pepper mills and reassembling them for a better, firmer twist, scattering peppercorns across the table. I sweep them quickly into my hand. I have no idea what to talk about. I don't want to ask about their families, or why they came into care.

'My family used to own this place,' I say.

'Wow!' says Joe.

'It was a café and *gelato* shop. That's ice cream. A *gelateria*.'

'Wow!' says Joe again.

Blake looks up briefly from his phone. 'Nice,' he says, and there's more than a hint of sarcasm in his voice. A sneer, almost. I say no more, wishing we were out of there.

The food arrives speedily and I'm grateful. I barely taste the soup as I watch the boys eat their panini.

'Blake, why don't you put your phone down while you eat?'

He sighs and puts it beside him on the table, but doesn't take his eyes off it.

Joe is inspecting his sandwich. He takes out the bacon, adds ketchup and carefully nibbles a corner. 'Excuse me?' he calls to Ed, as he passes with plates in his hands on his way to the kitchen.

'Yes?' Ed stops.

'Is this Heinz ketchup?'

'Erm . . . no,' says Ed.

'I can recommend it,' says Joe. 'This is not very nice.'

Ed looks at me, raising an eyebrow.

I'm about to wince but suddenly part of me feels

proud of Joe. He has politely put across his point of view. More than I managed when it came to the sickly powdery ice cream.

Joe abandons his panini with a sigh. Blake inhales his. Then, with no words, he checks that Joe has finished and eats his too.

Joe is happier when two small balls of chocolate ice cream arrive. He tries it with interest. Blake takes a look at the ice cream put in front of him – the same as Joe's. He tastes it, then puts the spoon into the bowl and picks up his phone, clearly having done what was asked of him, to stay off it while he ate.

Again I'm a stranger in the place that used to be home. There is still an uncomfortable silence around our little table.

Joe finishes his ice cream, then indicates Blake's. 'If you don't want it?' he asks politely.

Blake scowls and shakes his head. Joe finishes the ice cream.

'Okay, I have to get back for the cows,' I say.

'Oh, yes, I can do the cows,' Joe says. I wonder how milking will go with him around. Let's hope he doesn't take anything apart.

'You can help me, Joe, but you have to do as I tell you.'

He nods firmly. He has chocolate ice cream around his mouth. I hand him a paper napkin, which he uses to blow his nose.

'Blake? Do you want to come and help with the cows?'

'No, you're all right, thanks.'

I stand to pay.

'Guests, eh? Not family?'

'Yes and no,' I say to Ed, as he rings up my bill. I'm not ready to share any more. He tells me the total and I do a double-take. His prices make my eyes water.

'I've given you mates' rates,' he says, and I want to tell him we're not mates, anything but, but I'll take the price reduction. 'What about that drink? Catch up. For old times' sake?' My stomach starts to fizz. Damn you, Ed Wildes.

'I'm tied up at the moment,' I say, gesturing at Joe and Blake, grateful for the distraction and desperate to leave now.

He's intrigued. 'Another time.'

Over my dead body. The last thing I need is the complication of dating again. I've had my fill of that. And especially not Ed Wildes again. I learnt my lesson last time.

I turn to leave with the boys.

Outside, the sun has disappeared behind the clouds, and I shiver. The lunch hasn't lifted the mood like I wanted it to. I have no idea why I thought I was cut out for this. I haven't any experience with teenagers, but I've been one. I'd thought that would be enough. Clearly not. I'd be far better off sticking to cattle.

Back at the farm, the cows are lying down. Looks like there could be darker clouds on the horizon. I shiver again.

In the house I get Joe to help unpack boxes in the kitchen and he starts finding homes for things which I may never find again. Blake sits and stares, wordless, at his phone. At four thirty, I interrupt him. 'Blake? We're going down to the milking parlour now. Are you sure you wouldn't like to come with us?' He doesn't reply, just stands, helps himself to a can of Coke from the fridge and walks back towards the table, staring at his screen. To be honest, I'm feeling really frustrated by his attitude. I mean, he's only here for the weekend. He could put in a bit of effort. This is a beautiful place to be.

'You might like it?' I say, with an edge I'm not proud of in my voice.

Still nothing, head down, ignoring me. I'm rattled. I'm sure if I could just get him away from his phone he'd enjoy it here.

'Blake?' I repeat, this time a little louder.

'What?' he barks rudely, making my hackles rise even higher. I've worked with plenty of difficult customers and, at times, with tricky staff members who haven't lasted long. I'm not going to let Blake and his phone rule things here. This is my home, I remind myself. I lower my shoulders. And this is my job for the weekend. I have to be professional and take control of the situation.

'Maybe some time off your phone would be good,' I say.

Then I stand up a little taller and stare at him steadily, letting him know that I'm saying it like it is, not asking, but being polite, waiting for him to put away his phone and join us by the back door to go down to the cows. Milking waits for no man, woman or teenager. I can hear the herd mooing loudly. It would be a good lesson for him to learn, that some things in life are more important than his phone. It might help him – and I just want him to enjoy being here. From where I'm standing, Blake isn't.

'Look, Blake, I just wanted to give you a chance to spend some time in the countr—'

He cuts me off. 'A chance?' he says quietly, slowly looking up from his phone. 'You think I need a chance?'

There's something in his tone that tells me I've stepped on one of those eggshells. Actually it's more like an unexploded bomb. That's the impression I'm getting from him.

'No, I just mean – I meant, look, you're here, I thought you'd be grateful for the chance.' And I've said it all wrong again. 'Look, why not come and . . .'

'Yeah, a chance would be nice!' He looks around the kitchen, anger in his voice, and I wish I'd just let him stay on his phone. He wasn't harming anyone. Why did I have to push it?

'Look, don't worry.' I turn towards the back door where Joe is waiting, clearly hoping the situation will just die down.

'It's all right for do-gooders like you, in your big houses, thinking we should be grateful for a chance to stay with you. You don't know anything about me, or the chances I've had. Not one of them good!' His voice gets louder. 'You're getting paid for us to be here. What does it matter what I do?'

'Look, I'm sorry!'

'Sorry? I'd love a chance, and if I had what you've been given in life, I'd have one. We weren't all born into families who owned restaurants.'

The proud part of me wants to tell him my grandparents started off with a bicycle and a cool box, and how I built up my own business, made my own money when all my family's went on care-home fees, but the grown-up part of me says, 'Don't,' and instead I listen.

'You think you're doing something good, having us here! Why are you doing this? It's not like we're grateful. And it doesn't look like you need the money. What are we? Some replacement for the family that isn't here or you haven't got? Think you can make a difference in a weekend to poor kids who deserve a chance?'

'No! I know I can't make a difference. I just wanted

to . . . I thought you or other children might enjoy being here.' I blink several times. My eyeballs are hot. I'm hot. I want to get outside. I take a deep breath. 'Look, we're going to do the milking. You stay here, it's not a problem!' I'm trying to calm things down, as I would with an irate customer whose cleaners haven't arrived.

'No, I'm not your problem.' He's twisted my words. 'I'll be gone in another day. On to another do-gooder thinking I should be grateful for the chance,' he makes quotation marks in the air, 'they've given me. Or someone who's just happy to take the pay cheque they get from me being there. Well, stick your chance!' he says, and kicks out at the box from Wildes that's on the floor, sending it spilling its contents all over the floor and knocking over a lamp. I step back, shocked, but also telling myself I'd have done much the same when I was a wilful teenager and it's just frustration. With that he clatters up the wooden stairs and I hear the door to his bedroom slam.

From experience, mine, I know the best thing to do is leave him to calm down. And, with the cows waiting, I decide not to try to deal with any of the mess on the floor, even though I want to scoop everything up and put it right.

'Come on, Joe. Let's go and see the cows,' I say, opening the door and letting in the welcome breeze, making the papers and photos flutter about.

Clearly used to scenes like this, Joe joins me cheerfully as we walk down to the waiting cows. In contrast, my hands are trembling after the drama that's just unfolded. I know I should have handled things better. Perhaps I'm really not cut out for the responsibility that comes with caring for these children. I wanted to make a difference to a child's life. Well, I've done that, and not for the better. In fact, by the look of it, I've made things a whole lot worse for Blake and how he feels about his life.

It's hot when we leave the milking parlour after hosing it down. Really hot. The air is close and muggy, and clouds are building over the sea.

'Let's take some milk back to the house for hot chocolate,' I suggest. 'It might cheer Blake up.'

As we walk back to the house, the sky darkens. The clouds are about to burst and take the heat out of the day.

14

'Blake?' I call up the stairs. 'We're back! Do you want something to drink?'

There's no response.

'Blake?' I call again, and picture him on his phone, ignoring me. I wonder who he's messaging.

'We're making hot chocolate!' shouts Joe.

'Blake?' I go upstairs and knock at the door. Still no response. I knock again, then open it slowly, hoping not to provoke another confrontation. 'Blake?' I push the door wide and poke my head in. He's not lying on his bed with his shoes on, arm under his head, phone in the other hand, like I expected him to be.

I wonder if he's in the bathroom. The door's ajar. The seat is up. There's no sign of him.

I double-check Joe's room and then, with a sick feeling, trying to swallow a rising sense of betrayal, I check my own room. But he's not there either and I feel a small sense of relief. I go back downstairs to the living room. Maybe he's watching TV, a small step on from staring at his phone.

I walk into the room and stop. The television isn't on and Blake's not there. I head back to the kitchen.

'Joe, have you any idea where Blake's gone?'

'Nope,' says Joe, still unperturbed. 'I think out of all the cows Sarah Jane is my favourite.'

'Which one is she?'

'The one with the white mark here,' he points to his forehead, 'and the one black ear.'

'Joe?' I say. 'I can't find Blake anywhere.'

'Oh, he's probably run away, now that he's got the lie of the land,' he says. It sounds like something he overheard in the past and is repeating.

I'm gripped by panic. 'Run away?'

He nods and shrugs. 'It happens a lot. The ones who want to go. They wait until they can work out where they are, then disappear.'

'Oh, no, no, no . . .' This can't be happening. All I had to do was keep them safe for one weekend. How can I have got it so badly wrong? 'Where would he go? Who does he talk to on his phone?'

Joe shrugs.

'Sorry, sorry, Joe.' I can't risk upsetting him too. It's not *his* fault Blake's run away. Run away! I repeat the words in my head. What do I say to Mo?

My hands are shaking as I pick up my phone and dial her number. It rings. Then goes to voicemail. I could cry. But I won't, I tell myself. I have to find him.

'Joe, are you sure you've got no idea where Blake might have gone?' I ask again, as calmly as I can.

'Nope,' says Joe, preoccupied. He's started to take apart the standard lamp that was sent flying when Blake kicked over the box. There's still debris every-where. But I can't worry about that now, or Joe and the lamp. Actually . . . 'Make sure it's not plugged in at the wall,' I say, just in case. I can't afford any more mishaps this weekend.

I try Mo's number again and this time I leave a mes-sage: 'Hi, erm, Mo, it's Beca, Beca Valentino. From Sŵn y Môr. I have Joe and Blake staying with me.' I've lost the child you left in my care! I upset him and he's run away! He's probably with a drug gang by now! Oh, God! My anxiety increases by the second. What made me think this was the change of life I wanted? I'd take on a hundred difficult clients right now rather than deal with this.

'Could you ring me back as soon as you can?' I say and hang up, as my throat tightens.

Now what? I have to find him and bring him back. Do I ring the emergency number Mo left me? Is this an emergency? Yes! They'll never let me foster again if I've lost the first child in my care! Surely someone has seen him. He can't have got far. I look down at my phone.

There's Ed Wildes's number. Maybe Blake went back to the café. I doubt it. I don't even know if he has any money. I do the one thing I always did, and promised I'd stop doing once I left the town. I'd sworn to myself I'd stand on my own two feet. And I did. But now there's only one person I can turn to for help.

15

My hands are still trembling as I try to scroll through the numbers in my phone. Where is it? My eyes are hot, burning and blurry.

Finally I see it and press 'call'.

'Griff!' I say, as soon as he picks up.

'Beca? You okay?' My number must have flashed up on his screen. The familiarity of his voice brings a lump to my throat and my eyes prickle.

'It's Blake,' I mutter. 'He's gone.'

'Take a deep breath,' he tells me. I do. 'What happened?'

'We had . . . a disagreement, and now . . .' the lump makes my voice crack '. . . now I can't find him anywhere.' I tell myself to breathe. 'I think he's done a flit, or whatever they call it. Run away!' My voice rises as I say the words. Could this weekend have gone any worse?

Griff doesn't miss a beat. 'Okay, don't worry. I'll be there in a few.'

The phone goes dead.

Joe seems totally unfazed: he has plugged in the lamp and is turning it on and off with satisfaction. But that's good. Good that he's not upset. He's talking, but I don't really hear him. He's explaining that this can be a regular occurrence with flight-risk kids.

'Joe, are you sure he didn't tell you anything?' I repeat.

My heart is racing. It's banging in my ears. I had to keep these kids safe for a few days and I couldn't even manage that. I'm panicking now, really panicking.

Joe shakes his head. 'Blake doesn't talk to me. I don't think he likes me.'

'Oh, I'm sure that's not true.'

'It is,' says Joe, with certainty.

I feel for him and want to reassure him. But first I need to find Blake. Then I'll talk to Joe. It's like I'm writing a list, prioritizing the items in my head. How do parents manage this full time?

I look at the mess. The box of my grandparents' belongings. Mostly rubbish, but spilt all over the flag-stone floor. I pick up the photographs carefully, then scoop up everything else and put it on the table. Why didn't I just let him stay on his phone? He's only here for a few nights! I can't change his life, only make his time here nice. Was he talking to people who made his flight possible? Should I have taken the phone away altogether and got him to step back from whoever he was messaging?

I should have done the courses Mo talked about. And now I have to tell her I've lost the child she put in my care. I check my phone again. She hasn't called back.

I'm still trying to get Joe to remember anything Blake might have said when Griff appears at the back door. I feel like throwing myself on him to weep. In fact I do, a bit, but quickly pull myself together. Griff's here, I think, feeling reassured.

'It'll be all right. We'll find him,' he says. 'Come on, Joe, get your shoes on. We're going out. He can't have got far. Even if he went to the station, there isn't a train for hours.'

'It's all because we had an argument about his phone,' I tell him.

'It's nothing any other parent or carer isn't doing.'

I'm so grateful to him for being here and making it feel almost normal.

'Nia's looking for him in town. Tell anyone you can think of,' he tells me. 'Get them to keep an eye out.'

With shaking hands, I message the Sŵn y Môr Mermaids WhatsApp group, giving a description of Blake and asking them to let me know if they see him.

'I've messaged my swimming group,' I say, 'and I've told Carys. She's passing it on to Alys in the post office, so word should be out by now.'

He chuckles. 'You know what gossip is like around here,' he reminds me, in an attempt to lighten my mood. And it works. Griff has always been able to make me smile when life is chaotic. 'So, let's start the search. Where have you looked so far?'

'Just the house. He must have run away while I was out doing the cows. I asked if he wanted to come but he didn't. Joe came with me . . .' I trail off.

Griff nods. 'Come on, then, Joe. Ready?'

'Ready!' says Joe, cheerily.

'Let's go and find Blake.'

And with that Griff ushers me, Joe and Cariad out of the back door. His truck, its windows still open, is parked in the middle of the drive. I say parked, more left in haste where he pulled up.

'You check the barns and fields,' Griff instructs me. 'We'll head down the coast path.'

'He hated the coast path . . .' I say. It's still hot and close. The sky is getting darker all the time, the heavy cloud having moved in from the sea.

I check the cowshed and the milking parlour, then scan the fields, striding across them, not knowing where else to look. I'm sweating, trickles running down my back. 'Blake!' I call. 'Blake!'

There is nothing but the sound of the seagulls and the occasional moo from the cows as they lie down. I've turned to go back to the house when my phone rings, making me jump.

'Griff?'

'I think we may have found him.'

'Where?'

'I saw one of your swimming friends leaving the cove after a dip.'

'And?' I ask quickly, fearing the worst. More sweat rolls down my back. What if . . . The worst thoughts run through my head, scenarios tumbling over each other as they rush in. I feel the overwhelming weight on my shoulders of having let this boy down.

'Where did you go when you wanted to hide away from it all?' Griff asks.

'I don't know!' I snap back, frustrated and scared.

'Yes, you do . . .' I hear a smile tugging at the corners of his lips and, like the plug being pulled out of a bath, the worries drain away.

'The old boathouse!' The answer dawns on me as the same small smile tugs at the corners of *my* lips.

'Exactly!' I hear his grin.

'But how did he . . .?'

'Just come on down,' he says. 'Joe and I are here. Joe's discovering the rock pools.'

I don't need telling twice. Ending the call, I head, as quickly as my painful knee will allow, for the gate onto the grassy coast path and the wooden steps. The clouds are thick overhead and I can feel rain in the air. It's not always sunshine and sandy beaches here, I remind myself, but I love the rain too, and the magnificent thunderstorms. I run quicker down the steps as heavy raindrops start to plop around me in big round circles.

There are blue double doors at the front of the old boathouse and one is standing ajar. I run towards it as the rain starts in earnest. The waves are building and rolling up and back, like the manes of galloping white horses.

'Eek!' I shriek, as the rain falls heavier.

'Quick, in here!' Griff says, sticking his head out of the blue door he's holding open. 'Joe's with me!'

'And Blake?' I say, reaching the boathouse.

He's there! Thank God! He's standing in front of me, his head bent, his hair hanging over his down-turned eyes, shielding him. Relief washes through me all over again, just seeing him and knowing he didn't go too far.

'Blake! You're here!'

'Yeah ... I know ...' he says, circling a toe in the dust and sand on the floor. 'I know how this works. I'm supposed to say sorry, then you confiscate my phone and call the social worker.'

For a moment I have no idea how to respond. And then I realize I can only follow my heart. 'I'm just glad you're safe.'

He looks up at me, just as there's a flash and an almighty bang from outside. The door of the boat-house slams shut.

'Whoa! What was that?' Joe jumps, terrified.

'Don't worry, Joe. It's just thunder,' Griff reassures him. The old boathouse whistles different tunes as the wind whips through all the holes in its roof and walls.

'We'll be fine, Joe.' I put a hand on his shoulder and discover that Griff's is already there. I drop mine as we touch. 'We'll just wait here until the storm has passed,' I say, and see Joe visibly relax. Suddenly I feel a rush of excitement and realize it's the relief of finding Blake and that we're all safe, here, in the boathouse that was Griff's and my refuge while we were growing up. Where the old boat used to be there is now an empty space and oil stains on the floor. There are boxes on the wonky shelves, with rags, plastic bottles, ropes, faded orange buoys and broken lobster pots.

'We used to come here all the time when we were kids,' Griff says to the boys. There's another bang. Joe jumps again, and I think Blake does too.

'We did!' I smile mischievously. 'No one ever found us. There used to be a boat here and we'd hide in it, if anyone ever looked for us.'

'I could have done with a boat,' says Blake, and I think he's helping to lighten things, making me see him in a new way. There's another flash, followed by a bang, and this time I definitely see him jump.

'I wonder . . .' Griff says, looking around the big draughty shed. 'Yes! There it is!' He goes to a corner and pulls out a ladder, dusty and covered with cobwebs. He places it against the opening to the loft. He puts a foot on it and tests it.

'Coming?' He grins at me and I grin back. Another crash of thunder startles us both.

'Oh, I don't know. Maybe . . .' I look at the boys, reminding myself that I already nearly lost one today.

'Come on, it'll be fine,' Griff says. 'It'll be fun!'

He's right. We could do with some fun, and at least I didn't actually lose Blake. Things could have been far worse. We're here together. And it *is* just a bit of fun.

'Okay.' I turn to the boys. 'Come on,' I say, and smile to them both.

'I'm a b-b-bit scared,' Joe stutters, and I remember Mo telling me to look out for this. I start to tell him it's okay, he doesn't have to, but Blake beats me to it.

'Go on, mate. I'll catch you if anything happens.'

Tears spring to my eyes again. This time they're happy ones, as Blake guides Joe up the ladder to the loft. I put my foot on the first rung of the ladder. Is this really the same sullen boy whom Joe thought didn't like him? There's clearly more to Blake than meets the eye.

As I poke my head up into the loft, the memories are overwhelming. The smell of the place, of engine oil and salt, is still exactly the same. I can smell petrol and sacking too. And there, lying on their stomachs on layers of sacking in front of the triangular window, just like we used to do, are Griff, Joe and Blake. A big flash of lightning cracks across the sky.

'Whoaaaa!' the boys exclaim, and then they laugh. Griff turns to me, beaming, and there's nowhere I'd rather be right now.

'Come on! Come and join us.' I watch them all shimmy up a bit to make room for me to lie on my tummy too and watch the storm. I climb up through the loft opening and instinctively crawl to the other side of Blake. It doesn't seem quite right to be lying next to Griff on sacking in the loft now that we're grown-ups.

The waves are rolling and crashing on the rocks, like fireworks exploding skywards. There's another flash of lightning and I start to count. The boys look at me, questioning. And then we hear a rumble of thunder. 'You can tell how far away the storm is,' I explain.

'Really? Wow!' says Joe. With the next flash, he starts to count. When the thunder comes, his grin is as wide as it can be.

'Now do it again and we can tell if the storm is getting closer or moving away,' Griff says. In that moment he looks just like he did when we were teenagers. He's wearing his blue woollen hat like only sailors and fishermen do, as if it should fall off but somehow doesn't, his curly fringe poking out at the front.

There's more lightning, and Joe laughs before he starts to count. So does Blake, I notice, barely mouthing the numbers. The thunder rolls out like a low baritone reaching its audience.

'It's closer!' says Joe, excited, grabbing Griff's arm.

Suddenly they seem like children, a glimpse of how they should be at their ages.

We count together again and again, until the storm starts to move away, we count again. It's as if we're waving off a travelling parade of performers, enjoying the spectacle and distraction they brought. When the storm has finally rumbled off into the distance and the waves have calmed, we climb back down the ladder.

I glance around the empty boathouse. 'So, how did you get in?' I ask Blake.

''S not hard,' he says, with a shrug, retreating to his shell.

I'm reliving the memories when he says, 'So, you going to ring her, tell her about the box and me running out? Guess I'll be moved on by tonight.'

'What?' My attention snaps back to Blake. 'What do you mean?'

'You'll ring that bitch—'

'Blake!'

'That social worker. Tell her I'm trouble. Get me moved.'

'No!' I say, appalled. 'What makes you think that? It was just a bit of a kick-off, and you're here, safe and sound. No harm done.'

''S what happens. I mess up. Do things without thinking.'

'I know,' I say.

'What do you know?' he spits angrily.

'I know, because I did it too,' I say calmly. Griff is watching and I know he could back me up.

'Lucky you! Big house, rich family . . .'

'No. A working family. But I was loved. I know I was lucky. But I kept messing up.'

'What about this place? The house, the farm.'

'I . . . ran away too.'

'Yeah, right. What – to the end of the road?'

'No. I left, actually. I was twenty and was let down by a boy I thought loved me. I behaved badly when he hurt me. Did something stupid – I graffitied his car and then I was ashamed of myself. I'd let my parents down. I'd broken their hearts and I couldn't bear to hurt them any more. So I ran. Went to London. Worked as a cleaner. Worked hard. As hard as I could. It was like a distraction.'

'Did you come back?'

'Not for years, and then not for long periods. Just quick visits. I couldn't leave the business I was building up. But I should have moved back a long time ago. Shouldn't have left it so long.' I take a deep breath. 'I shouldn't have left.' I look at Griff. 'So you see, I do know how it feels to mess things up. To feel you have to keep running. But do you know what? Failure isn't the end of the journey.'

'What self-help Twitter feed did you get that from?' Blake laughs and so do I. It's the first time I've seen him smile.

'But it's true. The journey doesn't end just because you mess up. Not unless you give up,' Griff joins in.

'We shouldn't feel guilty for being angry over what's happened, or what we've done. It's all about where we're going,' I say.

'If you can stay in one place long enough,' Blake replies.

'Well, I'm not going to be ringing anyone, not this weekend.' I try to put my arm around him but he stiffens and I drop it. 'I won't be telling anyone about you running off if you don't tell anyone about me letting you up into the loft of this old place to watch thunderstorms. Deal?'

He gives me a little smile. A tiny glint in his eye. 'Deal,' he agrees.

I take one last look around the boathouse. 'It hasn't changed a bit.'

'Still as it ever was,' Griff says. 'Apart from the missing boat.'

'Who owns it?' asks Blake.

I look at Griff. 'Well, I think I do.' I'm still surprising myself with everything I've bought.

'You?'

I nod. 'It was all a bit rushed. I need to check the deeds but I'm pretty sure it comes with the house.'

'Technically, yes,' Griff says.

'And was it your boat?' Blake asks quickly.

Griff shakes his head. 'It was Carys's father's boat –

Carys Thomas in the fisherman's cottage, with the two Jack Russells.'

'I remember,' I say, as the memory of that awful day comes flooding back to me.

'Her father and her fiancé went down in an accident at sea.' He looks around. 'This place was closed up and has never been opened since. No one wants to revisit the memory.'

And that's why the boat is missing.

Griff looks up at me, sadness in his face.

'Are you two in love?' Joe asks.

'*What?*' we say in unison.

'No.' Griff laughs. 'No, not in love, more like really old friends.'

I'm still struggling to find the words and Griff has already explained it.

Joe sighs. 'I'd like to be in love,' he says. 'Super-heroes always end up in love. People love superheroes. I'd like to be a superhero. Get a medal for doing good. That would make me a superhero.'

'Well, I'm sure one day you will be.' I turn to Griff, hoping I've said the right thing.

He smiles. 'You never know when love is going to find you, Joe,' he says.

'Or not,' I say. 'Some of us are happy to be on our own.'

'Rubbish,' says Griff. 'Everyone wants to find love eventually.'

'Not necessarily. Some of us thought we'd found it. Once, even twice, and are never going there again.'

'You will.'

'I won't!'

'This sounds like a m-m-marital,' says Joe. 'They had them a lot in the last place I was in.' Again, it sounds like the sort of thing he's overheard someone say. And I can see him scratching himself. He's clearly feeling anxious.

'Oh, no, Joe, honestly. We're just talking,' I say.

'Really, mate, it's fine.' Griff squats beside him.

'Now, who fancies some ice cream?' I say.

'Is it the stuff from this morning?' says Joe.

'Yes!' I hope that'll help lift his mood. 'I could go and get some.'

'No thanks,' he says, and I feel as deflated as he sounds.

I look around the boathouse once more.

'I own this,' I say out loud.

'Well, as I was saying, technically you own it,' says Griff. 'But . . .'

'What do you mean?' I frown.

'Carys rents it. It's a lifetime rental, passed on from her father, paying a peppercorn rent.'

I frown deeper. 'How did I not know this?'

Griff shrugs. 'Maybe it's not written down. A precedent set years ago. All I know is, Carys has the right to this place for as long as she lives, and after the accident she closed it up and vowed it wouldn't be used again.'

'So,' I say slowly, 'even though I own it, I can't use it.'

'Well, unless you want to upset one of Sŵn y Môr's oldest families, I wouldn't. You want to fit in here again, don't you?'

'I do. I want it to be my home,' I say. 'I've realized what I left behind.'

Blake and Joe are now looking bored.

'It's all about the *hiraeth*,' says Griff. 'The longing for home.'

I stare at him. 'It is,' I say, and drag my eyes away. 'Right, come on, let's get back.' I'm keen to get out the deeds to Tŷ Mawr and check that what Griff said is right.

'Are you coming, Griff?' Blake asks.

'I'd better. I've left my truck on Beca's drive.'

We start to make our way outside. A ray of sunshine is pushing through the clouds, which are rolling away, lighting up the rock pools. Suddenly a rainbow appears over the cove. Along the coastal path come the Mermaids, waving as they arrive.

'Oh, lovely! You've got the family with you!'

'Oh, they're . . .' I bite my tongue and say nothing. No need to.

'Hello, Griff!' They wave.

He waves back.

'You coming in?' they call.

I shake my head. 'Not today. I've got—' Suddenly my heart plummets. 'Oh, no! Quick! We have to get back!' I run up the steps from the beach towards the farm, my heart thumping, hoping against hope I'm not too late.

16

Out of breath, I stand on the drive. Griff's truck is in the middle where it was left. I'm too late.

'I'm sorry, I should have thought,' he says, having belted up the steps behind me.

'It's not your fault. It's mine!' I say. 'I knew the truck would be coming for the milk. I've got seven missed calls from the driver.' My phone pings as the signal returns now we're back from the cove. 'Eight!' I listen to the message and swing the phone down by my side. 'He couldn't take the milk. He couldn't get the truck down the track, so the pipes couldn't reach the tank.'

'Like I say, my fault,' says Griff.

'No, it's not! It's mine!' says Blake suddenly. 'I always screw things up for me and everyone else!' He's back to being angry and begins to stalk away.

'Blake! It's fine,' I say. 'I just forgot the milk truck was coming. It's okay to make mistakes. It's not the end of the world! I'm still going to be up and milking tomorrow. Life won't stop because of one mistake. I just have to work out what to do about it.'

He stops and turns back.

'It just means we've got a lot of milk to drink!' I smile at him.

'Oh, good! I can do that! I love milk!' says Joe.

'Then let's fetch some and go inside. We can work out who else to give it to as well. There's no way I'm throwing that milk away.'

'Joe, you get the glasses from the cupboard.'

'I'll help you, Joe,' says Griff.

'Blake, you help me tidy up.'

We start to gather up the papers and photographs that had come out of the box, while Joe and Griff gather glasses.

'I'm sorry,' says Blake, quietly.

I get the impression that's not something he's used to saying. 'Thank you,' I say. 'I may not know how you feel, Blake, but I do know something about trying to work out where you fit in, where you belong . . . and about feeling you've let people down, and missing them.'

He humphs. 'Wish I'd been given up for adoption. That would have been the kindest thing my parents could have done,' he says, picking up some photos. 'But they decided to fight to keep me with them. Until my mum ended up in psych care and my dad got me to sell weed at school as soon as he was let out of prison. And I did it because I wanted to make him proud . . . He was my dad.'

Tears fill my eyes and threaten to spill. I rub my nose and sniff, hoping he hasn't noticed. The last thing Blake would want is pity.

He's looking at the photos. 'Who are these people?'

'My grandparents. Like I say, they owned the ice-cream shop in the town. I divided my time between theirs and the little house I shared with Dad . . . until I was twenty, when I left. My mum died when I was eight, so it was just Dad, Nonno and Nonna.'

'Hope their ice cream was better than today's!' Blake smiles.

'It was!' I wish they could taste it. 'It was proper homemade *gelato*.' I wish my dad could still enjoy his favourite: strawberry when strawberries were in season. I wish he was here now, all of us around this table.

'Even the seagulls didn't like that ice cream, Blake,' says Griff, helping Joe to carry glasses to the table. 'I found Beca trying to feed it to them, throwing it into the air for them to catch.'

'You caught me at a bad time.' I keep a straight face as I turn to Griff. 'I was upset. And the ice cream was dreadful. It was just everything, me being away for so long, missing being here, wishing I'd come back more. Missing Mum, Dad, Nonna and Nonno . . . missing all of it. And then that so-called ice cream! It's like their memory's being erased from this place.'

'Well, you being here means it's not,' says Griff.

I sweep up the rest of the papers and photos to make room on the table . . . and a battered exercise book falls to the floor. I pick it up and see pages of handwritten recipes for all of the *gelato* flavours sold in the shop. I run my hand over it, then stack the photos on top and put the whole lot into a pile with the other scraps of paper at one end of the table.

After all the excitement of the day – losing and finding Blake, the thunderstorm and cooking fish fingers for tea, washed down with fresh milk – the boys fall into bed, showered and tired. For the first time, I think Blake sleeps.

I go downstairs, scoop up the photos at the end of the table and put them back into their box, then head straight for the bottle of wine on the side. I take out two glasses. 'Want one?'

Griff consults his watch.

'Or do you have to be somewhere? I'm so sorry. You've been such a help with the boys.'

'It's fine. It can wait.' He pulls out his phone and sends a message. 'Done.' He smiles. 'She'll understand. We . . .'

'She?' I ask, then add, 'You don't need to explain anything to me. I just don't want you to be in trouble.'

'There's no trouble. I've explained something came up.'

His phone pings. He looks at the message that's come in and texts back, a smile on his lips.

I'm feeling more than a little curious.

'I'm spending time with an old friend. It's not a crime!'

He's right.

'And what about you and Nia? I didn't realize you two were still so close.'

He shakes his head. 'Why would you? You left and it was like you just forgot about this place.' The slight edge has returned to his voice. 'And once your grandfather died, I didn't think we'd see you back here.'

'And Nia?' So much has happened since I've been away and I want to make up for lost time.

'It wasn't a long thing. We're still friends. It helps to stay on good terms in a small place like this. I'd hoped she'd be the one. But she wasn't.'

I pull out a seat at the worn kitchen table. And he does the same.

I set down the glasses and pour the red wine.

'But there's someone now?' Curiosity getting the better of me.

'There've been . . . a few. No one serious. Well, not yet, maybe.' He flushes, and I decide not to ask any more.

We lift the glasses.

'Thank you for your help today. I couldn't have done it without you.'

The lighthouse further down the coast is flashing gently in the distance over the headland.

'What help? Messing up your milk collection?'

'I meant with the boys. You're a natural.'

He sips the spicy red wine. 'Not a natural. Just had experience. And you did great today,' he says. 'You should be proud of yourself.'

I let out a long sigh. 'I didn't realize . . .' I'm twisting the stem of my wine glass.

'What? That it would be so hard?' he asks.

I nod. I wanted to do something that *mattered*. I just didn't expect not to be very good at it. 'I'm going to need some help,' I say, and he frowns. 'With the cows,' I qualify.

'Ah.' He nods. 'I know someone . . .' He pulls out his phone and types. A ping comes straight back. 'Sorted. Help will be here in the morning for milking.'

'Really?'

'Yup.' He has another sip of his wine.

'Who?'

He taps the side of his nose. 'Wait and see in the morning! Talking of which, I'd better go. I need to be out there first thing to pick up the lobster pots before anyone decides to help themselves.'

'And I have to work out how to distribute all of this milk. I could give some to my swimming friends . . .'

'That's six pints, then!' He laughs, standing. 'They used to sell it to passers-by from the end of the drive here. You could sell it too or . . . make cheese?'

He waves at the pile of photos and papers in the box. 'They were great days,' he says, pointing to a photograph of the annual regatta by the jetty. 'We looked forward to it for weeks in the summer.'

'Highlight of the year!' I say.

The regatta comprised competitions for rowing, sailing, swimming and, of course, crabbing, which Griff and I always won. There was a huge barbecue for everyone and, always, Valentino's *gelato*. Nonno would come down to the beach with his bike and cool box, dressed up for the occasion in a straw boater. There was bunting blowing in the breeze and in the evenings, as the sun set, music and dancing. They were great days.

'It was!'

'Will it be back this year?'

'It will. Same week, before the start of school.'

I look up and Griff is smiling at me. 'Of course,' he says, 'you could make ice cream.'

'What? No. I was good at eating it. But I've no idea how to make it. Especially not like Nonna's. And it was never ice cream . . .'

'. . . it was *gelato*!' we sing, and laugh at the memory of Nonna correcting anyone who dared called it ice cream.

Then Griff says, a little more seriously, 'Bex, you've worked out you could give away a few pints to your swimming friends. Maybe sell a bit at the end of the lane. That's still a lot of milk you'll be pouring down the drain. At least with *gelato* you can freeze it. I'll help – I feel I should. It was my fault the milk truck couldn't get through.'

'We've established it was no one's fault. If anyone's it was mine. I was distracted.'

'And that's what makes you good at this. The fostering. You care. You cared about Blake today.'

'Really?' I say, feeling wrung out.

'Really. You're good because you care,' he says, and for a moment I feel like I could cry again. I'm tired, exhausted even. But, yes, I cared. I do care. I have just one more day with the boys to make it mean something, let them leave with some sort of memory.

'*Gelato*, you say.' I chew my bottom lip. 'But I really don't know where to start.'

'You'll work out a way. From what I remember, you always do! And, like I say, I'll help.'

I look at the pictures on the kitchen table again. 'Okay. It won't be of Valentino's standard, but it might just be fun. The boys will be leaving on Monday. It could be something to do with them tomorrow. Why not? The milk's only going to waste otherwise.'

'Good. I'll be here tomorrow.'

'It's a date!' I say. 'I mean . . . obviously not a date.'

I'm suddenly reminded of the day I decided to leave and how we left things.

'No!' He laughs. 'We don't want Joe getting the wrong idea.'

'No.' I feel so much more relaxed. I yawn.

'Sleep well, Bex. Tomorrow is another day.'

I see him to the door and open it.

'Like I say, it's good to have you back,' he says, then lightly pecks me on the cheek.

'Good to be back,' I say, meaning it, and watch him drive off as the bats flitter to and fro, diving and weaving overhead. I take in a deep breath of Sŵn y Môr air and head up to bed, where I collapse, images of *gelato* dancing in my head.

17

There's a *phut, phut, phut* underneath my bedroom window, in the early-morning light. My clock tells me it's 5.30 a.m. Nearly time I got up for the cows. But what's that noise?

It stops. I throw back my thin duvet and head to the open window at the back of the house, feeling the warm breeze on my face, and hearing the dawn chorus. I look around for the source of the noise and see someone walking down the track from my driveway in a motorbike helmet.

I yank my towelling dressing-gown from the hook behind the door, then race down the stairs, pulling it on as I go, heart thumping. Please tell me this has nothing to do with Blake and another attempt at running away. I thought we'd got over that. But maybe he was just trying to throw me off the scent. When he apologized, I believed him. I thought we'd had a lovely evening, that today would be a good day . . .

My hands grapple with the back-door lock. Why do our fingers never work quickly when we need them to? Who is it and what are they doing here at this hour of the morning? Has Blake organized a getaway on the back of a motorbike?

My mouth is dry and my throat tight. At last I manage the bolt on the door and fling it open.

'Hey!' I shout, without thinking. It's an automatic reaction. 'Hey!' I start to run, the stones crunching under my feet.

The slight figure stops and turns towards me.

'Beca?' Joe is at his window, sleepy-eyed, his dark red hair standing on end.

'It's okay, Joe, nothing to worry about,' I lie, trying to keep my voice steady. 'Go back to bed. It's still early. I'm just going to do the cows.'

'You want me to help?' he asks sleepily.

'No, it's fine. You go back to sleep.'

He disappears from the window.

The figure hasn't moved.

'Where are you going?' I ask. 'What are you doing on my land? If you're looking for Blake, he's not coming with you!' I hiss in a low whisper.

Blake's room is at the front of the house and I don't want him to hear this. But if he knows about the visitor he may not even be in his room . . .

The figure doesn't say anything, but wrestles with the clip under their chin and slowly pulls off the crash helmet.

I see a shock of bright pink hair on a young woman's head. Not what I was expecting! She peels off her gloves and throws them into the helmet. She has a small ring in her nostril, which she adjusts. 'I don't know who Blake is, but I'm here to do the milking.'

I narrow my eyes. 'I don't think so,' I say. 'They're my cows. And Blake is . . .' I'm confused. She's not here for Blake. But who is she?

She raises a plucked eyebrow, with another small piercing in it. There's something about her I recognize. 'Griff sent me. Said I was to help with the cows here. For as long as you want me. But if you don't need me, I can go again,' she says, turning back towards the drive, where she's parked a small moped with L-plates on it.

'Griff sent you . . .' The conversation about him finding me help with the milking is coming back to me through the foggy recesses of my mind. I'm not sure if it's the deep sleep I was woken from, or that I thought a kidnapper had come for Blake, or relief that this has nothing to do with him that made me slow to catch on.

'Of course. Sorry.'

'Clearly.' She smiles and, once more, I'm reminded of someone.

'So, did you want me?'

'Oh, yes, please. I'll show you the cows.' I step forward, stand on a sharp stone and shout in pain. 'Actually, I'll just get my wellies on. If you don't mind waiting.'

'Carry on.' She smiles again.

I run to the back door, step into my boots and pull the door to behind me. I'm in my towelling dressing-gown and wellingtons but who cares? I don't. And the young woman with pink hair doesn't seem to mind.

'I'm Beca, by the way,' I say.

'Yes, Griff said.' She's striding towards the milking parlour in the early-morning light. The sun is rising behind us, throwing its first rays over the fields, pink, purple and orange streaks in the sky over the sea, where already a few small boats are out. I don't think I'll ever tire of that view.

The day smells fresh after yesterday's thunderstorm and feels full of hope.

'So how do you know Griff?' I ask.

'He's my dad.'

'Your dad!' It's strange to think of Griff as a dad. In my head he's still the young man I left behind. The friend who always had my back. And now years have passed and this is his daughter. It's like Sŵn y Môr is a familiar yet unknown land.

'Of course he is!' I can see it now she's said it. That smile. How did I not know straight away?

'Nia's my mum. And you're Beca, Dad's friend from when he was growing up,' she says.

Jo Thomas

I hear footsteps behind us. It's Joe. 'I thought you'd gone back to bed.'

'Couldn't sleep,' he says, staring at Griff's daughter with her pink hair.

'This is Joe. He's staying for the weekend,' I say.

'Hi, Joe.' She holds out a fist for him to bump, which he does, smiling.

'You and Dad were besties growing up,' she tells me, as she walks into the milking parlour and starts setting up as if she's been doing it here all her life. Joe follows and leans on the top of the metal gate, where the cows are in their holding pen.

'Um, yes.' I'm marvelling at her confidence. 'And?' I ask, wondering what else she knows about me.

'And you left, made money and now you're back,' she says.

I like this young woman. And, clearly, so does Joe from the way he's watching her work.

'You here to help, Joe?' she says, turning to him.

'Yup!' he says, puffing up his chest, like a superhero with a mission.

'And me,' says a quiet voice from behind.

'Blake!'

'Thought you might need another pair of hands, what with all the extra milk, and it being my fault,' he says, a little awkwardly, and I can hear the apology in his voice.

'I've told you, it wasn't your fault. It was mine,' I

reply, but I'm delighted he's here and not on the back of a motorbike, as my overactive imagination had him.

'Okay, Joe, let's get the ladies in!' says Griff's daughter, my smile growing on my face. I could be watching a younger me, I muse, helping Dad or covering milking shifts.

'Thank you, erm . . .' I don't know her name. I can't remember if Griff ever told me. But it might be among the scrambled mess of my morning mind.

'Everyone calls me Scooter.'

'Because of the bike?' I ask, gesturing towards it in the yard.

She shakes her head. 'I used to travel everywhere on a push-along scooter. Managed to get funding for a skate-and-scooter park in the town. Turned out I was quite good at it.'

'Cool,' says Joe.

'Kept me out of trouble – mostly.' She winks at Joe, who beams.

'Okay, well, in that case, if you two are happy . . .'

'No problem,' says Scooter.

'Very happy,' says Joe, and I hear him sigh loudly.

'Come and find me when you're done, Scooter, so we can organize your wages. And, Blake, I have a job for you.'

'What is it?'

'Have you ever made ice cream – or, rather, *gelato*?

Never call it ice cream. *Gelato* has more milk than cream. And we have a lot of milk.'

He looks at me warily, as if this is punishment for yesterday's behaviour. 'Me? I don't know how to make anything!'

'In that case, we'll learn together,' I tell him. I put my arm around his shoulders, and this time he lets me keep it there as we walk back to the kitchen.

'We're really going to make ice cream?'

'*Gelato!*' I correct him.

'Oh, yeah, *gelato!*' He laughs unexpectedly. His whole face lights up and I feel a little rush of happiness.

18

'I know I saw it in here,' I say, going through the pile of photographs, old shopping lists scribbled on the backs of envelopes, splashed with the ingredients of the day and stamped with coffee stains and receipts that are well past their useful date but I'm not quite ready to throw out.

Blake bites his lip nervously.

'It's fine, Blake. It'll be here somewhere,' I say, hoping I'm right and it hasn't got lost in the chaos of yesterday.

'Here!' I pull out the exercise book from the pile, bits of paper falling from it – more envelopes repurposed as ingredients lists. The staples barely hold the pages together. There are ink splashes and sums roughly added up on the outside. It smells musty, but also slightly sweet, with just a touch of perfume. I lift it up and hold it to my nose, shutting my eyes. It smells of the *gelateria*, the café. It smells of home. Tears prickle my eyes.

'Er, are you okay?'

'Oh!' My eyes ping open. 'I was just remembering my grandparents. It reminded me of them.'

'Must be nice to have loved people so much you miss them like that,' he says shyly, and my heart twists.

'Do you miss anyone?' I ask.

'Not really.' Then, after a little more thought, 'It's more missing what you'd've liked them to be. Having someone there. I wanted them to love me. But my mum loved her drugs more, which was why she ended up in a psych ward, and my dad . . . He was sent back to prison after he got me to deal to the kids in school. They brought in sniffer dogs and I got done.' He takes a moment. 'And do you know? The thing that hurt most was I thought I'd let him down. Mad, isn't it?' He sniffs and rubs his nose. 'I wanted him to be proud of me. But maybe . . . I wish I could have been proud of him.'

I say nothing. There is nothing to say that could make this any better.

'He went back to prison and I went into care.' He shrugs and I feel the barriers go back up, as if he's said more than he usually would. He knows how to protect himself. He's had to learn.

'As Nonno always said, you can't change the past or where you've come from but you can create your future.'

He nods slowly, as if he's taking it in.

'You'll find your own path one day and work out where your parents fit into it, if you want them to. I don't know what it's like to be in care. But, as I said before, I do know a bit about feeling lost, especially as a young adult,' I say.

'You were lucky, though, having a proper family,' he says. 'Like I told you, I wish I'd been adopted. Instead my parents fought to keep me because I was useful to them, running errands and stuff. And the social worker thought it was best for me to be with my family.'

'I know I was lucky,' I say quietly. 'But . . .' I'm ashamed. '. . . I didn't realize it at the time. I thought I needed to work out who I was, who the real me was. Everyone here knew us, knew the family, knew who I was. Or thought they did. Nothing was private. I dreamt of a life outside Swn y Môr, and ended up being a right pain.'

Blake gives a snort of laughter.

'Then one day, when I couldn't stand being the subject of gossip in a small town any more, I left to build a life for myself in the city, where I could be anonymous. I kept in touch with my family, but I wanted to have a life away from here.'

He nods, like he understands. 'I try to avoid my family at all costs.'

'I realized I'd been lucky and I didn't want to let my parents down. But I was forever messing up in school.

I hated being inside, in lessons. I loved being on the beach. I wanted my parents to be proud of me, more than anything, but I kept screwing things up.'

'I thought you had life sussed,' Blake says.

'Maybe I do now. But not then. Griff kept me sane. I'd get into some fight or argument in school, usually stepping in if I felt someone was getting bullied. I hated unfairness. Then the school would ring my parents and I'd run off to the boathouse.'

'Like I did?'

'Yes. And Griff would find me there. My parents were never particularly cross. I'd end up at Nonna's, eating *gelato* at this table,' I put my hand on it, 'and feeling that the world was all right again. I felt safe there. Like life was fine. But I was always in some sort of trouble at school. I really didn't like it. And then I met someone and life became good. For a while.'

'What happened?'

'He was a second-home owner down here. It had been his parents' place and his grandparents' before that.'

'How come you haven't got any kids of your own?' he asks.

'Left it too late,' I say, as candidly as I can. 'And I never met the right bloke.'

'Not everyone has that approach,' he says. 'So, now you're going to foster? If we haven't put you off.'

I smile at him cracking a joke. 'You haven't put me off. I just wasn't quite ready for teenagers.'

'You're going to foster younger kids, yes?'

So he had overheard me on the stairs when they arrived.

'That's the plan. Children who will benefit from being here, on the farm, with the cows.'

He nods. 'I like your thinking,' he says seriously. 'It'll be great for loads of younger kids. And you could get some small pets too, rabbits or some such. Kids love to cuddle them. But you have to watch them . . . If they're not used to small animals they'll hold them the wrong way. A lot of kids will talk to animals when they won't talk to grown-ups, though. I was in a home where they had a dog. This kid would tell the dog how his day had been, what he was thinking. It was the only way the social workers knew how he was doing.'

'A dog?'

'Yeah, a dog would be good,' he says, nodding. 'Oh, and another thing . . .'

He goes on to give me a list of tips about how to deal with difficult kids and what to remember.

'You'll be fine. You're doing okay with us!' Eventually he smiles.

And I say something I'm probably not allowed to: 'Can I hug you?'

'Yeah.' He's embarrassed but happy. 'You can.' So I do, and I get the feeling he hasn't had a hug for a long time and he's tucking it into his memory bank to remember when he's gone. In a way, I am too. This difficult lad who has come out of his shell in just a couple of days and who I worry will retreat back into it when he leaves.

And before I burst into tears, I say, 'Right, what about this *gelato*?' There's a crack in my voice but he doesn't seem to notice, or if he does, he ignores it. People like Blake are used to turning a blind eye to emotion.

'Just one thing.'

'Yes?'

'Could we have that pasta sauce again for tea? I really liked it. Just was determined not to eat it. You know how it is.'

I smile. 'I do.'

I flick carefully through the thin pages of the exercise book. The paper is so aged, I'm nervous about handling it, but seeing Nonna's handwriting makes me feel like she's here with me. However, I'm not sure if it's my vision, which is temporarily blurred with unshed tears, or the old-fashioned handwriting, but what I'm reading barely makes sense.

'I'm not sure this is much help,' I say. 'Typical of Nonna, she always kept something to herself. A secret ingredient she'd include and not tell anyone. Until one day she'd pass it on like a prized family ornament. I loved it when she did that. But what we need right now is to make a basic *gelato* with the milk. Then we can think about other flavours.'

I put the book down and turn to Google. 'Look, there's a basic recipe here.' I show it to Blake. I don't know how well he can read, but as he's always on his phone, I presume he can. 'Let's start by making some of this and see how it turns out. We'll go with our gut instinct. We'll make a *fior di latte* first, then a flavoured one with eggs and vanilla. I'll go and get some eggs from the next-door farm.' I pick up my purse, shaking it to check for change to leave in the honesty box by their front gate. 'You go and get a couple of buckets of milk.' I point to the empty metal ones by the sink.

'Okay!' He picks them up and sets off to the milking parlour.

'And check on Joe while you're there!' I call after him, as if this was all perfectly normal. I smile as I watch him go, swinging a bucket in each hand, a spring in his step that wasn't there before. The sun is beating down on the green of the grass, which contrasts with the blue sky and the sparkling sea beyond.

I can't help thinking about what Blake shared of his home life and how he came to be in care. I know I can't change their lives in one weekend, but I hope I've made a difference to his day. I pull my arms around myself as he disappears into the milking parlour.

'You left your phone behind,' says Blake, when I get back with the eggs, his earlier good mood having vanished.

'Oh, it's fine, I'm sure no one was after me. Especially not on a Sunday,' I say, wondering what's happened to upset him in the short time I'd been gone. I put the eggs in their cardboard boxes on the table, next to the buckets of milk.

'You had a call. I saw it come in,' he says.

'It's fine.' I pick up my phone and flick to see who called just as it rings again.

'Hi, Beca, it's Mo, Blake and Joe's social worker. Sorry I missed your call yesterday. There was no reception where I was in the Lakes. Is everything okay? Did you need to use the emergency number?'

'No. Everything's fine,' I say, looking at Blake, a dark cloud over him, despite the sunshine outdoors and the smell of sea air. I try to give him a reassuring smile but my happy bubble has burst. I know what's coming. She's going to arrange to pick them up. I feel quite sad and tell myself not to get so attached so quickly next time. I need to be professional.

I see Blake focusing hard on the *gelato* recipe on my iPad, staring intently at the screen. These boys will always have a special place in my heart. They were the first.

'I'm on my way back now,' says Mo. 'How are the boys? Not giving you too much trouble?'

'No, they're fine,' I say again, and I see Blake's face, a glint of anxiety in his eyes as if he knows what's coming.

'Really? No problems? Blake's . . . doing okay, is he?'

'Yes, really good.' I can't bear to look at him now, knowing what she's going to say.

'Right, well . . .'

I swallow.

'. . . I was wondering if they could stay on with you for a bit. We're still so short of long-term care, but we're getting it sorted. It would just be for a little while,' she pleads.

'That's fine,' I say, quicker than I meant to, my back to Blake. And I feel a strange sense of relief. They're going to stay, just for a bit longer. I want them to leave feeling I've made a small difference. Looks like I might get that chance, after all.

She pauses. Then: 'Are you sure?' she asks, as if checking whether I've misheard her.

'Yes, quite sure,' I confirm.

'It would just be for a short while,' she repeats. 'I promise.'

'Fine.'

'Great, well, I'll be in touch when I have more news,' she says. We finish the call and I turn back to Blake, phone still in my hand. He's staring at the iPad, his fists clenched, the hard-faced youth who first arrived here.

'I'll go and get my stuff together,' he says, 'and fetch Joe.'

'What?'

177

He turns to leave the kitchen.

'No, no!' I say. 'You're staying for a bit longer. They haven't got anything else organized yet.'

He stops in his tracks. 'Really?'

'Really,' I say.

'How long for?'

'She didn't say. But . . .' I should have pinned her down on how long it would be, but I wanted to get off the phone. I was glad: I just wanted to enjoy a little more time doing this, making *gelato* with Blake and seeing Joe enjoy the cows. I stare at the kitchen table.

'So . . .' His eyes are on the ingredients.

'Yes, we have *gelato* to make. Come on!'

'Erm, what about Joe?' he says, all traces of the hard mask gone. 'He likes to know the plan. He's not good with uncertainty. Maybe tell him it's another week.'

'Good idea,' I agree.

'No need to get him overthinking things.'

'You're right,' I say, my heart melting at his thoughtfulness. The two boys couldn't be more different and they're not related. They were barely on speaking terms when they arrived and now, behind the hard exterior, Blake is kind, thoughtful, scared of being hurt, and protecting Joe from thinking about 'what next'.

'Right. Pass me that bowl. First, the *fior di latte*. Milk, sugar and a little cornflour.'

We warm the milk.

'Never boil.' I hear Nonna's voice. 'Never let it boil. Keep stirring!'

'This is the purest form of *gelato*. Made from the milk of grass-fed cows,' I say, hearing Nonna's voice. 'A little cornflour and a pinch of salt.'

I fish out the kitchen thermometer that Joe had unpacked and put into a drawer. 'It has to reach eighty-five degrees centigrade . . .' I refer to my iPad for the technical stuff I never knew. But when it's at the right temperature, I'm back in my comfort zone.

We watch and smell.

'Now for the ice bath. We have to get it really cold' – I put ice cubes into a stainless-steel bowl – 'as quickly as we can. And then into the freezer.'

We shut the door and stare at it.

'Now what?' says Blake.

'*Gelato* with eggs,' I tell him. 'First, we need to make a custard, so to speak. We'll make a plain one first,' I say aloud, but in my head I'm talking to Nonna. 'Warm the milk, but it mustn't boil. Then whisk the egg yolks and sugar in a separate bowl.' I point to a bowl.

'I thought you said you didn't know how to make *gelato*!' Blake raises his eyebrows.

I stop what I'm doing and chuckle. 'Looks like something went in, after all. I grew up around *gelato*. Right,' I say, more to myself than to Blake. 'We heat the milk . . .'

'But it mustn't boil!' Blake repeats. We wait for foam to form around the edges of the pan.

179

'Then take it off the heat and pour it into the sugar and egg mix,' I say and watch as Blake pours it slowly in while I whisk it all together. 'Then back in the saucepan and heat it up again. Just a medium heat,' I tell him. 'And maybe add some vanilla?'

Blake nods.

The two of us watch the milk, egg yolks, sugar and vanilla as they slowly heat.

'Now the ice.' Blake is ready with it, feeding more ice around the pan in its bath. I nod to the freezer and as Blake opens the door I push it in. He shuts the door again firmly.

'That it?' Blake asks.

'Now comes the hard part.' I hear Nonna's voice. 'The churning.'

We work together, studying the iPad and the exercise book, whisking up the mixture every thirty minutes to stop ice crystals forming. Churning, churning.

Five hours later, with Scooter back for afternoon milking, we leave her and Joe washing down the parlour and make for the kitchen. I pull the *fior di latte* out of the freezer and place it on the table where we sit, opposite each other, gazing at the bowl between us. It looks like *gelato*.

I hand Blake a spoon and take one for myself.

'You first,' I say, and he doesn't need asking twice. He dives in for a spoonful and tastes. I quickly follow. I put the spoon to my lips, feeling the cold, and then into my mouth. The soft creamy *gelato* sits on my tongue, and slowly melts. Plain *gelato*, no frills. Then we get out the next, made with milk, a little sugar, eggs and vanilla and try that too. It's a soothing, comforting sensation on my tongue. I swallow.

'Well?' he asks.

'It's good, but it's not quite as I remember,' I tell him. I sit and think, letting the cool, creamy *gelato* flavour sit on my tongue, with a longer lingering taste of vanilla. What if it's me? What if my memory's off? Am I remembering something that never existed? I've dreamt of being here for so long, believing I'd step back into a simple way of life. Instead I've got sixties wallpaper, can't find a decorator who'll actually turn up, and the town I remember seems to have turned into Chelsea-on-Sea with huge four-by-fours and second-home owners taking over. Next they'll be opening a Waitrose. There are gardens with neat rows of flowers, and everyone seems to talk about sourdough and home baking. The restaurants are becoming more about foams and veloutés, instead of fish and chips and ice-cream sundaes. What happened to the seaside town I left?

I take another spoonful and so does Blake. 'It still reminds me of being a child,' I murmur.

'You're lucky,' he says. 'There's nothing I'd want to remember about being a child.'

'Sorry.'

'It's fine. If anything, this is the exact opposite, and it's making me forget.' He speaks with the hint of a smile under his dark fringe and digs in again.

I follow suit. It's good, but not quite the same as Nonna's.

'So, what happened between you and that Ed bloke?' Blake asks, out of the blue, surprising me.

'How do you know anything happened between us?'

He taps the side of his nose. 'Instinct.'

I laugh. 'Yes, he and I had a thing. Well, more than a thing. I thought he was it. My big love. I thought we were making plans to go travelling. Then he turned up here, as his uni finished for the summer with . . .' I gulp '. . . Portia in tow.'

'Portia?'

'Uh-huh. Met her at uni. He brought her down for the summer, got engaged. Treated me like the cleaner I was. Him and his friends, laughing and joking as if what he and I'd had was nothing. Just a fling, and I needed to move on.'

'Twat!'

'Language, Blake.'

'Sorry.'

'I was mortified. I felt so used. I was the talk of the town. Everyone was gossiping, or so I thought. I hated feeling that people were talking about me. "Look at the Valentino girl. Always in trouble." I felt everyone thought I was trying to split Ed and his girlfriend up, trying to steal her boyfriend. But I had no idea about her! I thought Ed and me were together! I didn't want to cause my parents any more trouble. Or be the centre of any more gossip. So, to my shame, I graffitied Ed's car, the one he loved so much. Covered it in shaving foam, wrote rude words right down the side. Packed up my belongings and moved to the city. I left.' I shake my head. 'I shouldn't have. My parents loved me for who I was. That should have been all that mattered. But I was young. Hot-headed. I didn't see it. And I didn't . . . want to let anyone else down.'

'But you made money. You bought this place, or was it your family's?'

'I bought it. Cash. When I ran off to London I got a job as a cleaner. I was used to cleaning cottages and caravans. I'd done it all my teenage years, in the holidays and weekends. It was second nature. But there was more work than I could handle and I saw how much demand there was for hardworking, reliable people. So I started to accept jobs and contract them out to other cleaners. I'd keep an eye on them, check their work and get them to redo it if it wasn't good enough. I started running my own cleaning business and . . .' I hold out my hands '. . . when I finally discovered I wanted to come home, I couldn't. I had the business to run.'

'And now?' He's intrigued.

'I'm home. But I wish I hadn't run in the first place. If I'd stayed, things could have been different.'

He looks at me as if he's about to say something more, when the back door opens. 'Hey!'

It's Griff and my stomach does a little dance. 'Just in time!' I say.

'We're making ice cream,' says Blake. '*Gelato*,' he corrects himself. His phone has been on the table all this time and he hasn't checked it once.

'Come and try it!' I say, grabbing another spoon for Griff.

He tucks in. 'Hmm,' he says. 'Like we had at the *gelateria*!' His eyes widen. 'Simple ice cream. A baby one! *Bambino*!' he says, enjoying the memory. 'This is what the babies would have. A small, simple *gelato*. A *bambino*!'

My eyes blur. 'It's not quite right yet.' I frown to distract myself from the memories swirling in my mind.

'Oh, she'll work out what's missing. When Beca wants to do something . . .' he says to Blake.

Something in me stirs. He's right. If I'm so worried about the town losing what used to be at the heart of it, I should put my money where my mouth is and do something about it. But what?

'Are we talking about the *gelato* or the town?' I ask.

He smiles. 'Both! If anyone can stop us losing our town, its identity, to second-home owners and holidaymakers, it's you, Beca Valentino!'

'Oh, I don't know . . .'

'Can we start to make different flavours now?' asks Blake.

'We can!' I enthuse.

'Well, you seem to have made the *gelato* without the need for me to be here, but I popped in anyway with these.' Griff holds up a bag. 'I was having a turnout. A few bits that don't fit me any more.' He holds his hand to his stomach, a small mound rather than washboard flat. 'Thought Blake and Joe might like to take them when they leave. If not, hang on to them for other youngsters around the farm.'

Blake peers uncertainly into the bag, pulling out a hat like Griff's. Griff takes it from him and places it on Blake's head. Blake doesn't remove it, as I'm expecting, but carries on looking through the things Griff has brought. 'I'll share all this with Joe. Thanks. But I'm keeping the hat!' He smiles, surprising me again.

'All okay?' Griff asks me quietly, as Blake continues rummaging through the bag. 'Looks like he's enjoyed his day.'

'They're staying a bit longer. The social worker just rang.'

'That's good. Isn't it? Or not?' Griff looks concerned.

'It is,' I confirm. 'Blake doesn't seem too unhappy about it.'

'He seems happy about it to me. And how's Scooter

doing?' He smiles, lines appearing in his cheeks that mark the years I've missed seeing him.

'Scooter is brilliant! She's great with the cows. And with Joe – he loves being with her.'

'Great! She's really good . . . well, now anyway.'

I cock my head.

'Oh, you weren't the only one around here to be a handful. I don't know what I ever did to deserve two feisty teenagers in my life.'

I flush. I'm not sure why – the fact I was a youthful pain in the backside or because he sees me as part of his life.

'You staying for dinner?' asks Blake. 'Oh, sorry, is that okay, Beca?'

'It's fine. You're more than welcome, Griff. We're having spaghetti.'

'Nonna's?'

I nod.

'Ah, I'd love to, mate, but I can't. I have to be somewhere. I've got a date!'

Just then Joe and Scooter come in through the back door.

'Who's got a date?' says Joe.

'Griff,' says Blake.

'Hi, Dad!' says Scooter, and kisses his cheek. They're so alike. I wonder if they know it. Suddenly I feel a pang. Did I miss out, not having children? I didn't mean to. It just never happened. After the miscarriage and Josh leaving, I wanted it more than ever. But there's only so many frogs you can kiss before you realize they're all just frogs.

'So did I hear right? Another date? You must really like her,' says Scooter, helping herself to some of the *gelato* and handing Joe a spoon too.

'I do.' Griff nods.

This must have been who he was talking about last night, when he said maybe he had found someone. Suddenly, I'm a little flustered. I was enjoying it being me and Griff, as we used to be. But that was twenty years ago! We're grown-ups now. And Griff is glowing.

'I'd love to meet her sometime,' I say.

Griff beams. 'That's a nice idea! But maybe give it a while, eh?'

Why did I say that? The last thing he needs is me crashing in on his dates. My cheeks burn. I can't just expect to move back here and pick up exactly where I left off: life has moved on for everybody.

'I'd like a date.' Joe gazes at Scooter with his big eyes and leans his chin into his hands. Scooter ignores him.

'One day, Joe,' says Griff.

'Any tips?' asks Joe, in a loud whisper.

'Well, always shower beforehand. I think girls like clean men. And use deodorant. And be yourself.'

Joe nods seriously. 'I'd like to be a superhero.' Then, 'What about flowers?'

'Flowers are nice,' says Griff.

'So is *gelato*,' says Blake, licking his spoon.

'Now, that's a good date. Who can turn down *gelato*?' Griff checks his phone. 'Right, I have to go. Save me some of that.'

'Will do!' says Blake.

And with that, he's gone.

'He seems happy,' I say to Scooter.

'Yes. He met this woman a few weeks ago. She's bought a second home down here.'

'She doesn't seem Griff's type,' I say, then wonder how I would know anything about Griff's type.

'He's into her.' Scooter helps herself to another spoonful of *gelato*.

'Well, good!' I say firmly. I may be trying to convince myself. 'Now, who's ready for spaghetti?'

'Me!' say Blake and Joe at the same time.

'You guys have fun! I'll see you for milking in the morning,' says Scooter, pulling on her helmet and taking the cash I hand her.

'Thank you so much,' I say.

'No problem. It's a lovely place to work. And, Joe, you go and shower,' she says.

'Yes, shower. Scooter? Are you sure you wouldn't like some more *gelato*?'

'Maybe another time, Joe,' she says, and he beams.

19

It's Monday, and market stalls are dotted up the main street again, clearly a regular feature for the summer. It's busier than ever.

'Right, let's choose a few flavours and see what we fancy having a go at,' I say, at the ice-cream counter in Wildes. And how we can make them better, I think. 'We've still got milk that needs using up.'

The boys point to the ice cream. The young waitress offers us cheap wafer cones or pots. We go for pots. Three scoops each. There are no wafer biscuits on offer here, or sprinkles, or thick chocolate or strawberry syrup. No knickerbocker glories, ice-cream sundaes or waffles with maple syrup and vanilla ice cream melting into the pockets.

I'm glad there's no sign of Ed. I'll have to get used to bumping into him in such a small town but not today. I double-check the café, because I really don't want to see him. A memory of him is scratching at the back of my brain, reminding me of the excitement I used to feel when I was with him. I try to push it away. That was then, and this is now. Focus on the *gelato*, Beca, I tell myself firmly. It was twenty years ago. You can't recapture that excitement. It's gone, like a lot of things around here. Life has moved on. We just have to accept it.

We sit at a table outside and watch families going about their business in the little market as others enjoy their summer holidays.

We try the ice cream and, once again, I'm disappointed. I have no idea why I thought it would be any different. There's no flavour of rum and only two raisins in the rum and raisin. It doesn't justify its name. Joe has bubblegum flavour. It's turned his lips blue but it hasn't brought a smile to them. Blake is trying the coffee, the pistachio and the chocolate. They've started to melt into an unpleasant sludge.

'What do we think?' I ask.

"S okay,' says Blake. 'But it's not like the *gelato* we made.' I experience a swell of pride that he can tell the difference.

'I don't think bubblegum is a flavour I want to try again,' says Joe, having eaten it all. He burps, taking me by surprise. Blake and I giggle.

'Come on,' I say. 'We can leave these. Let's go and see

what there is to add to our *gelato*.' I point towards the market stalls. 'See what we can come up with.'

'Hi,' says a voice behind me. This time my heart leaps and dips and my stomach does an excited dance.

We turn to see Ed Wildes, standing by our table, his newly washed blond hair falling forwards.

'Hi,' I say, as casually as I can.

Ed puts a hand on the back of Joe and Blake's chairs. 'How is everything?'

Blake lowers his head.

'Lovely, thank you,' I say, getting up and gathering my bag, ready to leave. I find myself standing face to face with Ed, wishing I couldn't see the young Eddie in his eyes, his smile.

'The ice cream is terrible,' says Joe, and I don't know whether to laugh or cringe. I do both.

'Well, not terrible . . .' I try to climb out of the hole that Joe's just dug for us.

'You said it was and no wonder people aren't stopping to buy any,' Joe says truthfully. 'Beca made *gelato*!' He beams. 'It was delicious.'

I clear my throat, which seems to have tightened.

Ed looks down at my pot of uneaten ice cream, the sludge Blake has left in his. 'Well, we're more of a restaurant, these days. People come for lunch, afternoon tea. Share a glass or two of wine. Would you like to see the wine list, Beca? Our customers have discerning palates when it comes to their lunchtime tipple.'

Joe pulls a face, 'Yuk,' and Blake gives a barely suppressed snort.

'No, really. We have to be going,' I say, trying to hold down the bubble of a giggle rising up in me before I explode, too.

'So, you up for meeting sometime, like I suggested? I could show you the wine list then. Just to . . . well, for old times' sake.'

'Oh, I don't think . . .' My head, heart and stomach are squabbling. Yes! No! Don't be ridiculous. This is Eddie! People change! For old times' sake! Never!

'Like a date?' asks Joe, interested. My head, heart and stomach stop bickering and pay attention.

'No, definitely not.' I squash any thoughts in that direction.

'Griff's got a date,' Joe carries on. 'I'd like a date. With Scooter,' he says, dreamy-eyed. Oh, no, I think. I really need to manage his expectations there.

'When shall we say?' says Ed.

'Sorry, what?' My attention is back with him. 'No, I can't.'

'There's Griff!' says Blake, seeing him at his stall, selling seafood and paintings.

But Griff hasn't heard him. He has his arm around the waist of a very attractive woman. They're nose to nose, talking quietly to each other.

'That must be his date,' says Joe.

'Griff!' Blake calls, and I go to stop him. We can't crash in on his private life.

Griff turns and spots us. 'Hey, guys!' he calls.

The boys are on their feet, clearly intent on joining him. Griff and his date let each other go and smile at them. I'm so grateful to him for making the boys welcome.

'Boys, wait!' I remember Griff saying maybe we could meet her but not quite yet. He needs some space. But as she's at the market with him, it must be fine to say hello. I just don't want him to think I'm checking her out. Which I'm absolutely not. At all. I have enough on my plate, making my own life here.

'Beca, come on. It would be good for us to talk.' Ed breaks into my thoughts.

Joe and Blake turn back to look at him, then me.

'Sorry, what?'

'What about tomorrow?'

'For what?' I say, confused, still thinking about Griff and whether he'll want us going over to him.

'For the date!' Joe says, in a loud whisper.

I look at Griff, who raises an eyebrow.

'Tomorrow is fine,' says Joe, and I wish he hadn't. 'We don't have to leave for another week.'

Ed's clearly a little taken aback. 'Er, okay, great. Why not come here after we close at five? I'll show you the wine list and you can give me some tips on my ice cream.'

193

'We can certainly do that!' says Joe. This time Blake and I both laugh.

We leave the bowls of melting ice cream, which seem to be attracting the attention of a nearby seagull, white and grey, his bright yellow eyes on the molten mess we've left behind.

'Hey, guys, how are you doing?' Griff asks, as we cross to the other side of the road. Blake's wearing the hat he gave him, despite the July sunshine.

Blake turns to Griff's companion. 'Hi, I'm Blake, and this is Joe,' he says to the woman, smartly dressed in a striped long-sleeved top, knee-length denims and leather boating shoes. She smiles at him, a friendly smile. And I'm astonished. Not by Griff or his partner, but by Blake, who comes out of his shell when he's around Griff.

'Hi,' says Joe, straightening up from greeting Cariad, stroking her and giving her tummy tickles where she's basking under the table. Blake may be right. It would be good to get a dog.

'I'm Annabelle,' she says.

Griff looks at me. 'Of course, where are my manners? Annabelle, this is Beca.'

'Ah, the Beca I've been hearing about.' She smiles again.

'All good, I hope!' I'm praying the old gossip that made me leave in the first place isn't about to come back and bite me on the bum. Beca the boyfriend

194

thief! The floozy! The mistress! I didn't know! How could I?

I cannot let Griff's new partner think there is anything more than friendship between us. I'm not a threat in any way. I ran away the last time I was branded the local tart, when Ed arrived with Portia. I'd felt like the bit on the side, trying to steal her man off her. But I'd had no idea he and Portia had been together throughout uni. Griff's right: I need to meet more people, not just rely on him being there for me.

'Well,' I'm determined to show I have plenty more friends than Griff, 'nice to meet you, Annabelle.' They still have an arm around each other's waist, and I'm presuming her being here this morning means she spent last night at Griff's. Why am I even thinking about that? It's none of my business. I hate gossip!

'How was your date?' Joe asks Griff, in a loud stage-whisper.

'Oh, Joe, maybe you shouldn't . . .' I try to stop him. But Griff's my friend – used to be my best friend and maybe still is. Why wouldn't I be interested?

'Very good. Thank you!' Griff smiles, as does Annabelle.

'You like her,' Joe says, with the back of his hand to his mouth.

'I do!' Griff says, holding the back of his hand to his mouth, too, and my heart twists a little. I'm not sure if it's because Griff seems so happy or because he's looking at Joe with such kindness.

'We're going to make some more *gelato*,' says Joe.

'More?' Griff laughs.

'We are!' I start to turn away. 'And we need to get going,' I tell the boys.

'Come and try it later,' Joe says. 'It'll be like another date!'

Griff blushes. 'I'd love to, Joe. You'll need a bigger freezer at this rate, Beca.'

'I have to get back to London. I just popped in to say goodbye,' Annabelle says to Griff, 'but another time would be lovely.'

'Oh, we won't be here another time,' says Joe. 'We're just staying while they find us new foster accommodation.' And suddenly no one knows what to say. Annabelle seems worried that she's put her foot in it.

'Come on,' I say. 'Let's find some ingredients to put in the *gelato*.' I'm trying to distract them, and Griff gives me a small smile, as if he's letting me know I'm doing okay at this. I say we'll see him later.

'Oh, and Beca has a date,' Joe tells Griff.

'Really?' Griff's eyebrows shoot up. 'That's fast work.'

'It's not really a date, just catching up.'

'It is a date. They're going to have wine as well as ice cream. So that's definitely a date.'

I stare at Joe, stunned, not sure what to say next. I look at Griff and Annabelle, happy together. I can't hang around Griff all the time. We may be friends, but he's in a relationship and I really don't want to be the third wheel. 'Yes, you're right, Joe. It's a date. Tomorrow night. With Ed.'

Joe nods and folds his arms, with a satisfied smile.

'Ed, as in Eddie? Ed Wildes?' says Griff. 'Your ex. The one who—'

'Yes.' I cut him off. My throat tightens and my cheeks flush. 'We're going to clear the air. Have a drink. Just . . .' I swallow '. . . put the past to rest. Like grown-ups.'

Griff takes a moment or two to process the information. 'Well, brilliant,' he says, evidently surprised. 'Hope it's a good one.' He's staring at me as if I've gone mad. And maybe I have. I didn't mean to agree to it. It was Joe. I look back at the café, to where Ed is talking to customers on the terrace, being his charming self. I remember that. Suddenly he catches my eye. My cheeks burn again. Maybe laying the ghost to rest with Ed will help me settle here. It's just a drink. And I can tell him he needs to sell better ice cream.

'Oh, yes, nothing like finding someone you just click with after a time in the wilderness.' Annabelle draws my attention away from Ed and back to her and Griff. 'The right man often turns up when you least expect it, and in the most unlikely places.'

'Oh, it's not like that. We're old friends.' I'm trying to make the words more palatable to myself. 'Me and

Ed – Eddie, that is.' Why am I flustered? It's true. We're old acquaintances. Just like Griff and I are old friends. It's okay.

Annabelle smiles, and I wish I could say I don't like her. But I do. I'm pleased for them. Maybe I shouldn't be so quick to put my dating life on hold after a time in the wilderness. Maybe she's right. Maybe there is still hope for me to find someone when I least expect it.

'Here, take these for dinner later.' Griff hands me two large crabs.

'Oh, lovely.' I pull out my purse.

'No, they're a present. For all of you.'

'So, what do we fancy putting in our ice cream?' I ask the boys, having thanked Griff, said goodbye to Annabelle and, despite my reservations, waved to Ed, just so Annabelle can be sure that Griff spending time at the house tasting *gelato* is nothing more than that. We wander around the green-and-white-covered stalls.

'What's that?' Blake asks, pointing to bags at a honey stall.

'Honeycomb! Great idea!' I say.

'What is it?'

'You've never had honeycomb?' I say, and instantly regret it. I'm sure there are many treats these boys have missed out on over the years. 'Let's get some.' I fish out my purse and point to a bag.

'Really? Honeycomb could be a flavour?' he asks.

'Let's take some honey too,' I tell the seller. 'We'll see which one works.'

'This comes from my bees up on the mountain,' she says. I gaze up at the mountains behind the town, where Griff and I used to walk on days with nothing else planned. We'd take a picnic and amble up the pathways, looking out for the wild ponies. Griff always swore he'd catch one, train it and keep it. But he never could.

'Have you been there long?' I ask.

'About twenty years, I love it,' she says, handing us the honey and the honeycomb. I can see why.

We walk on through the stalls, around people stopping to chat in the sunshine, wearing straw hats and boating shoes, much like Annabelle's, and holding cockapoos on leads.

'What's that?' Blake points.

'Fudge,' I tell him.

'Could that be a flavour?'

'Let's try it.' He's on a roll. We stop, taste, then buy the creamy fudge, again made locally.

I can feel the excitement as we add to our shopping. 'Salt!' I point at a stall.

'We're buying ingredients for *gelato*,' Joe tells the seller.

'Yeah, Beca wants to put salt in it!' Blake grimaces.

'Well, it's excellent salt. From the seals' bay,' he says, from beneath the brim of a battered straw hat, holding up a little dish for us to try.

'Did you collect it?' I ask.

He nods.

'You'll want to put Griff's crab in the *gelato* next,' Blake says drily and Joe pulls his disgusted face, making us all laugh.

'Salted caramel,' I correct him happily.

'Chocolate!' Joe says.

'With the crab?' Blake carries on joking, but Joe is pointing at the stall with locally made chocolate from a factory run by a young woman in colourful patchwork clothing and odd shoes.

We walk over to the stall and accept the offer to taste.

It's some time before Joe is happy with our choice, but once we've agreed, we head back to the farmhouse to whip up more *gelato*.

20

'I feel sick,' says Joe, chocolate *gelato* around his mouth. He's making no attempt to wipe it off.

'I can't eat any more either,' says Blake, leaning back in his chair and holding his flat stomach.

I stare at the pots of *gelato*, hands on hips.

'It's still not quite the same,' I say, practically to myself. 'I wonder what I'm missing.' I look at all the old ice-cream-seller magazines on the table from the box of my grandparents' belongings, with pictures of men in boaters pushing carts and bicycles on the front cover. If I go through them all again, like I did last night, I might find the answer. But it's getting late.

Joe burps. 'I liked it as it was,' he says.

'Me too,' says Blake.

'It was good.' I look at their empty bowls. 'But I wanted it to be the same as Nonna's.' I'm re-reading her exercise book but there's nothing in it. No secret ingredient. Nothing I haven't put in already. A spoonful of this and two of that. On the back page there's a recipe for rum and raisin. It states exactly what I put in. What am I missing?

'Come on, let's sleep on it,' I say, and we put the lids on all of the pots and squeeze them into the freezer, which is almost full. 'Griff's right. I'm going to have to get a bigger freezer.' Then, not for the first time, I remember I may not be doing this again, once the boys leave. It was something to keep them entertained and use up the milk, rather than pouring it away. But, my goodness, it was fun.

Joe is twisting the old wooden spoon from the box of my grandparents' belongings in his hand and goes up to bed using it as a magic wand to battle dragons and wizards, making me smile.

'Goodnight, Blake,' I hear Joe say.

There's a short pause before Blake replies, ''Night, Joe.' My heart swells.

I finish clearing up and make my own way up to bed. I peer in through the slightly open doors – the boys have obviously been talking but now they're fast asleep.

The following morning I wake with the birds chattering and the sun streaming in through the windows. There's no need for the alarm. I throw back my covers and look out to see Scooter heading along the track, bang on time, to milk the cows. I hear Joe next door, getting up to go and help, no doubt.

I stare out to sea. I've tossed and turned all night trying to work out what's missing from the *gelato*, the *fior di latte*. The taste is still on my tongue, soft, sweet, milky, but not quite right.

The sea looks so inviting. Why not? I grab my swimming costume. I may see some of the Mermaids at the swimming-hole. Might be just what I need.

I grab my bag with a towel and head down the track, waving to Scooter and Joe and motioning that I'm going for a swim.

I love the smell of early-summer mornings, the scent of the fresh dew on the grass that I can almost hear groaning as it grows so fast.

I stop at the gate and peer out. Early-morning boats are sailing past as if there wasn't a care in the world. The sky is a glorious baby blue and the water sparkles as if handfuls of crystals have been scattered on its surface. I take a deep restorative breath of fresh sea air and walk down to the cove, slipping off my flip-flops to feel the sand on the steps beneath my feet and between my toes.

I'm halfway down when I see that someone has beaten me to it. They're swimming.

I hurry the rest of the way down the steps, realizing I'm not twenty any more, my knee twinging on each step.

'Good morning!' I smile.

'Hey! *Bore da!* Morning!' Griff turns and stands up in the sea, just revealing his chest and shoulders, pushing his dark hair back and running his hands over his face, the bracelets on his wrist visible. He always used to wear those friendship bracelets, as we used to call them. Friends for ever, and that's how it feels, despite the time apart.

'You coming in?' he asks.

'Thought I would,' I say, dropping my towel onto a rock and slowly stepping into the water. It's cold but gloriously refreshing.

And then suddenly, feeling a little self-conscious, I do as the sea swimmers told me: 'Just dive in.' I surge forward with spray splashing, and take the plunge, catching my breath before I enjoy the sensation of cold water on my warm skin, the salt and the minerals washing away my sleepless hot night.

'How's things?' Griff says, as I come up for air. 'How are the boys?'

'Fine. Joe's with Scooter, doing the cows. She's great.'

'She's a good kid, but,' he shakes his head, 'as I say, it hasn't always been easy.'

That still surprises me. 'Really?'

'Really,' he confirms. 'She was angry.' The memory shadows his face. Then, like a passing cloud, it moves on, letting the sun in. 'Reminded me a lot of a friend I once had.'

'Have!' I correct him, and we soak up the ease of each other's company.

'She didn't like it that Nia and I weren't together. Always trying to fix us up. Wanted that textbook happy family. But we were happy as we were. It wouldn't have worked any other way,' he says. 'And you're doing a great job with the boys. You should be proud of yourself.'

'I'm just so scared of getting it wrong.'

'Kids don't come with handbooks. They're all different,' he says, but I don't really hear him. I still feel out of my depth, as I tread water over the deepest part of the swimming-hole, by the rocks we used to throw ourselves off as youngsters.

We swim in silence, enjoying the peace of the cove, with only the seagulls and two buzzards, calling to their young, for company.

On the shore, we pick up our towels. I use mine to rub my face and then, as I pull it away, I see movement and realize a pod of dolphins is travelling through the undulating water further out at sea. Griff follows my gaze. It's sheer joy, and the pleasure never goes away no matter how many times you see it.

'So, you're going to meet up with Ed?' he asks, breaking the moment as the pod passes on its way. 'See if you can clear the air? A date?'

'It's not that.' I'm feeling . . . I'm not sure how I'm feeling. 'It's just a drink to put the past behind us and, well, move on.'

205

'Joe seems to think it's a date.' He gives a teasing laugh.

I jab him with my elbow and he grabs his side, pretending it hurt.

'Stop it!' I flick my towel at him, and he retaliates.

'So, tonight's the night. The big date with Ed!' he carries on teasing.

'I'm just going over to—'

'Talk things over? A little wine? See if the old spark is still there?'

I nudge him again, feeling like a teenager, laughing and play-fighting. I think of Joe last night, going off to bed carefree and happy, zapping dragons and wizards with the wooden spoon . . . and suddenly I remember.

I remember what Nonna always used to say: 'It's not about what you put into life, but about how much you put in! That's the secret to a successful recipe.'

And then it hits me, like Griff flicking me with his towel and this time catching me.

'Ow! That's it!' I say.

'Is it?' He looks confused but is still smiling. 'Because I don't know about you, but I've got lobster pots to check.'

'It's not what's in the recipe . . . it's how much! Joe, you're a genius!'

'Joe?'

Griff drops the towel.

The Mermaids are arriving at the beach.

'Hey, you beat us to it!'

'You staying?' Leah asks.

'No, I've got to go! I'll be back later!' I say, gathering up my clothes.

'Beca?' Griff calls, as I start to make my way up the shingle to the steps.

'The spoon! Nonna's spoon! That's what was missing!'

'What?' he calls.

'In her recipes, she lists ingredients but I couldn't get it right. It's the spoon, the measurements. She always used that spoon. The spoon that came from Italy, she told me. Her grandmother's spoon! A pint of milk and a spoonful of sugar. That spoon!'

I look back at him and grin. 'I have to go! I have to get the spoon! There's *gelato* to make!' I'm slipping on my flip-flops and running up the steps.

'Take it easy.' Griff laughs. 'And enjoy your date!'

'It's not a date!' I shout back, as I tear up the weather-worn wooden steps.

'Joe!' I call, as I catapult into the cool of the kitchen on the terracotta-tiled floor, out of breath and salty from the early-morning swim.

Joe sits up straight in surprise. 'Have I done something wrong?' he asks, looking up from his bowl of Coco Pops, surrounded by little white splashes, with the small urn of milk on the table. 'I was going to put the milk straight back in the fridge, like you showed me. And I know I've made a mess but—'

'No, Joe, it's fine. You haven't done anything wrong, but I do need you to find that spoon for me, the wooden one you had last night . . .'

He sits and thinks. I hold my breath.

'You still have the spoon, don't you?' I ask, and take a breath.

'Spoon?' he says, and looks at me from behind his glasses.

'Yes. The wooden spoon with the deep bowl. You were playing dragons and wizards, and you zapped Blake with it,' I say.

'Hmm.' He puts a finger to his lips.

'You remember? You took it upstairs. Did you do anything else with it? Take it milking? It's very important I find it.'

'The one from the box. Your nana's spoon.'

'Yes, Nonna's. That's the one.'

He doesn't reply.

'Is it upstairs? Maybe in the cowshed? Or in the field?'

I can feel my high spirits deflating, like a burst balloon. He's lost the spoon. Oh, well, it was just an idea. Just a thought, a memory I wanted to hold on to.

'Oh, the spoon!'

'Yes, the spoon!'

'You mean a teaspoon?'

I hold my head in my hands. It's gone. I should have read it all more carefully, should have thought. She always used that particular spoon. Her grandmother's. It was the measure of sugar to milk.

I pull my hands from my face. Never mind. I don't know why I was so determined to get it right.

Joe is beaming. 'You mean this one?' He pulls out Nonna's spoon from behind him and holds it up. 'Of course I've got it! Got you!' and he bursts into peals of side-splitting laughter. Suddenly I'm laughing too, until tears are rolling down my face.

'I tricked you!' he says, and points at me. I don't know when I've laughed more.

'What's all the noise?' says Blake, in the doorway, his hair on end.

'I've got the spoon!' Joe and I laugh more and, without knowing why, Blake joins in, and it feels so good.

'Come on.' I sniff, as the laughter settles, my sides aching. 'We've got *gelato* to make.'

'More?' asks Blake.

'Much more.' I beam.

'With the spoon!' Joe holds it up, and for no reason we're all laughing again and I can't remember when life felt so good. Maybe Griff was right. Maybe I can do this.

21

'Whoa! What's going on in here?'

Griff appears at the back door, barely knocking. Or if he did I didn't hear it. And I love that the earlier awkwardness of my return hasn't stopped us being the friends we used to be.

'Griff!' says Blake.

'We've made more *gel-gel-gel* . . .' says Joe, waving the spoon excitedly and stuttering.

'*Gelato*,' Blake and I join in, with huge excitement.

'I can see!' He waves at the tubs on the table, the dribbles of honey, the crumbs of honeycomb, then notices the open bottle of rum.

'It's for the *gelato*,' I say quickly, 'for soaking the raisins, like Nonna did.' And now that we've found the wooden spoon, it tastes just like Nonna's, just like I remember. The measurements are right. I look at the bottle and the mess and start cleaning up, still worried that people might judge me while I'm in charge of two children. And that's what they seem to be today. Children. And that's good.

'No one's judging,' says Griff, as if reading my mind, and I relax. 'In fact, I could do with one myself!' And I pour him some rum.

'Can I have some?' says Joe.

'Not rum, but you can have Coke,' I tell him, and he seems happy with that. 'Or what about dandelion and burdock?' I produce a bottle I bought at the village shop for their arrival and have yet to offer them.

'Oh, wow!' says Griff. 'I haven't had it in years! We used to drink it all the time.'

'That and cream soda,' I say. 'I remembered when I saw it in the shop. Want to try some?'

The boys nod. Blake shrugs, clearly thinking rum might be a better idea.

'Here.' I hand them a glass each.

'Weird,' says Joe, and shakes his body. 'But more-ish!' Making us all laugh. Blake sips his and says nothing. Griff holds out another glass, and I put a splash into it.

'Ah . . . summer!' he says. 'Oh, I forgot. I met the postman coming in.' He holds out a letter.

'Thanks,' I say, stretching out my hand to take it.

'Actually, it's for Blake,' he says.

Blake's face darkens, like a stray cloud floating across

the sky, and I decide not to say anything. He takes the envelope and puts it beside him. I can't help but be intrigued. Who knows he's here? And why would they be sending him a letter?

'You know what?' Blake says.

'What?' I swing round to him, thinking he's going to say something about the letter.

He bites his lower lip. 'I think this could be a really good ice-cream flavour,' he says, tipping back on his chair. I look at him. We all do.

'He's right!' says Griff, taking another sip.

I help myself to a glass. 'It could be brilliant,' I say.

'And cream soda,' Griff adds.

'Memories of summers in Sŵn y Môr,' I say.

'Let's do it!'

We start another batch. 'That's practically all the milk used up,' I say later, brushing my hands down my apron.

Scooter joins us in the kitchen, and I barely notice Joe go out with her for afternoon milking as Blake and I start on more *gelato*.

'Hey, Scooter, want some *gelato*?' Joe calls, returning to the kitchen after milking. Behind her, through the window, the cows are grazing as the sun dips over the sea and the neighbouring headland.

'I'm fine, thank you, Joe. You were a great help today, by the way. He could make a great farmer,' Scooter says to me, and Joe physically blooms, then serves himself more *gelato*.

'Whoa! Look at all this ice cream!' says Scooter, and joins us in the kitchen.

'*Gelato*,' we say together, and laugh.

'You'll have to sell it at this rate,' she adds.

'Oh, no, it's just a bit of fun,' I say.

'You'd make more money selling this than the milk,' says Scooter, seriously, helping herself to a spoon.

I look at her.

'Not that hard. We're not getting a great price for the milk, are we?'

I move to the kitchen table, grab an envelope and write down the figure. 'And how much did the *gelato* ingredients cost?' I wonder aloud. Joe has memorized the prices from the market. I write them down. 'But what could we sell it for?' I look at the figures.

'Wildes' ice cream is sold mostly by the scoop.'

Joe's right.

'But would anyone really pay that for ours?' I ask.

'It's Valentino's *gelato*, isn't it?' says Scooter, licking her spoon. 'Hmm, that's amazing. What flavour is it? Dad says people came from miles for it.'

'That's salted caramel,' says Blake.

'They did,' Griff says.

'They did,' I echo thoughtfully.

'Well,' says Scooter, 'there's only one way to find out.' Could she be right? Just for a bit of fun. Not a

Jo Thomas

business, because I'm not going back into business, but just to see if people do remember. A pop-up! Maybe at the end of the drive.

The letter is still sitting on the table where Blake left it.

'Hey, Blake!' she says. 'Who's writing to you?'

Griff and I glance at each other, thinking about Blake now, not *gelato*, worried that this could set something off.

'Ah, no one,' he says. He picks up the envelope, walks over to the bin and tosses it in.

'It must be someone,' Scooter says, and I'm on tenterhooks but he just goes back to stirring another batch of ice cream.

Scooter pulls the letter out of the bin.

'It's a card. Open it,' she says, holding it out to him, and the words are on the tip of my tongue to say I think we should leave it. Although I'm as curious as Scooter is.

'Nah!' He shakes his head. 'You open it.'

'Okay,' says Scooter. She looks at me and Griff. Then she rips open the envelope. 'It's a birthday card!' she says, and opens it. Blake doesn't look up. 'Who's Mo? They've sent you a card.'

Finally he meets Scooter's eyes. 'Mo, the social worker,' he says flatly. 'When you're one of us, you don't get cards from people you hope will remember.'

And my heart tears right down the middle.

214

I look at Griff, who's wide-eyed.

How did I not know? I should have spotted it in Mo's notes about Blake. I've been too busy just getting through the days. And I say the first thing that comes into my mind. 'We can do better than that! Let's have a picnic! With *gelato*! On the beach!'

'Yes!' says Joe, doing a little fist pump into his side.

'And a barbecue!' says Griff.

'If you're sure . . . I mean, do you have to be any-where?' I ask.

'No, it's fine. Annabelle's back from London any time now. I'll invite her along.'

'Good idea! The more the merrier.'

'And I'll invite Mum,' says Scooter, pulling out her phone.

'Great,' says Griff, texting. 'And I'll check the lobster pots. Who wants to help me?'

'Lobsters?' Joe's eyes are wide.

'Yes, we can have lobster rolls, on the beach,' says Griff.

'I've got some burgers,' I say.

'Surf and turf! What could be better?' Griff beams.

And I couldn't feel more grateful or happier.

'Okay, let's make salads, get the cold box out and take some *gelato* down to the beach.'

We all jump into action, Blake on *gelato*, me on salads. Scooter organizes drinks to take and Joe sits at the table. Griff goes ahead to check the lobster pots, with Joe telling him he'd like to come but he has some 'important business to do first'.

'Right! Is everyone ready?' I scan the food, the drinks and the box of *gelato*. We have enough to feed an army.

Blake looks happy.

'Come on, birthday boy!' I say, determined he'll leave here with a happy birthday memory at least.

We head to the back door.

'Um, Blake?' says Joe.

Blake turns to him.

'I made you a card,' he says, and holds it out, drawn with the coloured pencils. It's a picture of all of us, on the beach, me, Griff, Scooter, with a little heart on her, Blake and Joe. My heart breaks all over again in the knowledge that this will soon be a memory.

'Thanks, Joe. It means a lot,' Blake says. I see a tear at the corner of his eye. He brushes it away and I pretend not to have noticed. I think I got that right.

22

When we reach the cove with the cold box and the bags, Griff already has a fire going. His boat is moored a little way out on the estuary that leads back to the harbour and the town. His trouser legs are rolled up and he's barefoot on the sand and shingle.

The Mermaids are in the water. 'Happy birthday, Blake!' They wave and he blushes, smiling. The seagulls squawk overhead, the waves roll back and forward from the shore beyond the cove, and the sun is still warm. It's like stepping into a happy memory while making a new one.

On the beach Griff has created a circle of stones, and in the middle, the fire is burning brightly to match the orange ball in the sky as it starts to set.

'Give us a hand, Scooter, lads,' he says, and jogs to the edge of the cove where there's driftwood, lots of it from the storm still, a couple of big branches. Between them, they lift and carry them to the fire, placing them around it like benches.

'I've left the *gelato* in the boathouse,' says Blake, and I nod, shielding my eyes from the sun. 'I put plenty of ice packs in the cold box.'

'We'll wait for the fire to die down before we cook anything,' Griff tells Blake, who is standing beside him, almost imitating his stance.

'Hey,' Griff says, seeing Nia and Annabelle coming over the hill of the coast path, carrying bags with clinking bottles, and folding chairs.

'Happy birthday, Blake,' says Annabelle, and hands him a cactus.

'Cool!' he says, his eyes lighting up. 'Thanks!'

'And from me, *Penblwydd Hapus*,' says Nia, giving him a bar of chocolate from the man in the market.

'I didn't have a chance to get you anything,' says Griff.

'Nor me,' I say.

'You two did this. Thank you!' says Blake, beaming.

'So, how old are you today?' asks Griff, and I realize I'm not sure.

'Fifteen,' he says.

'How about a shandy? Would that be all right, Bex?' Griff asks.

'I'm sure a shandy would be fine,' I say and, out of the corner of my eye, I see Joe stripped off to his boxers, heading to the sea.

'Joe, what are you doing?' I accept a plastic beaker of rosé from Nia.

'Going swimming!' Joe shouts over his shoulder. He carries on into the water, striking his superhero pose once more. The Mermaids call him on: 'Go for it!' And he does, plunging in, then splashing, coughing, choking. I thrust my drink at Blake.

'Joe!'

'It's okay, we've got him!' says Mair.

I'm at the edge of the water. 'Joe, I thought you said you could swim.'

'I didn't say I could swim, I said I was going swimming. But I don't know how.'

'Here, I'll teach you,' says Leah. She soon has him lying flat in the water.

Blake hands me back my drink. 'Swimming lessons aren't high on the list of priorities where we come from,' he says. It's a painful reminder that this is just a visit, and soon they'll be going back to where they've come from, or a new children's home.

'Come on, let's get some food,' I say, and start to lay out the food on one of the rocks at the edge of the cove.

There's a bowl of sweet cherry tomatoes, a rice salad with crunchy peppers and French dressing that Nia has brought. Annabelle bought sourdough rolls from the baker in the town, just as he was closing for the day. I've made a green salad and coleslaw, with sliced cabbage, tangy onion, raisins and grated carrot in mayonnaise. There's Heinz ketchup for Joe, and big bowls of ready salted crisps.

The women start to leave the water as the sun is setting.

'Thank you for the lesson,' says Joe, shivering. I grab a towel from my bag and wrap it around his shoulders, noticing a scar, a burn, on his chest. A mark from the past. I rub him to warm him up as my dad did for me when I got out of the sea.

'You'll be ready for the regatta at this rate,' says Griff. I look at him, and give a tiny shake of the head.

'What's a re-re-regatta?' says Joe, teeth chattering.

'It's a day of events at the harbour, sailing races, rowing and swimming too,' says one of the swimmers. 'And sandcastle competitions.'

'I'd love to make a sandcastle,' says Joe.

'Lots of food stalls,' says another. 'Hot dogs, pasta, pizza.'

'I'd like that,' says Joe. 'I'd like to win something at the regatta.' And I'm back on shifting sand, not knowing what to say.

'When is it?' he asks.

'End of the summer,' says Tilda.

'Oh.' Joe is downcast.

'What's up?' says his swimming teacher, Leah.

'We won't be here then,' says Blake, quickly and bluntly, and the mood darkens around the circle.

'Maybe not, but there's the crabbing competition soon,' Griff says, saving the situation. 'Maybe you'll still be here then.'

Blake and Joe look at me. I nod and they beam, and the roller-coaster is taking my spirits up again.

'And the good thing is, me and Beca know all the good places.' Griff grins.

'Go, Team Tŷ Mawr!' says Scooter, shaking her fist in the air, bracelets jangling.

'Now come on, it's Blake's birthday. Have a drink and something to eat,' I say to the women. I'm nearly back in my comfort zone.

'Will there be cake?' asks Leah.

'Better,' says Joe, with a beam. 'Ice cream! Home-made! I mean *gelato*! Beca's family used to own the café in the town, before it was Wildes. Did you know that? Her *gelato* is way better than what they sell now. Would you like some?' Joe asks.

'Have you got enough?'

'Loads!' says Blake, and sets off to get it from the cold box in the boathouse. 'Is that okay, Beca?'

'Of course! Share it round, the more the merrier,' I say.

'What if they don't like it?' Blake is nervous.

'We'll feed it to the seagulls!' I say. 'Let's have the barbecue first, with *gelato* for pudding.'

Everyone finds a rock or a place on the driftwood benches to sit as Griff starts to serve up a tray of burgers and lobster. Paper plates are handed round along with all the forks I could find in the kitchen. And there in the setting sun, with new friends in towelling dressing-gowns and wet hair, Nia, Scooter, Griff, Annabelle, Blake and Joe, I feel the happiest I've felt in a long time. I lift a piece of lobster dripping melting butter to my mouth and bite. I close my eyes as I taste the sweet flaking white meat, while the melted butter rolls down the inside of my wrist. Eyes open now, I have to lick it off. I see Griff smiling at me and my stomach flips in a happy dance.

'Thank you,' I mouth to him, and he nods.

'*Gelato!*' calls Joe, as Blake brings the cold box down from the boathouse.

'This one is Joe's chocolate dream date,' Blake says, scooping out the *gelato* and putting it into jam jars I found in a box and washed, while Joe gazes up at Scooter.

'And this one is Blake's honey and honeycomb from the hills.' I point to them behind us.

'And the last is Sŵn y Môr's salted caramel,' Blake says, with a flourish. He's a far cry from the sullen boy who arrived here, I think.

There's silence as we watch the group hold their jam jars and dip in with teaspoons Joe has handed round. I grab Blake's hand and squeeze it tightly. Some shut their eyes, tilting their faces to the setting sun. Others keep the spoon in their mouths, savouring the moment. There is the occasional grunt of satisfaction.

'Are they okay?' asks Joe.

'I think they like it,' I whisper.

'I love it!' says Leah, holding up her spoon like a flaming torch.

'I think I've died and gone to Heaven!'

'This is what this place should taste like – the sea, the mountains.'

'And chocolate!'

'And the milk one . . . so simple but bliss!'

'You really have to sell it,' says Leah.

'Oh, no,' I reply. 'We just . . . we had too much milk and wanted to do something with it.'

'Honestly, it's so good. You have to sell it.'

Blake looks at me.

Scooter raises her eyebrows in a way that says, 'I told you so.'

'Do you think?' I ask tentatively.

'I don't think, I know. It's wonderful,' Leah says, and the others agree.

They finish their jars and have seconds, trying all the flavours and agreeing that ours is the best *gelato* they've ever tasted. I could burst with happiness. It's like my grandparents and parents are with me, enjoying the moment, surrounded by happy faces, just as they always were at the heart of Sŵn y Môr. I'm really proud of everything we've done here this evening.

The day is cooling. We sit and gaze into the fire, the glowing embers, as the Mermaids gather their belongings, wish Blake the happiest of birthdays, which he agrees it has been, and make their way home before it gets too dark to walk along the coast path.

Griff and Annabelle are sitting side by side on a driftwood log, smiling at each other, hands touching, she brushing crumbs from his lips. I catch Nia glancing at them every now and again. It must be hard when a new person comes into your child's life and you have no say in it, however old the child is.

'He looks happy,' I say, sitting next to her.

'For now,' she says, and I cock my head, surprised by her answer.

'Don't get me wrong, I hope it lasts. It's just they don't seem to. But this one looks to be going well so far,' she says, with a smile that doesn't quite make it to her eyes. 'The *gelato* was amazing!' she says.

'Oh, wow! Thank you!'

'My childhood,' she says, and tops up my glass with prosecco.

I'm blushing with pride. 'Well, it's my grandparents' recipe, I just . . .'

'It's amazing. They're right, you should be selling this. You should bring it to the market maybe.'

'Oh, yes!' says Joe, as if he's seeing the start of his career as a businessman.

'I'm not sure Ed Wildes would like that.'

'Well, he should make better ice cream,' says Joe, blunter than usual.

And something in me seems to click. Joe's not wrong. Good *gelato* was always at the heart of this town. Ed should make better ice cream. And if he won't, maybe someone else should.

Griff raises an eyebrow as if he knows exactly what I'm thinking.

'Valentino's has always been here,' he says.

I try to stop my thoughts going down that road but they collide in that direction anyway. I didn't come here to make *gelato*. I came here to farm and to foster. Griff is still looking at me, as if he's laying down a challenge, a gauntlet thrown in front of me.

'Who better to bring *gelato* back to the town than a Valentino?'

Blake and Joe's eyes are on me.

'We've lost enough of our local businesses and houses,' says Griff, flapping a hand in the direction of the town, where almost every house is a holiday home. 'Maybe it's time we took something back.'

Scooter cheers.

'It was just a one-off. I'm not looking at going into business. Like I'm not looking for the right man any more.'

And they laugh.

'Oh, my God!' I squawk. 'Ed!'

'Ed Wildes?' asks Griff.

'I was supposed to be meeting him.'

'Your date!' says Joe, and I blush.

'It wasn't a date,' I say, brushing off my embarrassment.

'It's okay to date someone while you're looking after youngsters,' Griff says quietly. 'You might actually have fun.' He winks at me and smiles, like only Griff can, making me feel better about life.

Maybe fun would be good.

'Like you did making the *gelato*,' he adds.

That night, 'What if . . .' goes round and round in my mind. And I'm not sure if it's dating Ed I'm thinking about or *gelato*.

23

'I'm so sorry. I . . . It was Blake's birthday. I completely forgot what we'd arranged,' I say the next day, as Ed is closing.

'No worries,' he says, and smiles. Eddie's smile. 'Join me now. Have a glass of wine,' he says, putting the closed sign on the door to the disappointment of a family of four with their wet Labrador, straight from the sea.

He directs me to a table and two chairs in the window and pulls one out for me. I hesitate but, frankly, what harm can it do? It might be fun. I should remember to have fun. The boys are back at the farmhouse helping Scooter clean up the yard. Just a quick drink, I tell myself.

I sit down.

He joins me with two glasses of chilled white wine. 'Still drinking white?' he asks.

I'm impressed he remembered. Although back then I probably drank anything that was on offer or cheap. I don't tell him I'm more of a red wine drinker these days. Lots has changed over the years. I sip the wine. And this definitely isn't cheap.

'So, how are you finding being here?' he asks.

'Being back, you mean?'

'Yes.'

'Good,' I say.

He twists the stem of his glass and I sip my wine. Definitely not cheap.

'So, you got Tŷ Mawr,' he says. 'You always loved that house.'

He remembers that too.

'Always said that one day you'd buy it.'

I smile. 'And I did!'

'It's a big old house, though. You going to do some-thing with it? B-and-B? Events?'

I shake my head. 'No, I'm fostering.'

'Fostering? The two lads who are with you?'

'Uh-huh,' I say, taking another sip of the dry, cold wine.

He frowns. 'Really?'

'Yes,' I reply. 'That's what I'm doing with the house. Fostering. And running the farm, of course.'

He frowns again. 'Can't see the locals being happy about that.'

'Pardon?' I'm not sure I've heard him right.

'Well, you know, bringing all sorts into the area. They'll probably worry about their property prices plummeting and begonias being vandalized.'

I heard him right. 'This town has always welcomed people in. No reason for that to change,' I say stiffly, wishing I could leave now.

'Yes, but that place would make a great boutique hotel.'

'It's not for sale,' I say quickly.

'I understand.' He drinks some wine. 'But, as I said, it's a big old place and fostering probably doesn't pay that well. I mean, I was interested in the house.'

'You were bidding for it? Against me?'

'Looks like it.' He smiles.

Suddenly that smile is the last thing I want to see. No wonder the price kept going up. He wanted it and had deep pockets. But so did I.

'Look, why don't I help you out? Buy that piece of land, with the boathouse, off you. It's just sitting there, doing nothing. You could probably use the money to do the place up.'

The penny drops. This wasn't about old times' sake, or any kind of closure on what he did to me. 'So,' I take a deep breath and push away the wine glass, 'it's the boathouse you're interested in. I get it,' I say, picking up my bag.

'Well, yes . . . no.' He gives what could be close to a

nervous laugh. 'Look, I'm just saying, we're two out-siders here, old friends, here to do business. I'm looking to invest.'

'Old friends? Is that what we are?' There's steel in my voice that has only ever appeared when I needed to put my business hat on, and make sure I was getting the best for my clients and my company.

'Yes!'

I feel queasy. Betrayed, all over again.

'We were close, and if you wanted to, we could be again.' He places a hand over mine. I look down at it, longing for it to feel like the touch of his hand all those years ago, to have the effect on me that it once had. But I feel the opposite. It's warm, slightly damp from the chilled glass.

'We had something, Beca.' He rubs his thumb over mine, and part of me wishes it didn't feel like a cold fish.

'And that's why you were bidding on Tŷ Mawr?' I say, sliding my hand away.

'That's what I was thinking. You know . . . that little boathouse. I mean, it's not much to look at, but it could make a good hot-dog stand.' He shrugs. Like he did when he tried to explain to me that there was never anything between us when I finally collared him about Portia . . . A shrug, to brush off the lies that were fall-ing out of his mouth. A lot like now. And just like when I went to London, through a sea of red mist as

Ed and his friends were gathered on the beach, drinking beer, calling for me to join them, like I was free for hire. That was when I left, their cat-calls and laughter in my ears. I saw my grandparents' and father's worried faces and promised to call and come home if I didn't like it. I was never going to do that. I was going to show Ed Wildes and his friends. Just like now! He hasn't changed a bit.

I stand up and rummage in my bag.

'No need to decide now,' he says, his confident smile returning, as I find what I'm looking for. I take out my purse and put twenty pounds on the table.

'That should cover my drink,' I say, 'at these prices.'

'No, really, on me,' he says, wrong-footed and standing to join me.

'I can see now why you look after Carys so well. You're after the boathouse, one way or another. For another of your retail enterprises.' I'm fuming. I can see red mist at the rims of my eyes, just like before. I need to get out of here now.

'You've got this all wrong,' he says. 'Really, I wanted to meet you, put everything behind us. Put things right! I heard your marriage broke up.'

'Well, whatever you've heard . . .' I sigh, my spirits plummeting to the floor '. . . about me, my marriage and my plans for Tŷ Mawr, it's probably all true. And one thing you'll remember about me, Ed, is that I always do what I say I'm going to do.'

I leave.

'Bex . . .'

'It's Beca,' I correct him.

'I really didn't mean to offend you. I wanted to invite you here for a drink, something to eat. There's more to me than business,' he says.

I look at him. And, just for a moment, I realize that was what I was hoping too. That there was more to him, and me, than business. That what we'd had all those years ago had meant something. That I wasn't just a summer fling. But it seems, for Ed, it was just about business. And I'm not here for that. That's what this whole move was meant to be about. More than just business.

'You may live here, Ed, but you'll never be a local. Locals look out for each other. They don't try to cheat. Goodbye, Ed.'

I walk down the hill, towards the shore and Tŷ Mawr. It's over. For good. The water under the bridge just became a torrent.

That evening, we take fish and chips into the field, looking out over the sea. I watch the boys tucking into theirs. I imagine telling Nonno about Ed, the *gelato*-making and how angry I am that Valentino's is being erased from the town. I should have bought the place when you offered it to me, I think.

'You had your own life, your own business,' I hear

Nonno say, with the slur the stroke brought. 'It wasn't the right time. Sometimes, the things you love, well, it's not the right time. But it will be.'

'What do you mean?'

'You need to up your game,' he says, with a twinkle in his eye.

'How?'

'Do what you always do. Think bigger! Do what you know how to do.' Nonno smiles with the right-hand side of his face, and I grin with satisfaction as the sun sets over the sea in a blaze of golden glory.

24

The front of the cottage in a row on the way to the harbour is a visitor attraction in itself. Dripping washing hangs from a line with each end tied to the window handle at either side of the front door. Brightly coloured cotton trousers, vests, T-shirts and large pants hang across the front of the little two-up-two-down, leaving puddles of water on the footpath as hikers and holidaymakers pass on the narrow pavement.

There are window boxes of tomatoes and courgettes, and small scarecrows, which look like they've seen the worst of the weather at the front of the cottage, also hanging from the washing line. There's a stepladder that doubles as a seat propped up against the peeling blue door, for when Carys wants to sit and watch the world go by, as she often does, the dogs at her feet barking at those passing her little fisherman's cottage that has been in the family for generations. The only one in a row of cottages not sold off or gussied up, standing out for its worn, eccentric exterior.

I knock on the door and hear the dogs barking, like a call to arms.

Nothing.

I knock again, and the dogs start up once more.

This time the door opens. Carys looks at me, surprised that anyone should be knocking at her door. A large drip falls on me from the wet washing. I hope it's from the T-shirts, and try to ignore it. 'Carys,' I say.

She doesn't respond, just stands and stares at me.

Another drip from the wet washing.

'Actually, Carys, could I have a word?'

'Yes,' she replies, but doesn't move.

'I mean,' I look up and down the busy footpath, families moving out into the road to walk around me, cars and cyclists passing by, 'may I come in and have a word?'

For a moment I wonder if she's going to say no and shut the door on me, but just when I think I shouldn't have come, she steps back and lets me in. I shut the door behind me and follow her into the small front room. The dogs jump up onto the settee beside her.

'So, I hear you're taking in waifs and strays?' she says, before I've even sat down.

'I'm not taking in waifs and strays, Carys. I'm fostering.'

'Looks like you've got your hands full there. Teenage boys?'

'Well, I'm not going to be fostering teenage boys as a rule. Younger children.'

'Right. More of them coming, are there? Not sure which is worse, second-home owners or kids who could be stealing from us and murdering us in our beds.'

'Carys! These kids have had a hard time.'

'All the more reason for them to make other people's lives a misery. You watch yourself. Lock up your valuables. There's talk in the town. People are worried. I heard them after church, muttering about your place and your visitors.'

'Well, they should be more worried about what's going on right under their noses, instead of tittle-tattle without any foundation.'

'I heard one of them ran away from your house, broke into the boathouse. Barricaded himself in.'

'That isn't what happened, Carys. This place is full of gossip. It's why I—'

'Left?' she interjected.

'Yes,' I say, clenching my fists and trying to see through the red mist colouring the edges of my eyes once more.

'So, what can I do for you?' she asks. 'As if I didn't know already.'

I look around the little room, with its fireplace. Even

on a hot day like today, it's chilly in here. There are pictures on the walls of boats at sea, her father and her fiancé.

Maybe this isn't going to be as straightforward as I'd thought.

'It's about the boathouse.'

'I thought it might be.'

My mouth goes dry but I'm not about to ask for a glass of water.

I look around for somewhere to sit, but there isn't anywhere. The only place is a footstool and it's piled high with newspapers.

'It's just that . . .'

'You want to take it off me, develop it.'

'I mean yes, no . . .'

'You and every other business owner on the make around here. You're as bad as that Ed Wildes. He thinks I don't know why he always lets me eat at his café for free. But I know it's because he's after the boathouse. I'm not stupid! He's doesn't look out for the elderly of this town from the goodness of his heart.'

'Are you going to let him have it?'

'Why? Should I?'

'Um . . . no,' I say.

'Well, what do you want, then?'

'Well, it is about the boathouse . . .' I wish I hadn't started this. 'As you know, I bought Tŷ Mawr and the deeds include the boathouse. If you're not using it, I thought we could terminate the lease and I'd take it back.'

'Did you? To do what?'

'I thought I'd sell *gelato*, like my grandparents used to make,' I say quickly, hoping mention of them will put her on my side. 'Small-batch artisan *gelato*. A pop-up *gelato* parlour. On the beach. Just for the summer. We'll make it from the milk we get from the cows. Different flavours every day. Open up, and when we sell out, we sell out.'

'So, to set up a business. Like every other newcomer around here. You want to cash in on this place, where the rich come to use our home as their playground.' She strokes one of the dogs.

'Carys, you know me! I'm not like that!'

'Aren't you?' She stares at me with a shrew's eyes.

'No! I grew up here. This is my home.'

'When it suits you. You left, went off to make your life somewhere else, and now you want to try to pick up where your parents and grandparents left off.'

My eyes are prickling. I hadn't anticipated this.

'Sorry, I shouldn't have come,' I say, turning to the front door, taking in the pictures of the boats again.

'Some things shouldn't just be forgotten,' I hear her say. 'Someone has to fight for the memories of what brought this place alive.'

'That's what I'm trying to do,' I say quietly. I open

the door, go outside, and turn back to her. She's followed me into the dark hallway.

'Like the *gelato* shop, you'll change the boathouse so it will be unrecognizable. All the memories of the place will be gone. I'm sorry, but no.' She shuts the door behind me.

I walk back up the main road, cars and camper-vans whizzing past me.

Back at the farmhouse, the others are waiting, Joe, Blake, Scooter and Griff, who said he'd keep an eye on the boys for me but seems as keen as the rest of them on the idea.

'What did she say?'

'Are we going to do it, set up a pop-up parlour on the beach?' they clamour.

Slowly I shake my head. 'I'm sorry, boys, she said no.' I feel I've let everyone down. 'She said I was like all the other incomers, wanting to make a profit from the place.'

'Maybe she thinks you need to prove yourself as a local,' says Griff.

'But I am a local,' I say crossly. Because if I'm not a local, what am I?

25

That evening, I sit down at the cove, in front of the boathouse, after all the swimmers have left, listening to the waves rolling back and forth.

'Guessed I'd find you here,' says a voice behind me. It's Griff, with two cans of lager. 'Thought you might like a drink.'

I smile at him. 'I was just going to head back and check on the boys.'

'I poked my head in, looking for you. They're showered and watching TV, said I'd find you here. They wanted to know how you were.'

'They were watching ordinary TV?'

Griff smiles. 'Blake's watching some cookery show. Something to do with baking.' He hands me a can as he sits on the driftwood bench next to me.

I can smell the salt in the air and in the seaweed on the rocks.

'You always did come here when you needed to think,' he says, cracking open a can. I do the same, a small amount of froth bubbling up.

It's true. I always did.

'So, what's on your mind?' He sips his beer and looks out to sea. 'Carys?'

'I was thinking about what she said about someone having to hold on to the memories. She's right. We have to remember the past. So much is changing, so quickly. We can't let everything be wiped out. She lost her father and her fiancé in that fishing accident when the boat went down.'

Griff's elbows are resting on his knees, his hands around his beer can. 'I remember,' he says. 'There was an assembly in school.'

'I remember us singing, but that was it. There's nothing now to say that we remember what happened here. That's why she won't give up the boathouse. It's the only memory she has left.'

Griff doesn't reply.

'We should do something,' I say.

'I had a feeling you were going to say that. You can take the girl out of Sŵn y Môr, but you can't take Sŵn y Môr out of the girl.'

'But we should. She's right. We can't let these things,

these people, just be forgotten, like they didn't happen and aren't part of our town's history. Just because people come and go.'

'So what are you thinking?'

'I'm not sure yet. Some sort of memorial. Something permanent that will stay and remind us of the ones who aren't with us any more. For all the fishing families who lived here.'

26

'Do you think people will come?' I say nervously.

We've done everything we can to pull this event together over the last couple of weeks. The boys have been brilliant. Blake watches cookery shows whenever he's not suggesting and trying out new flavours. And Joe has been practising serving *gelato*, mostly by tasting it and giving Blake his genuine opinion, which is usually very positive. Apart from the basil and olive oil. He didn't like that, and Blake says it's still a work in progress, but he's watching Heston Blumenthal a lot. He's even taken to ditching the black jeans and hoodie and is wearing some of Griff's hand-me-down T-shirts. Joe's enjoying milking with Scooter and drawing when he's not in the milking parlour, which is an improvement on taking things apart. And it's distracted them from worrying that we haven't heard anything from Mo since she phoned and said a place still wasn't sorted for them, she'd be back in touch soon, and was I happy for them to stay? It's been like a ticking time bomb, waiting for the phone to ring and jumping whenever it does.

'People have bought tickets!' Griff says firmly. 'Lots of people.'

He lights the firepit, just like last time, and shows me the box of lobsters he's caught and plans to serve in rolls, with Pembrokeshire new potatoes. They're in a huge pot ready to go on the fire and to cook in salty water. Joe and Scooter are on salads with Nia. Annabelle and I are on fairy-lights, battery-operated, which we hang from long poles we push into the sand, with hooks at the ends.

Blake has everything organized for the *gelato*, which is in the freezers at the house: he'll collect the tubs when we're ready to eat it.

With just half an hour before the barbecue, the choir have arrived and are setting up under a sail, with more fairy-lights. The stonemason is here, a friend of Griff's, giving the stone one last final polish: a huge rock beside the cove, remembering those who fished here, and those who lost their lives when the boat went down.

Griff's right. We've sold tickets to go towards the cost of the stone. People understood and wanted to contribute. I'm sure they'll come. Then I see a figure, bent over, with a stick, two small dogs bouncing at her feet, coming unsteadily down the coast path. I take a deep breath, hoping this will meet with her approval. When I tried to talk to her about my idea, she slammed the door in my face. I hope I'm not about to get another earful and be told to stay away from the boathouse.

'Carys,' I say, as she stands outside the boathouse and looks at it. She hasn't been to visit for a while. 'If you're here to check, I'm not using it,' I reassure her.

She says nothing, her breathing getting more and more snatched.

'Carys? Are you okay?'

She pulls at the scarf around her throat, stressed.

'Carys?' I put out my hand to steady her and she dips into it. I take a firm grip and guide her to one of the driftwood benches.

I grab a bottle of water and pour her a plastic glassful. She takes it with shaking hands. 'I . . .' She coughs.

'Just drink,' I tell her. 'I promise you, we haven't used the boathouse at all. You could have trusted me.' Gradually her breathing seems to settle.

She's a small woman, and she looks as if the wind has been taken out of her sails. 'I wanted to see this place, just once more. It's a long way to walk these days.' She stares up at the boathouse and then around the cove, bright with fairy-lights and the fire.

'Would you like to see the stone?' I ask.

She nods, just once, and I put out a hand to help her

up. Usually strong and independent, Carys takes it. I lead her to the rock where she stands and gazes at it. Slowly, as the gentle sea breeze lifts the ends of our hair, she reaches out a hand and touches it, placing her palm against the cool stone.

'*Diolch*,' she says, and the stonemason nods. 'Thank you,' she says to me, her eyes full of tears. 'I didn't express myself right when you suggested this.'

'It's fine,' I say.

'I was scared . . . I was scared that, if anything changed here, I would forget. But this . . . this is perfect,' she says. 'And I'm sorry for what I said about what you're doing.' She looks at Blake and Joe. 'You're doing a good thing. A very good thing.'

Her words take me by surprise. The gossip I've heard has been nothing but derogatory, especially from the churchgoers, worrying that my foster-sons are going to bring down the neighbourhood, wondering why they couldn't go elsewhere, making my blood boil. 'We all need a chance in life. And, from what I hear, these boys have been helping on this event.'

'Yes,' I say, feeling very proud. 'And Blake has helped make the *gelato*.'

'May I try it?' says Carys.

Blake races off, returns with a pot for her and hands it to her.

She takes it. Blake and I are watching her. She dips in the waffle wafer, says nothing and then, slowly but surely, smiles. 'Just like it used to be. Don't ever change it.' She finishes the pot, then stands to leave.

'You can join us if you want,' I say. 'Be my guest.'

'I'd like to pay my way. Pay for my ticket.' She hands me a twenty-pound note. 'And please do use the boathouse. It has electricity and water. It just needs a good clean.'

'Really?'

'Do. This is a good thing.'

I call to the others and together, Carys watching, we push back the big blue doors to the boathouse, turn on the lights, and set up a *gelato* counter with a bar. Very soon, I have no time to worry whether anyone will come because people are trailing over the top of the coast path, carrying chairs, cool boxes of booze, bags of plates and cutlery. I rush around from the makeshift bar to greet them, and organize the seating.

Joe and Blake give me a thumbs-up, and Griff moves towards the fire, his face lit by the flames as the music starts.

When everyone is seated at the long trestle tables we've borrowed from the town hall, we serve the supper. Trays of seafood that Griff has caught and cooked on the fire, new potatoes and samphire. And then the *gelato*. And when the last scrapings have gone, the choir stands by the stone and begins, their voices blending, rich and deep and harmonious.

'*Ar lan y môr*,' the first voice sings, '*ar lan y môr*,' and others join in. 'Beside the sea . . .' Beautiful, touching, as softly undulating and as deep as the sea they're standing beside.

There's not a dry eye as the choir finishes. I look at Griff and know we've done something today to keep our community together. I just wish my family could have been here with me. Maybe they are, I think, looking at the animated faces as more *gelato* is handed round.

27

'So, that went well,' says Griff, stretching his legs in front of the fire's embers, his back against the log and elbows resting on it.

'Because of your brilliant cooking,' I say, sitting on the log, hugging my knees.

'Here.' He hands me a glass of prosecco.

'Can I have some?' asks Blake.

'No.' He tuts playfully.

'I'd like some more *gelato*,' says Joe.

'Come on, Joe, let's get you some,' says Scooter.

'We could do prosecco *gelato*,' says Blake thoughtfully as he, Scooter and Joe make their way up to the boathouse and the ice boxes there.

'Where's Nia?' I wonder.

'Helped take Carys home. She had a good time.'

I hold the key Carys has given me, not knowing

what to think now it's real. It was a big moment. Just as she left, thanking me again, she slipped the key into my hand, on its lifebuoy key-ring.

'It's yours to do with as you want. I'm giving up the tenancy,' she said. 'Make sure you do something that matters.'

I look around, realizing it's just Griff and me.

'And Annabelle?'

'Gone home. Got to leave early in the morning.'

'She's nice,' I say.

'Nice?' Griff laughs.

'I'm glad you're happy.' I don't want to get into it.

'Maybe it's time I settled down.' Griff's looking into the fire, sipping his drink.

'So it's that serious?' I say, surprised. I can feel the sand and shingle between my toes, and I wriggle them, loving the comfort it brings. I love the sound of this place, too, the waves lapping the shore. The seagulls, circling for scraps earlier, have left along with the oyster-catchers. And, in the distance, I hear the call of the owl waking up in the trees above the cove.

'I don't know,' he says, the moon throwing out a long silver strand across the water, as stars start to pop out. 'Maybe . . . maybe it's time to accept what we have and not wait for what might be.'

'Might be?' I say, not sure what he means. Something inside me shifts. A memory tickles at the back of my mind.

'Annabelle wants me to move to London, to her house there.'

'And will you?' I'm shocked. I can't imagine Sŵn y Môr without Griff.

'I don't know. Perhaps,' he says thoughtfully. 'Scooter will be going to uni. This place is changing. Maybe I should go and see what's out there for myself.'

'We all think there's something else out there, don't we?'

'I didn't,' says Griff. 'You did. You went out and looked for it. You left to find out what it might be.'

'Doesn't mean I found it. Maybe I lost what I was looking for along the way.' I gaze at the fire and the cove.

'Well, lucky for us you came back!' He turns to me, his face lit up in the golden glow of the embers. Something inside me flips again.

'So . . .' he's going to ask me something '. . . what's it to be?'

I'm tongue tied. Is he asking what I think he's asking? Is he asking . . . me?

'Are you going to do it? Take Carys up on the offer of the boathouse? Bring back Valentino's *gelato* to Sŵn y Môr?'

I grip the key in the palm of my hand. What was I thinking? Of course he wasn't talking about me and him. There never was a me and him. We were always friends, the best of friends, and only ever that one time

251

an inkling. A little bubble of excitement rushes up inside me. It was nothing, I remind myself, feeling my lips tingle. It was the cider, just before I left. It was a moment, leaving me wondering what-if. But by the morning I had gone to London and a whole new beginning, leaving behind the feeling of what-if on the beach where it happened. And that was it, a fleeting moment. It was washed away when the tide turned and covered any trace of that moment.

This is now, a lifetime away. He'll never remember it, even if I do, the taste of something that felt a lot like home, *hiraeth*. There's a chill in the air now. I shiver. The key is giving me the sharp focus I want. Not that I needed it to get into the boathouse. But it's the reminder I need right now. The reason I came back here. I look at the boys coming back from the boathouse.

'Yes, I am. Just for the summer. I'm going to bring back Valentino's *gelato* right here.'

And I hear the boys' whoop of excitement. That's enough for me.

28

There's a crackle in the atmosphere as the boys regard each other. Three of them with scooters, lounging against the wall outside the small supermarket. There are whispers and sniggers and I know they're talking about Blake and Joe. I'm uncomfortable and cross.

They look at Blake, who doesn't drop his eyes and instead gives them a defiant glare. I hurry the boys into the hardware shop next door, decorated with crabbing buckets, nets, kites and spades, bags of charcoal, and wetsuits dancing in the light breeze, like a Eurovision song-and-dance act.

I seem to have spent the last couple of weeks covered with dust as we've cleared out all the junk from the boat-house, cleaned it, and Griff has helped create a counter. I've had a plumber in to make sure the sink works, then an electrician, and sourced second-hand freezers. Getting

them down to the boathouse hasn't been easy but I nego-
tiated with Dewi the farmer to use his field for access in
return for a bit of grazing, which made it possible.

'I need paint, brushes and rollers,' I say, picking up
pots and putting them on the counter. 'I'll pick them
up later if that's okay.'

My phone rings. I jump, and so does Blake.

It's Mo.

'Hi, yes . . .' My stomach twists at how I'll tell the
boys they won't be here for opening the boathouse.
But Blake must be dying to get back to the city. And
judging from how he eyed up the lads outside, I'd say
it was no bad thing. For me too. This was just short
term. I have to keep reminding myself of that. I can't
get too involved or attached, if this is what I'm going
to do from now on.

I have one eye on Blake, who is looking out of the
crowded front window, full of fishing equipment and
hats, and the other on Joe, who is bewitched by the
crabbing buckets and is trying to get Blake's attention
to show him.

'It's about the boys,' Mo says, as tentatively as I feel.

'Yes,' I reply, trying to watch Blake, as he stares at the
lads jostling and sniggering outside, and Joe trying to
get a bucket down from the display – the whole thing
is about to fall like a house of cards.

'Blake,' I say, in a loud whisper – I need him to help
Joe.

I have a plastic basket over one arm, and am trying to move out of the way of a family of five, all keen to find themselves wetsuits and body boards.

'So, you see, it would be for a little longer, while the children's home we're hoping the boys will go to gets the insurance money to pay for the damage . . . for the fire. A pizza, left in its box, in the oven.' I don't really hear what she's saying.

'Sorry, what was that? Blake!' I hiss loudly. Too late: Joe has tugged at a bucket and the whole display is teetering, then toppling, buckets and spades crashing down around the holidaymakers wanting wetsuits and startling Carys's two Jack Russells as she stands by the dog-food bins.

'Oh, shit!' I say into the phone.

'Look, I understand it's not ideal but it would really help us out. As soon as the boys are in their new home, we'll place some younger children with you.'

I'm not really listening.

Joe is mortified. 'It's fine, Joe,' I say. 'Don't worry.'

'I promise I'll sort it as soon as I can,' says Mo, at the other end of the line.

'I'm so sorry,' I say to the shop owner, one of the Mermaids.

She smiles. 'It's no problem. Happens all the time. Maybe I should find a different way of displaying them.'

'I could help,' says Joe, and starts restacking the buckets.

'So, is that okay then?' says Mo.

'Oh, sorry, what were you saying?'

'The boys, if they could stay on for just a little longer. I und—'

'Fine. Is that it?'

'Yes.'

'Sorry, got to go,' I say quickly, and guide Joe towards the till with all our shopping.

'Well, I think we got everything,' says Joe, dusting off his hands as we leave the shop in chaos.

The local boys are still outside sniggering, clearly talking about us loudly behind cupped hands. I feel Blake bristle. I bristle too.

I need a distraction. And then I see Ed. That's the last thing I need.

I try to hurry the boys along.

'Hello, all! Still here, boys?'

I wince.

'Yes, off to the crabbing competition,' I reply.

'And to paint the boathouse,' says Joe, carrying his crabbing bucket. It's much the same as all the others, but clearly it spoke to him as he removed it from the centre of the pile, as if he was playing Jenga.

'Must go!' I say, chivvying them down the road. Not the distraction I had in mind. I don't really want people to know what I'm doing at the boathouse until I'm ready. Especially not Ed Wildes. That's the problem with this place: nothing stays secret for very long.

'Beca,' he calls. I turn back. He wipes his hands with

a tea-towel. 'I'm off this afternoon, heading down to the harbour. Perhaps I'll see you there.'

Is he for real? He's the last person I want to see.

'After we win the crabbing competition,' Joe says. Blake is silent, still eyeing the lads outside the shop.

'Come on, guys,' I say, keen to move Blake on. Does Ed really think I'm interested in him? Or is he still trying to get his hands on the boathouse? Either way, he's not going to succeed.

As we move down the hill, the women from the Zumba class are heading in the same direction. I nod to them and move away quickly before I become the subject of their chat. I hope they didn't hear any of my conversation with Ed and get the wrong idea. They lean in and whisper.

'Beca, there's a sourdough-making class in the memorial hall this afternoon, followed by master-classes in baking banana bread and growing dahlias,' one says. 'They'd look lovely in your front garden.'

I smile tightly and carry on past the little row of terraced cottages.

'No doubt the car park will be full of day-trippers coming to the beach,' says another, and they tut.

'Shame no one can get that mess of a property tidied up down there. Prime location. If it was a holiday home, at least it wouldn't look like a squat.'

I stop. I'm telling myself not to get involved when my mouth opens and my brain tries to catch up.

'Do you mean Carys's home?' I say.

'The woman with the dogs?' says another.

'Carys Thomas. Her family have lived here all their lives. Generations. They were a fishing family, bringing in the very thing you say you love about this place, the seafood for the restaurants at the heart of the harbour you all love.'

'Well, yes, but you've got to admit the cottage is an eyesore.'

They look at it in disgust.

'Actually, I think it has character. A reflection of who lives there. And it gets the sun perfectly well where it is. And no, thank you, I don't want to make banana bread or sourdough or learn how to grow dahlias. And that beach is there for whoever wants to use it,' I say. 'Come on, boys, we've got a crabbing competition to win.' My competitive streak rises, like a phoenix from the ashes. 'See you there, ladies!' I call back as we march past. So much for me wanting a quiet life and to keep my head down. At least in London no one bothered you or had their nose in your business. They weren't judging your front garden or commenting on you passing pleasant-ries with a man or wondering why you weren't making sourdough. But banana splits, or even banoffee pie, now that's a thought, and we walk on to the harbour swinging our buckets.

29

'Phwoar!' Blake and Joe recoil.

'What's that smell?' They screw up their noses as I produce the tinfoil parcel Griff had sent with Scooter that morning.

'This is from Griff. Some of the best bait you can get. It's been rotting for a while,' I explain, but the boys don't look convinced.

'It's all about the bait,' I grin, 'and knowing the best spot. Come on,' I urge, a feeling of fun flooding back into my world even though Blake doesn't seem to be enjoying himself.

'Can't I just go back to the house?' he asks.

'No, we all have to join in!' I say, with good-humoured bossiness. Just as good-humouredly, he harrumphs but follows me. 'Now, we need to get to the edge of the jetty over there without everyone spotting us.'

There are families along the edge of the harbour, just along from the pub where pints are being drunk and where we'd go as kids for Coke and crisps outside when our parents took us. Outside the yacht club, there are bottles of prosecco in coolers and craft beers in jugs on the table.

There are Panama hats and deck shoes, knee-length shorts and jumpers slung over shoulders as families and friends gather and chat in the afternoon sunshine, making me feel on the outside again. I'm not a local any more. I'm not a newcomer or a second-home owner. I'm not sure where I fit in here. I'm looking around for Griff, but can't see him.

'Beca!' I suddenly hear his voice. The sight of him confuses me and makes me smile at the same time.

His hat is missing. He's smarter than usual. Then I see Annabelle, dressed similarly to the group she's with, a pink shirt, white cropped trousers. It's not hard to see why Griff's smartened himself up.

'I hardly recognized you!' I say. He chuckles and kisses my cheek warmly, as does Annabelle. Cariad jumps up in greeting and Blake rubs her head.

'Scrubs up well, doesn't he?' Annabelle says, leaning into him, with a glass of prosecco. I smile, but somehow I feel slightly awkward. He looked fine as he was. Griff clears his throat and I wonder if he feels the same. They don't seem quite as comfortable as they did the other day at the beach barbecue, not quite the same couple. 'Would you like a drink with us?' Griff asks.

'Oh, no thanks. We'd better get our spot for the crabbing contest.' I can see Joe is frustrated, hopping from foot to foot.

'Great! Has Beca shown you where to go?' he says quietly.

Joe seems to settle. 'She's taking us there now,' he says, with the solemnity of passing a secret.

'I'll come and help,' says Griff. 'I'll be back,' he says to Annabelle, handing her his beer.

'Sure,' she says, putting the bottle on a nearby table and turning her back on it. 'Don't be long. We've got lunch in half an hour.'

'She'll be telling me not to get my trousers dirty next,' says Griff, laughing, and Blake joins in, happy now. It makes me feel as good as the sun on my face and the scent of the sea in my nostrils.

'Over here.' Griff beckons. 'This is where Beca and I would crab. Mind the rocks over there,' he says, as Blake steps off the jetty. The waves roll in and break against the rocks, with splashes and a shower of water, making Joe squeal excitedly.

'Come on, Joe,' says Griff, the bottoms of his trousers already wet, his shoes left on the wooden jetty.

Joe grasps Griff's hand, and Griff guides him onto the rocks.

'Bex?' he says, holding out a hand.

'I'm not sure there's enough room for me.'

'Of course there is! Come on!'

'Yes, come on, Beca,' says Blake.

Griff holds out his hand and I reach for it, then step over the swell of little waves between the end of the jetty and the rocky outcrop.

'Who's got the bait?'

'Phwoar!' Joe and Blake recoil again as I hold it up in the bucket I'm carrying.

'Beca?' I hear my name and Ed is on the wooden jetty, slightly out of breath.

'Look, I'm wondering if we could have a chat. Sort things out. I may have given you the wrong idea the other week when we met up.'

'It was the right idea,' I say. Griff still has my hand, holding me on the rocky outcrop, but I drop it.

'Team name?' says Lloyd Owen, with his clipboard and cheeks as red as apples.

'Erm . . .' I look to Blake and Joe.

'Family name? Valentino's?' Lloyd asks.

'How about Gelato Lovers?' Griff jumps in.

'Champions!' says Joe.

'How about Team Tŷ Mawr?' Griff tries.

'*Yesssss!*' says Joe, and Blake nods in agreement.

'Team Tŷ Mawr it is!' he tells Lloyd, who writes it down, looking between the five of us.

'Okay. Has everyone entered who wants to take part?' Lloyd calls, lifting his whistle.

'You know, you'd be better off on the jetty,' says Ed. 'Why don't you set up over here? Luke and . . . erm?'

'Blake,' I say, through clenched teeth, 'and Joe.'

'Of course.' He picks up one of their buckets and lines. 'We can all have lines off here,' he says. 'What do you think?'

'Griff?' Annabelle appears on the jetty, not looking happy.

'Be back there now,' he says, clearly having no intention of joining her just yet. Not when there's a crabbing competition on.

'Here's fine,' says Griff, unrolling one of the lines. 'Pass the bait, Bex.'

'I brought some bacon,' says Ed, putting it on the end of his line.

'I like bacon,' says Joe.

'Come here with me. I can show you how to do it.'

'He's fine where he is,' I say, not looking at him, and then I notice Joe is trying to climb back onto the jetty.

'Joe, stay here!' I say.

'It's okay! I'll get some crabs from here and we'll have loads!' says Joe.

'Joe, it's best we stay together.' I sound tense.

'It's okay, I've got him!' says Ed, just as Lloyd blows the loud whistle. Joe looks startled and turns back, not sure which way to go.

'Joe!' I say.

'It's okay, mate, jump!' says Ed, and Joe does.

263

'Joe!' I shout, as he lurches towards Ed, grabbing him and toppling backwards, taking Ed with him. Griff barely misses a beat and jumps in after Joe, who is gasping and flailing, gulping water.

'Joe!' I shout.

There is splashing and shouting, pleas to get out of the water in case it scares the crabs.

'Grab him!' I shout. 'He can't swim!' I flick off my flip-flops and undo my trousers to dive in.

But Griff is there, guiding Joe to the jetty. With me pulling him and Griff pushing behind, we get Joe out of the sea.

Ed is still treading water and brushing back his wet hair. Joe is safely on dry land. Griff turns to Ed. 'Idiot!' he says, and slaps the water in front of Ed. It hits his face. Ed slaps back at Griff, and Griff retaliates. They're like a couple of schoolkids.

Most of us feel her presence before we turn and see her.

Annabelle has moved to the steps leading to the jetty and is staring at Griff with a face like thunder. I'm in my knickers, shouting at Ed and Griff, who are attempting to push each other underwater in front of a crowd of families and a tangle of crab lines.

Annabelle's face tells Griff everything he needs to know right now. She's not happy, not happy at all.

'Come on, Joe. Let's get you home,' I say. He's shivering and dripping on the wooden jetty and I realize I've said 'home', but I can't take it back now.

30

'Hi.' Griff raises a hand in a sort of wave that I decide to ignore.

'I came to see if Joe was all right,' he says, standing in the kitchen. He's changed into his usual clothes and his hat is back on his head.

'I'm fine, thank you, Griff. Just making sure I don't get cold,' replies Joe, sipping hot chocolate and repeating what I said to him.

'No thanks to you,' I say crossly, under my breath.

'We're going to the boathouse to start painting it. Want to come?' Joe says.

'If that's okay?' Griff is contrite but he can't stop a smile.

I give him a serious look but I can't help the small smile that reflects his. 'Only if there are no silly antics!' I say, trying to sound like a schoolmistress, half joking, but half stern. Today could have been very serious.

'I promise.' He crosses his heart. 'Come on, we have a *gelato* stall to build.'

'Um, how's Annabelle?' I ask, biting my bottom lip. 'Will she mind you missing the lunch?'

'She's . . . not happy. And, no, she won't mind me missing the lunch. In fact, I was told in very firm terms to stay away.'

'Oh.'

'Yes,' he agrees, and we seem to decide without words to say no more on the matter.

Down at the boathouse, I study the empty space at the front. 'We need tables for people to eat their *gelato* at,' I say.

'I may have just the thing,' says Griff, and disappears with Blake in tow.

Scooter, Joe and I go on painting. Joe and I are doing the blocks of colour on the walls. Scooter is copying *gelato* and sundaes from the photos I've shown her that used to hang in Valentino's. We paint happily in our own thoughts.

'That's amazing, Scooter!' I say, admiring the paintings. 'You've certainly got your dad's artistic talent. You should do more.'

'Don't let Mum hear you say that.'

'She's not keen on you doing art?'

'She thinks I should do something more . . . solid.'

'Oh.' Then, 'And what do you want?'

'Pfff,' she says. 'I don't know.'

'Hey!' Griff is coming down the steps from the farm, Blake behind him. And between them they're carrying surfboards.

'What?' I exclaim. 'I thought we were doing up the boathouse, not surfing!'

'These are for tables,' Griff says, and Blake beams.

'A mate of mine has a surf school, and these are last year's boards. Old ones he can't use in the school. He's got more he can let you have for a small fee.'

'Really?'

'Yup!'

I breathe a sigh of relief. I hadn't budgeted for renovating a boathouse and making it into a business for the summer. 'They're amazing!'

'And I picked up some old rope, thought it might come in useful. We could hang it on stakes, to mark out the seating area. Oh, and I've got some old lobster pots and nets if you fancy.'

'We can weave fairy-lights into them!' My excitement is rising.

Finally, after a long day's painting, as the sun is about to set we stand back and admire our achievements. Scooter's artwork is fantastic.

'She's artistic, like you,' I say to Griff, amid the *gelato*

267

and swirls, the red cherries and yellow lemons he and his daughter have painted.

'Shame she doesn't want to go to college to use it,' he says.

'Really?'

Griff shakes his head. 'Nia thinks she'd be better at agri college. She's probably right.'

'Scooter's not sure,' I say. 'She wants time to work it out.'

He stares at the work. As does Joe, who is utterly transfixed by it . . . and by Scooter, if I'm not mistaken.

'Come on, who's up for a swim?' Griff whips off his T-shirt and runs towards the inviting water in the orange glow of the setting sun.

'Me!' shouts Joe. Scooter runs after him, leaving her T-shirt on over her shorts.

'Joe, be careful. Don't go out of your depth. And take your trousers off!' Not for the first time today he ends up in the sea fully clothed.

'You know, Beca,' says Blake, 'I might miss this place when I leave. Who knew there was life outside the city?'

'Come on,' I say to him. 'Let's enjoy this while we can. They can't take memories from us.' He gives me a small smile and peels off some clothes to join the others in the sea.

Then, once again, Griff lights the fire and I dash to the house to gather towels and the makings of a picnic, with crunchy bread, fat tomatoes, cheese, and sausages to cook on the fire. Right now, I don't think I could feel any happier as the five of us watch the sun go down over the cove.

'We need a name for the boathouse,' says Blake.

'Like . . . Beca's!' says Griff.

'Or Sweet Treats!' Joe suggests.

'Or . . .'

'Blake and Joe's,' Blake says.

'Like Frankie and Benny's!' Griff says.

And we all laugh.

'How about the Beach Cove Café?' says Griff. And our laughter peters out.

I look at him, lying next to the fire, then at the purples and pinks in the sky. 'The Beach Cove Café,' I muse.

'Valentino's,' says Griff, 'By the Sea.'

'I can't think of anywhere I'd rather be,' I say, thinking of my grandparents and how they must have felt, starting here, all those years ago, when anything was possible. 'Valentino's it is!'

We sit on the beach, with our picnic and the fire. I wonder what lies ahead for the five of us, come the end of the summer.

31

'I can't keep relying on friends to buy *gelato* from me.'
I look at the Mermaids tucking into it beside the water,
wrapped in towels. It's been more than a week now
since we opened and business is a slow trickle, occasional dog-walkers – Joe keeps a bowl of water for the
dogs – couples looking for a quiet spot to picnic and,
of course, the Mermaids. Otherwise it's been deathly
quiet. The beauty of this cove is that people barely
know about it. Most of the tourists stick to the town's
main beach, by the harbour. What made me think that
was a good business model?

We've bought second-hand freezers from a charity
and moved them into the boathouse, filling them
with pots of *gelato* that we take home again at the
end of the day. We're doing everything that the Environmental Health team told me I must when I rang

them at the council, including keeping records of every *gelato* we make, the temperatures it's heated and chilled to, and for how long. The sink at the boathouse is clean and polished and we have a system in place for which scoops get used and how often they're washed. There's the counter, with spoons and napkins and a little blackboard with today's special flavours on it. It's all here, just not the customers.

'We need more customers,' I say.

'Well, you know the answer,' says Griff, fixing the bunting where it's slipped down over the open doors revealing the serving hatch in the boathouse.

'What?' I say, frowning.

'Yes, what?' asks Joe.

'You'll have to rely on the one thing you've always hated.' He smiles. 'Gossip!'

I throw a tea-towel at him. He catches it. 'I mean it,' he says. 'If you want people to come, you have to get them talking. You can't have a secret *gelateria* that no one knows about.'

I feel the breeze on my face, the sun and salt on my lips, which remind me of why I'm here. I love this place, and I want others to taste our *gelato*, here, by the boathouse, with its bunting and fairy-lights and surfboard tables. Everyone's worked so hard. He's right. I have to get people talking about this place.

'Okay. We need to get out there and spread the

word,' I say to Blake and Joe. 'Let's start with the market.'

'And social media,' says Blake, looking up from his phone. 'We need a Facebook page with directions on it. I can do that.'

'And we need to be able to get across that field, so people who can't walk the coast path can park and come that way.'

'We could put a sign on the road,' says Blake.

'And tell them about our great flavours,' Joe chimes in.

'We could do daily flavours. Not stick to the same ones,' I say, realizing how we could keep things fresh. 'You're right,' I tell Griff, and smile. 'We need the gossip!' We laugh and, just for a moment, I want to lean forward and kiss him, as if we were a couple. I have to remind myself we're not. We're just friends. Good friends. And my stomach flips again. I can't remember it doing that with other friends.

32

The following morning we head into town, with a cold box and flyers that Scooter designed and printed last night. We're armed to cause a stir.

It's market day, with more stalls than there are during the rest of the week, and the little town is buzzing. As we reach the end of the street, which is closed off for the market, I stop at the top of the bustling road, with green-and-white awnings at either side. For some unknown reason I'm nervous. Suddenly Griff is beside me from behind his stall and he's looking at the triangular sign in the road outside Wildes.

'Gelato and ice cream. Locally made, from the heart of the countryside . . .' it reads.

'Once people buy yours, they'll know the difference,' Griff says, seemingly understanding exactly how I'm

273

feeling. 'I've cleared it with the market organizer for you to sell here.'

'But how do we get them to buy it?'

'We give people a taste,' says Joe. 'I always like a little taste of something before I eat it all.'

We look at him. 'Of course! Let's buy some paper cups and start handing round tasters.'

Blake doesn't need asking twice. It makes my heart melt: the introverted, sullen boy with the shutters down has disappeared. Now he doesn't need to think twice about doing this. I give him the money and he runs into the little grocery store, returning with paper cups, wooden spoons and foil trays.

He and Joe put some spoonfuls of our homemade *gelato* into the cups, fill a foil tray each and start offering them to holidaymakers and second-home owners, wandering up the high street and pointing towards where I stand behind a small camping table with the cold box on it.

Blake turns to me with a thumbs-up as he directs some customers my way and I swell with pride. I know what people mean now when they feel real pride. I was proud of my company, the work we did, what I'd achieved, but this is the best feeling in the world. I'm selling something we've made with the milk from the cows grazing in the sun by the shore, just down the coast path: delicious *gelato* with local flavouring ingredients.

'Actually, make that three pots,' says someone in front of me, and I realize that a small queue is forming.

'Oh, of course!'

And Griff gives me one of his little winks, making my stomach flutter. This is it!

'Come and see us at the cove on the coast path in the old boathouse,' I say.

'We will!' says the customer.

Ed is standing on his terrace. He's not looking happy as people queue at my stall instead of making their way into the wine bar.

I don't stop for the next few hours. We've nearly sold out as lunchtime approaches.

I take a moment's breather. Seeing people walking through the market with pots of Valentino's *gelato* made at Tŷ Mawr, flyers in the other hand, makes my eyes prickle again. We did it.

Then I hear a shout. It's Joe. My heart leaps into my mouth.

There are three young lads around him.

'It's only one taster per p-p-person,' Joe is stuttering, trying to protect his tray.

'Come on, buddy. It's fine. We'll just take a couple more each.'

'No!' says Joe, stumbling back. I'm out from around the table within a split second. But Blake beats me to it.

'Back off!' he says, firmly but not loudly.

'Says who?'

'Me,' says Blake, eyes flashing.

There may be trouble and I move forward, but Griff comes out from behind his stall and puts a hand on my arm. I stop and we wait, ready to jump in. My heart is racing. I'm desperate to shout out and wade in. But Griff is there, ready if we need him.

'You're the kids in care, aren't you? What – your parents didn't want you?'

I can see Blake's fists clench.

'Okay, lads, that's enough,' Griff says, stepping forward.

'You his brother or something?' one says to Blake.

'No. I'm more than that. I'm his friend,' says Blake. I'm holding back a tear. The lads stare at Blake, who gives them one of his Blake stares. Slowly they peel away, with a look that says this isn't over.

As they stroll away, I breathe again. The tear escapes from my eye and rolls down my cheek, followed by another. I brush them away before the boys see me. But Griff has noticed.

'I know those boys,' he says, nodding towards the lads who've just walked off. 'They're okay. Just a bit boisterous.'

I look at him.

'Testing the boundaries,' he says. 'Like someone else I used to know.'

Then he reaches up to my cheek and brushes away a last tear, holding my gaze.

Around us the market is packing up. But right now it's just me and Griff, and the bond that seems always to have been there between us.

'Blake was a-*mazing*,' I hear Joe say, and the moment is broken.

'He was, I saw!' I say quickly, turning from Griff and seeing Joe glowing.

'He said he's my friend!' he whispers loudly, and Blake's face slowly softens.

'Well done, Blake. You rose above it. They're just idiots.' I'm trying not to embarrass him, but wanting to tell him I was proud of him.

A muscle twitches in his cheek.

'Sometimes you just have to prove to yourself that you're the better person. Stand up to idiots. Don't run.' I see Griff raise an eyebrow at me. 'Because the best revenge you can have in life is to be happy.' I'm remembering those words of advice, the ones I didn't take back then.

Blake glances at me and I wonder if he heard me, or if he's going to revert back to the sullen young man he was when he arrived, angry at the reminder of the unfairness of it all and the cards life has dealt him. I look at him. He looks back at me. Then smiles.

'Come on, we've got a *gelateria* to open!' he says, making me smile and filling me all over again with pride.

*

By late afternoon, back at the boathouse, a slow trickle of families is appearing over the hill on the coast path, like a line of ants heading towards the cove. They set up chairs, buy *gelato* and enjoy the sea.

'It worked! It absolutely bloody worked!' I cry. I clap, then hug Blake and Joe.

I wish Griff was there to see it. I think of staring into his eyes, and feel my stomach fizz. It would have been so easy to lean in and kiss him. But I can't spoil what we have.

By the end of the week, boats and paddleboards are appearing around the rocky outcrops to the cove as people pull up on the shore to eat Valentino's *gelato*. And I can't help but notice that when Griff has finished his lobster pots and boat maintenance he's spending more and more time here with us, helping. Annabelle is nowhere to be seen. Nia's been popping down too, sometimes helping, sometimes having a coffee with Scooter and Griff.

As the next couple of weeks pass, Blake works hard on blending new flavours. Scooter starts early in the morning with Joe in the cowshed, and they join me down at the boathouse to serve *gelato* and give the new flavours names.

'Hi, need a hand?' Nia arrives at the boathouse as she has done frequently after packing up her stall in the town. People are sitting at the surfboard tables, eating ice-cream sundaes and drinking bottles of cream soda or dandelion and burdock.

'Hello again!' I beam. 'Yes, I think it's fair to say that word has got around.'

'This place, once word gets out, there's no keeping it a secret.' She smiles but she looks tired.

'How's things?' I ask. 'Business doing okay?' She nods, inspecting the list of flavours.

'*Gelato*?' I ask.

'We have new ones today. Gooseberry and ginger!' Joe pipes up. 'I don't like it, but Beca says it's lovely.'

Nia laughs. 'I'd love to try it. Are you sure I can't give you a hand first?'

'No, we're fine. It's quietening down. Coffee?' I say, pointing to the new machine.

'Wow! Yes, please!'

While I make it, Joe hands her a pot of *gelato* with a wafer in it, and a spoon.

'I'll join you.' I step out from behind the counter with two cups of coffee from the machine.

'This is a great little business,' she says.

'It's just until the end of the summer. Until the boys . . . are back at school.' I find it easier to say that than 'leave'.

We sit at an empty table, watching the families on the beach, and I run my hand over the polished surfboard.

'How's Griff?' we ask at the same time.

Nia frowns. 'I hardly see him, these days. Only down here. I thought he'd be at my house more now Annabelle's gone back to London. And, from what I hear, they're not on good terms.'

I shake my head.

'I was hoping to chat to him about Scooter.' She sighs. 'I don't know what she's thinking about college or uni, but Griff's ideas aren't the same as mine.'

'You'll work it out, I'm sure. You two are so good at co-parenting. Is that the word? It's fantastic the way you get along and are there for Scooter. And you're still friends. I wish I could have made things work out with my ex like you two.'

I turn to Nia and see her eyes filled with tears.

'Nia? Oh, God, sorry, was it something I said?'

'No . . . no.' She licks the *gelato*. 'This is really good,' she tries to say, but I can tell she's got a frog stuck in her throat she's trying to clear.

'Nia?'

She lowers the *gelato* pot and holds it, the rounded peak dripping down the sides and over her knuckles. She's staring out to sea, where Griff is letting Blake steer his little boat into the cove. They've been putting out lobster pots for the morning. Blake is concentrating.

She looks down. A tear plops into her *gelato*. She sniffs and swipes at her eyes. 'Sorry, I just . . .'

'What is it?'

'Griff,' she says, looking out again to him and Blake.

Scooter is helping to moor the boat now and is up to her waist in the water.

I look at Nia. And in that moment I know the answer. 'You're still in love with him, aren't you?' I say quietly.

She sniffs again and laughs. 'It's that obvious? I try to hide it.'

'Oh, Nia!' I say, my brain working overtime. 'But surely you should tell him, especially now that he and Annabelle have split up. You have to tell him.'

'There isn't a happy ending out there for all of us, Beca. And with Scooter going to college now, I doubt he'll want to spend time with me at all.'

'But he's single, you're single, and you have a beautiful daughter. You get on so well . . .'

She shakes her head, and the *gelato* is dripping on the floor. Cariad is helping to clear it up and a nearby seagull is padding around waiting for his moment to dive in.

'Shoo!' I say, standing up and handing her a napkin from a pile weighed down with a painted stone. She thanks me and sighs.

'I don't understand,' I say.

'There can't be an "us",' she says, 'because there was always someone else.' She looks at me.

Griff waves as he and Blake wade in carrying a lobster pot.

'What? Who?'

She stares at me meaningfully.

'*Me?* No! Griff and I were always best friends. There was never anything between us!' Once again I push down the memory of that one moment when there was a chance that there might have been.

Still she says nothing.

'Honestly, Nia,' I say, feeling I should be crossing my fingers. Even if I felt something, he's never said anything. But I ran, didn't come back . . . I couldn't bear to have misread the situation between us.

'Maybe not for you.'

I look from her to Griff, who is now approaching us. Is what she's saying true? Did Griff really have feelings for me beyond our friendship? I mean, we were friends and neither of us wanted to do anything to spoil that. And years ago I thought I had. That one night before I left. I can't do that again.

'It's always been you, Beca. There was never any room for anyone else.' She peers up at me. 'I'm sorry, I don't know where this has come from.' She dabs at her eyes with the napkin.

The seagull is still keeping an eye on Nia's *gelato*, probably hoping for another puddle like the one Cariad has worked hard to clear up.

'But I never . . . We never . . . There never was,' I say. 'Never will be!'

She tilts her head. 'I just assumed that now you were back . . . and like you used to be . . .'

'Honestly, Nia,' I say, hating being the obstacle to her happiness, 'really, I don't have feelings for Griff. Never have.' And something deep inside me twists.

'Really?'

'Really. I promise you. There is nothing going on between Griff and me. Never will be.'

She sniffs and gives me a grateful smile. 'He's the only one I've ever loved,' she says.

I look at Scooter with her dad, laughing and joking. 'I promise I'm not here to stand in the way of that,' I say, and something inside me twists so hard it hurts. It's a promise I know I'll have to keep, however close Griff and I are and despite whatever may have woken up inside me.

I hope she believes me.

'Thank you,' she says, and licks the drips of *gelato* from the sides of her pot, to the seagull's chagrin.

I see someone approaching the boathouse and jump up from the wooden log I'm sitting on. 'Wait here, I'll just serve this customer,' I say to Nia. 'Hi, what can I get you?'

'Beca Valentino?'

'Yes? Oh, two secs,' I say, turning from the rented coffee machine, which is suddenly hissing and spitting at me.

'What can I get you?' I say again, wiping my hands. 'I'm still getting to grips with the coffee machine but we've got all the flavours of *gelato* on the board, plus *gelato* sandwiches made with fresh brioche buns from Baps bakery just up the mountain.' I point. 'And milk-shakes, frappés, Coke floats?'

I smile at him. He's hot in a suit and smart shoes that are hardly appropriate for trekking over the coast path.

'I'm Efan Rhys, environmental-health inspector, from the council.' He hands me a sheet of paper. 'I'm sorry, but I'm here to close you down.'

33

I slam down the hatch over the ice-cream counter that Griff and Blake had built together and close the newly painted boathouse doors with a bang. I know it was him, and I'm furious.

'Blake, keep an eye on things,' I call over my shoulder, screwing up the paper in my fist and tossing it into the bin I've put there for empty pots. Griff is walking back up the beach, looking confused. 'I'll be back!' I barely notice that Blake's talking to a boy of about the same age as him. And they seem to be laughing with each other.

It must be him! It can't be anyone else! I storm towards the coast path. Despite the heat, I'm thundering past families still making their way towards the beach cove, with Google Maps and Facebook directions.

How dare he? The red mist is simmering along my eyelids.

I stride up the main street towards Wildes.

It's empty now, shutting for the day. Families have gone home to shower off the salt and sand after a day at the beach.

I march into the café and slam the door behind me.

Ed stands up, startled, from the table he and I had sat at. His guest is clearly surprised by my arrival.

'There should be a bloody bell!' I bark.

'Beca! Hi!' he says.

I glare at him. 'It was you, wasn't it!'

'Sorry?'

'You rang the council and reported me because I turned you down.'

'Whoa, hang on. I have no idea what—'

'Rubbish!' I don't let him finish.

'Ed?' asks the woman still sitting at the table.

'This is Beca, Beca Valentino,' Ed tells her.

'Oh, hi! You own the boathouse,' she tells me.

'I was telling Lily, my business partner, about it,' Ed explains. 'What a great venue it is.'

And suddenly I feel a whooshing in my ears, like I'm back there, with him and Portia, laughed at, used, stupid. Just like last time when I had no idea I was being played for a fool. I can't believe I could let this happen again. Do I have 'idiot' written on my forehead?

'So . . . this is what it was really about.' My voice is

low and quiet, even slightly scaring me. 'I was right! You didn't want to talk over old times. You just wanted to get your hands on the boathouse, one way or another.'

He laughs, but I can hear the nerves in it. 'Wait, Beca, join us. We have a proposition for you.' He indicates a chair.

I can feel fury bubbling up in me. The injustice of it all.

'Lily has a proposition. To buy the boathouse.'

'I told you before,' I snarl, 'it's not for sale. I outbid you on the auction for Tŷ Mawr and its land, and I'm not selling any of it. However hard you try to push me out, I'm here to stay.'

'I can offer you a good price for the boathouse. It's just a shack, for goodness' sake,' says Lily.

I take a deep breath. 'Never. You haven't changed, Ed Wildes. You used me and treated me appallingly when we were younger, and you're still doing it now. You're only out for what you can get and you don't care who you hurt in the process. You are the very last person I would sell the boathouse to.'

I stalk out of the café, kicking the Wildes ice-cream stand, and march towards the beach, not looking back.

The wind has picked up, buckets and spades clattering against each other outside shop doors. Awnings flap and slap as gusts rush up through the town. I carry on to the harbour and along the coast path, welcoming the fierce breeze that cools my cheeks and my temper, slowing my pace, taking time to breathe in the salty air.

As I reach the headland overlooking the cove I'm surprised to see so many people on the beach still. I'd thought, with the change in weather and the day almost over, they'd be heading for home. But there are crowds on the beach, gathered along the water's edge. Curious, I hurry forward through the wind, which is whipping my hair across my face.

'Beca! I've been looking for you!' It's Griff, out of breath, hurrying up the coast path to meet me. 'It's Joe. He's taken my boat.'

34

By the time I get to the cove, the water's edge is bustling with people. Blake spots me, runs to me, throws his arms around me and hugs me tightly.

'It's okay, we'll find him,' I say.

His eyes are screwed tight shut and he doesn't let go of me.

'It's okay,' I tell him, wishing I knew that it was and hugging him back, scanning the cove.

Then boats appear around the corner of the cove, fishermen's boats, three, maybe more, I can't tell. Griff calls to them and waves. They're followed by a fast RIB with a young crew dressed in orange waterproofs, the RNLI lifeboat. And behind that, small pleasure boats, holidaymakers and second-home owners who have clearly heard the news. A local boy, Joe, is missing.

I'm rooted to the spot, eyes full of tears, clinging to Blake, Griff's arm around me, which I barely notice.

'They'll find him,' he tells me. 'I promise.'

'But why did he take the boat? Where was he going? How far could he have got?' I ask. 'I wasn't gone that long.'

'They think he might have been caught by the tide, dragging him out. The current's strong today.'

For once I feel utterly helpless. There is nothing I can do but wait.

A little girl is crying, being consoled by her parents.

'He said he'd get my unicorn back,' she sobs. 'He said he could get it. He was a superhero.'

'Stay here,' says Griff. 'We'll bring him home. He'll want you here.' He rushes off to join the search.

And I daren't utter the word circling inside my head. Not 'when' but 'if' . . .

All sorts of boats are out there now, sailing boats, kayaks with holidaymakers, local fishermen, and the young crew of the RNLI coordinating a plan, making their way out of our safe little cove, or that was how it had always felt, round to the rocky outcrops out to sea.

I'm hugging myself and Blake, praying that Joe comes back safely. I make a pact with myself that if he does, I'll give up the boathouse, sell it, stop trying to get one over on Ed Wildes. He can have it. I'll go back to the city. The earlier sunny day, with families enjoying themselves, has disappeared, like melting *gelato* on the stony shore.

I stand, swaying, with Blake next to me. Someone puts a fleecy jacket around our shoulders. Holiday-makers with small kayaks come in from helping out, shaking heads and looking sorrowfully at me. It's too rough for them out there now. I feel utterly desperate. Sick with a desperation I have never known before. Blake doesn't leave my side as I remember Griff's words: 'We'll bring him home.'

Eventually, as the sun is setting and darkness falls, the fishing boats appear round the rocks. It's the lights I see first, then the silhouette of the boats and finally I make out that they're towing Griff's. My heart leaps into my mouth.

Then I can see Griff on the boat, beside a smaller figure – Joe! He's got him! He's alive! Once more my eyes fill with tears.

Griff jumps out of the boat with Joe in his arms, carries him ashore and puts him down. Slowly, like a drowned scrap of a thing, clutching a towel that Griff must have put around him, he walks up the beach uneasily. I watch him, my hand over my mouth. Then I run to him. His glasses are steamed up. His hair is matted with sea water and he's shivering, his lips blue. He looks up at me, tears filling his eyes, just like mine.

Neither of us says a word as he throws his arms

around me, much like Blake did earlier. And I throw mine around his wet, cold, trembling body.

'S-s-sorry,' he stammers. I can't reply for the lump in my throat. 'I just wanted to help! When that man turned up at the boathouse in his suit, I thought it was my fault. It was like when they took me from my mum. A man in a suit came then too, once they realized I was looking after her on my own. They thought I couldn't cope and didn't let me stay. I thought if I could prove I was needed here, that I was a hero, they'd let me stay with you.'

My tongue ties in knots. I have no idea what to say.

'I thought if I saved the blow-up unicorn, everyone would think I was a superhero. That you needed me. Now they'll send me away again,' he says, and drops his head.

Suddenly I'm furious at the injustice.

I've spent my life scared of not being good enough, of people talking about me, judging me. That's why I left here. Why? None of it mattered. I was enough for my parents and grandparents, who loved me no matter what trouble I got into at school. It was Ed who wasn't good enough. And Josh, when he chose a life in the city without me. None of that matters. This is what matters, these boys. I've never felt anything mattered more than these boys.

'Don't ever do that again!' I've raised my voice and I

didn't mean to. I'm angry, relieved, and hurting like I've never hurt before as Joe pulls himself away from me.

'You're not my mother! You can't tell me what to do!' he shouts back, taking me by complete surprise.

I'm getting it wrong again. I take a deep breath, hold on to his shoulders and look him straight in the eye. 'No, I'm not your mother,' I say, evenly and slowly. I have no idea if I'm saying the right thing, but I'm going with what I feel and I mean every word of it. 'But I care about you very much.' I hold them both close to me. 'And about what happens to you. Wherever you go, you and Blake.' A lump rises in my throat. 'I love you both!' I say, surprising myself, my voice cracking. The boys are just as surprised. 'Remember that!' I well up again.

'I just wanted to help! I wanted to be useful so they wouldn't send us away again.'

And Blake and Joe throw themselves into a hug with me.

'You're a hero to all of us, Joe. Just keep being you. We love you for you,' I tell him, my heart breaking in two.

35

With the boys showered and in bed, I collapse into the old carver chair that was the subject of Carys's comments on the day I moved in, with its worn cushions. It's at the end of the table where Nonna would sit, her bottom spilling out of the sides of the chair. Once she died, no one sat in it. It stayed empty. But, right now, it's where I want to be, bringing me some sort of comfort.

I put my head in my hands and my elbows on the table.

Although I need a good cry, the tears don't come.

'I can't do this. I can't. It hurts too much.'

I hear a glass being placed on the table, the pop of a cork, the glug of wine from a bottle and the glass being pushed towards me. Still I don't move.

'You've earned it,' I hear Griff say. I take a big breath and look up. There he is. Griff. He always is when I need him. And my heart does a leap and it crashes again. I wish I'd realized it sooner. It's Griff, it's always been Griff, and now there's nothing I can do about it. And the tears are spilling down my cheeks.

'How could I have been so stupid?' It sounds as though I'm talking about Joe, but I mean Griff too.

'It wasn't your fault. Joe did what he always does. He wanted to help. He wants to be a superhero!'

I take a sip of the red wine.

'I know.' I run my hand under my nose. 'And I should have been there to see what he was doing! Instead I was chasing after bloody Ed Wildes.'

'You weren't to know.'

'About Joe or Ed Wildes?'

He sits on the chair next to me. The lamp from the corner of the room is throwing out an orange glow, lighting up his face. Outside, I can see the moon casting a silver sliver across the water now that the wind has dropped and the sea has settled. I look at Griff, his familiar outline, as if I'm seeing him for the first time, his angular jaw, smiling mouth and sparkling blue eyes.

'Both,' I say quietly. 'I shouldn't have let Joe out of my sight. And I certainly shouldn't have thought that Ed Wildes was ever interested in me for anything other than the boathouse. He didn't want to make up for the past, how he behaved. He just wanted what I've got. I hadn't grasped how low he'd stoop.'

'Ah, so that's what he was up to,' says Griff, his fists tightening. He gulps some of his wine.

'He was there . . . with his partner. Business partner! How could I be so stupid? Again! Just like last time.'

'Whoa, hang on. What do you mean "just like last time"?'

Suddenly all the anger I felt back then is in my burning cheeks.

'Just like when I was the talk of this town! When I met a lad, Eddie Wildes, and thought he felt the same way about me as I did about him, and all the time I was being played for a fool. I was just his bit on the side when he was down here from university. Everyone was talking about me. My poor parents, what did they do to deserve that?' I whisper, making sure not to disturb the boys.

I hiccup loudly and put a hand over my mouth.

'Wait!' He covers the other, which is holding the stem of the wine glass, with his own. 'It wasn't your fault. He was the one who was in the wrong. He should have been worried about how people saw him. You just fell for a guy who was promising you the world.'

I sigh. 'He did indeed promise me the world. And I believed him.'

'So it's Ed Wildes's fault.'

'It's foolish Beca again. Just like before when she was a silly girl. Nothing's changed.'

'Will you stop beating yourself up?' he says crossly,

taking my hands in his big, strong ones. They're rough but I like the feel of them.

'I can't, Griff.' My throat is tight. 'I can't do this. I shouldn't have come back. I can't do any of this. My every move is watched and gossiped about. Nothing has changed. My parents didn't deserve it then and neither do these boys now. I'm going to phone their social worker,' I say. 'Everyone saw how I failed them today. It'll be the talk of the town. I was chasing around after Ed Wildes when I should have been looking after Joe! I'm done, Griff. I can't do this. I'll get her to find other emergency accommodation for them and then I'll go back to London. The past is gone. I couldn't just come back and fit in. It's not my home any more.' This time a sob escapes and I cover my mouth with my hand.

'That's not true,' he says.

But I pick up the phone and dial.

'Is Ed really why you left, Beca? Truly?'

Another sob catches in my throat. His face looks a lot like home, a place I want to be, the *hiraeth*.

'What do you mean?'

'Is Ed why you left? Or was it me? Did I make you leave?'

'No!'

'Really?'

'Of course not. Why would you say that?'

'It was just one kiss, Beca. That night, after you found out about Ed, one kiss, and then you were gone.'

The phone cuts into answerphone and I quickly shut it off. 'No, no!' I grab his hands.

'You ran then, and you didn't know how much people cared about you.'

'I – I wanted to get away. Stop the gossip. I didn't want to hurt anyone else. My parents, my grandparents . . . I didn't want you to think I was on the rebound, or for other people to think I was using you, and ruin your life too. I'd had enough of letting my family down, getting it wrong. I didn't want you to think badly of me too.'

'No one thought badly of you!'

'Oh, they did. I was always the troublemaker at school. Messing up, getting into bother.'

We both laugh.

'And taking you down with me. Nonna despaired of us.'

He laughs again. 'She thought the world of you. We all did.'

Suddenly we stop laughing. Our eyes seem to lock onto each other's.

'So, no more talk of leaving. This is your home. You belong here.'

I drop my head.

'Promise me?'

'Okay, no more talking of leaving,' I say and, with all my willpower, slide my hands out from under his. 'You always could talk me down.'

'Not always. I let you go once. I wish I'd told you then not to run, to be proud of who you are. Whether you like it or not, you're a Valentino and this place needs you. Those boys do too.'

'You're right.'

'I know.' He smiles and his face lights up, as does mine. 'Good. Tomorrow is a new day.'

'And I'm going to put Valentino's back on the map!' I say.

'Yes!'

'I'll show Ed Wildes. Valentino's is here to stay! I'll have to find out what I need to do to reopen.'

'The boys will be delighted.'

'Yes!' The emotion catches in my throat and, with his face so close to mine and the sheer excitement of what tomorrow will bring, it's as though we're drawn together like magnets. We move towards each other so that our foreheads are almost touching. My lips ache and, as if it's the most natural thing in the world, I lean in as he leans in towards me, my lips nearly on his – and then I remember Nia.

'No!' I pull away. 'Sorry. I shouldn't have done that. I'm sorry.'

He looks confused.

'I shouldn't have done that,' I repeat.

He stands up quickly. 'I should go,' he says, grabbing his sweatshirt from the back of the chair.

'No, wait! I can explain.' I stand up too.

'No, Beca!' He twists the sweatshirt in his hands, frustration written all over his face. 'I'm in love with you. I always have been, and you obviously don't feel the same . . . You never did!'

'I c-can't, Griff. I just can't.' My mouth is dry. The words catch in my throat.

'You could take a chance on an idiot like Ed Wildes, but clearly I was never good enough,' he says, in an angry whisper, as he heads for the front door and pulls it back.

'Listen. It's not that. It's complicated.'

'It always is with you, Beca!'

He leaves, and I hear the truck roar as it disappears up the drive at speed. I slump against the wall and rub my face, trying to erase what just happened.

I promised Nia! I said there was nothing between us and that there never would be. I can't be the one to crush her dreams. I can't be the troublemaker again! Despite my head and heart battling it out between them, I have to step back, no matter how much it hurts.

I'm feeling a desperate need to run away all over again.

But I can't. It's tempting to leave this mess behind but I have to stay. I have to make this work. But how?

36

The following morning, I'm rummaging through rubbish bags. 'It must be here!' I say aloud. I remember being cross when Efan arrived at the boathouse, screwing up the paper, tossing it into the bin, and Griff bringing up the bin from the boathouse after I'd left the cove with Joe and Blake.

Griff . . . My heart feels as heavy as an anchor. I need to find him and put things right. But first I need to sort things out at the boathouse.

I keep rummaging through the bags of recycling, like a dog looking for a buried ball in the sand.

'Ah!' I pull out the piece of paper and wipe off a dollop of melted *gelato*. Lemon sherbet: another of Blake's inventions.

I take out my phone and dial the number. 'Efan Rhys? It's Beca Valentino here, from Valentino's, the *gelateria* on the beach in Sŵn y Môr. Tell me what I need to do to reopen, and how I can make it happen fast.'

'Okay,' says Efan, the environmental-health inspector. 'We're going to have to check your products for harmful bacteria and I'll have to spend a few days with you to observe your operating practices.'

'I need to get up and running again as soon as possible. In time for the regatta.' I'm going to end this summer on a high for all of us.

'Well, let's get started straight away. I'll come and meet you at the farm. Check out your premises, send off some *gelato* samples and then, if they're all clear, I'll spend some time watching your working practices.'

'Can you tell me any more about the complaint?'

'I'm afraid not. Just that someone rang to say they had become ill after consuming one of your products.'

I seethe. I know it was Ed. 'But if you test our products . . .'

'. . . and working practices, we can assume that the illness didn't come from you.'

'I've been following all the guidelines and regulations,' I say. 'I even rang your office when we set up to get advice.'

'Then we have a point to prove,' he says kindly.

'Okay. Let's do it!' I say.

37

'So, you managed to get access to the cove across the field?' Efan asks, on the phone. He's keeping me up to date with the results of the inspections. It's been three days since samples of the *gelato* were sent off and I've been keeping busy, cleaning and planning how to make the boathouse bigger and better than before. Trying to keep my mind off the test results and that I haven't seen Griff in as many days. He hasn't popped by and I haven't run into him. Nothing.

'In return for a summer's supply of mint choc chip, one of the local farmers has given me access so people with mobility issues can park on the road and come straight across the field to the boathouse. No need to go over the coast path.'

'That's great,' he says. 'Well, I have some good news.

The *gelato* samples came back clear on all the tests. No problems. You can reopen.'

A smile creeps over my face.

'But . . .'

'Yes?' The smile halts.

'. . . I'm afraid you'll have to put up with my company for a few days. Just to double-check your working practices. But from what I can see everything's in order. Whoever put in this complaint didn't get ill from your *gelateria*.'

'I know,' I say quietly.

After I've shared the good news with the boys and Scooter, who's scrubbing the milking parlour again, we all head down to the boathouse. As we arrive, Griff is heading along the coast path from the other direction.

'Griff!' call Joe and Blake, and Cariad comes bounding along the path to greet them.

'Griff,' I say nervously, hating myself for feeling like this around him. 'We got the all-clear.'

'I heard! That's why I'm here. Scooter told me.' He seems as awkward as I feel.

'Word travels fast,' I say, smiling tentatively.

'Get Cariad some water, can you, please, boys?' Griff calls, and they run off with the dog at their heels to find a bowl to fill.

'Now what?' he asks.

'Well, I can reopen, but Efan, the inspector, has to watch our operation for a few days, to check we're doing everything right. Using a different scoop for each flavour, making sure our serving area is clean, all rubbish in the bins . . .'

'It's spotless. Joe sees to that!' Griff grins.

'Yes, he does!' I laugh.

'Actually, Beca, I've come to say sorry. I should have kept my mouth shut. I'd hate anything to spoil our friendship.'

'Me too!' I want to tell him I feel exactly the same as he does, that I'm in love with him, but I can't. I promised Nia. 'And I've been thinking we should offer lunches, not just *gelato*,' I tell him.

'Thinking big, like you always do.'

'Fresh shellfish, cooked here on the beach. Lobster rolls. Crab salads.'

I have no idea what to say about the other night. I just want things to go back to how they were.

'I could buy directly from you, and other fishermen in the area.'

'Great minds!' he says.

'I'll show Ed Wildes. He's not putting me out of business and getting his hands on the boathouse. No way!'

'Good for you! I can do the lobster and crab, no problem. There'll be mackerel too, once it comes in. You could barbecue it. I'll spread the word to the other fishermen. They'll be glad of the income.'

'Well, it won't be much, but let's hope word spreads and people like it. And I need to put some more fairy-lights down the coast path. I'm going to do sunset opening hours from now until the regatta.'

'Good plan!' He beams.

It's so good to have him back in my life. Even if this is all he can ever be, the best of friends, the yin to my yang. We just fit and I don't want to give that up again, or run away and risk losing what I have. It's enough for me. If it's all I can have, I'll take it.

Cariad is lying in the shade, panting. Griff notices me looking at her. 'She's hot. And pregnant.'

'She's pregnant?'

'Just found out. Looks like she's been making out with one of the holidaymakers' dogs in the cottage.'

I bend down and stroke her.

'You'll make a great mum to your pups,' I say. 'Even if they try your patience, you'll be there for them.' I'm choking up. I have no idea where that came from. I shake it off and straighten.

'It's been a stressful couple of days. Don't beat your-self up,' he says, not needing to ask what's wrong. 'I didn't help.'

I can't talk about that.

'So, lunches.' I distract myself from the anxiety rattling at my fingertips and toes, avoiding the conversation about the other night and also checking my phone. There's been no word from Mo lately, and I'm wondering when she's going to call, how much longer the boys will have with me.

'Let's get the word out and people in,' I say.

'I'll organize the seafood.' Griff dips his head.

'Perfect.'

'And fish-finger sandwiches for the children. Every-one likes a fish-finger sandwich,' Joe joins in.

'Quite right. It'll be a great pull for families.'

'Let's get it on social media,' says Blake, starting to tap on his phone.

'Any new *gelato* flavours, Blake?' I ask.

He grins at me with black lips. 'Liquorice!'

We laugh.

'Be interesting to see how that goes down.'

'Glad you're back on track,' Griff says. 'And sorry again about the other night.'

I want to lean forward and kiss his cheek, but I don't. I can't. I pull away. I'm just happy he's still here, helping, being my friend. It's all I can hope for.

38

For the next few days, business booms as word gets around that we're open again, bigger and better than before. So much so that Efan has to join in serving at the counter when the queue gets too long as visitors arrive from the coast path and via the new route across the field.

'Nia!'

'I heard you could do with a hand,' she says, and looks at Efan.

'This is Efan, from Environmental Health.'

He waves at her. He's not wearing his suit or lace-up shoes today. Instead he's in a T-shirt, long shorts and deck shoes, blending in much better.

'Hi.' Nia waves back. 'I came to help.' She looks around. 'Heard it was busy here.' She sees Scooter, and Griff, who is barbecuing fresh mackerel, which we're serving with salad and new potatoes. Scooter is unpacking cold boxes with more *gelato* from the house. It's all hands on deck, and we're a real team at the moment. 'And to say I'm sorry. About the other day. I should never have made you promise what I did. Griff is his own person. It's not for me to decide who he should be with. I suppose I'm just sad at what has been. I know it won't happen again but I'm lucky we can still call each other family.'

I'm surprised by what she's just said. But is it too late for there to be anything between Griff and me? I put my hand over hers, telling her I understand.

'Well, as this looks like a family business, I'd better help out too!' She attempts a smile.

'Beca?'

Oh, no. That voice interrupts my thoughts and doesn't make my heart leap like it used to. My fists curl in anger. I turn slowly.

'I'm busy, Ed.' At the tables, people are enjoying the sunshine, the food and the *gelato*. Most of all the *gelato*. I wonder if we could start making our own cones, then shake off the thought. This place was just for the summer, and the summer is nearly over. But the sound of seagulls, laughter and the splash of the sea makes me happy. I'm not going to let Ed Wildes spoil it, not again.

'This was always going to be a great location. Look, Beca, can we talk?' he says.

'I told you, Ed, I'm busy, and I have nothing to say to you.'

'There must be a way we can work together here.'

'What? By trying to get me shut down? You don't think there's enough space in this town for two *gelaterias*?'

'It wasn't me.'

I raise my eyebrows.

'Business is good. I can see that.' His eyes sweep round the busy cove, with its bunting and fairy-lighting, the barbecue pit and my chilled-out customers.

'You mean you're losing customers to us,' I state the obvious.

He looks at the chalked menus, one for lobster rolls and fish-finger sandwiches in locally made bread. Thick white slices with butter, cut into quarters.

'Look, Beca, I'm going to do all I can to pull out the stops for the regatta. Make it a really big one. We'll need the income when the holidaymakers go home.'

He's right. It'll be quiet around here. And it's not just the holidaymakers I'm going to be missing, but the boys too . . .

'Why don't we pool our resources?'

I frown. 'You want us to work together?'

'Yes. A shared menu and ingredients that we both sell, then split the profits.'

I look at him. Twenty years ago, this would have been the dream. Ed and I building a business together.

But not now.

'No, Ed. You tried to have me closed down,' I say firmly.

'Look, I'm telling you—'

'Who was it, then, Ed? From where I'm standing, it was a very serious attempt to get me shut down and try to buy my business from me. Let me tell you this. You will never get my business. I'll make sure of that. You treated me badly twenty years ago, and it seems you still have no respect for me, or anyone who stands in the way of you getting what you want. I will never let you use me again. Everyone will want *gelato* at the regatta and I want to make sure that it's Valentino's *gelato* they're eating.'

He sighs. 'Believe what you want, Beca. But, I'm telling you, I didn't try to get you shut down. Yes, I wanted this place. But I didn't call Environmental Health. And, for what it's worth, I really did want to get to know you again.'

I watch him as he walks away. Business is definitely booming. It's not hard to see that.

A few days turns into ten as Efan takes holiday leave from his office, stays on and helps because he's enjoying being at the café.

On his last evening, as the sun is setting over the cove, the fairy-lights come on and it's time to start clearing up. It's been another good day. Blake is checking his stock and planning what he's going to make for tomorrow, while Joe is washing down the surfaces so they're spotless.

'Well, I think we can agree you have everything in order here,' says Efan, with a smile. 'I wish I could say I'll be back tomorrow, but I won't be. You don't need me here any more. You've had your clean bill of health. And I have to get back to work. But thank you for letting me be a part of this, just for a while. I loved it! Who knows? Maybe one day I'll break out of the office and do something like this myself.'

I beam. 'Thank you for everything, most of all for helping to get us open again so quickly.'

'Sometimes people get in touch with us for their own reasons. I'm sorry they do. But you have nothing to worry about from what I've seen.'

'Well, that's good news,' says Griff. He puts his arm around me and kisses my cheek. Nia's face tightens.

'Let's have a drink, if you're allowed,' I say to Efan. 'To celebrate and to say thank you for your help. And if ever the environmental-health thing doesn't work out for you, you've always got a job here.' What am I saying? I'm going to close at the end of the summer. I don't intend to reopen. But there's no need to think about that now. The sun is setting and one thing I've learnt from having Blake and Joe with me is to take each day as it comes. Each day they've stayed has turned this summer into one of the best I've had in years. Them, this place, and Griff, my best friend Griff.

I watch as he makes his way to the firepit, Blake behind him with more wood. He lets Blake feed it onto the burning embers, and my heart swells. Right now, I don't want anything to spoil this.

I open the fridge and pull out a bottle of white wine, plus a couple of bottles of beer. 'What's everyone having?' I call from behind the counter.

'Dandelion and burdock for me!' says Joe.

Everyone else gathers bottles and plastic glasses from the counter and we walk down to the firepit. The last of the holidaymakers are straggling back up the coast path.

'Bye. Thank you. The *gelato* was wonderful. We'll be back next year!' says a family, leaving with big smiles. If only I thought I'd be here next year too.

'*Nos da!*' says Griff.

'*Nos da!*' I find myself slipping into Welsh. Whatever happens, this feels very much like home.

'Here's to Valentino's at the boathouse,' says Griff, and we raise our glasses and bottles.

'To Team Tŷ Mawr!' says Blake, and Joe whoops.

We finish our drinks by the fire.

'I must be going,' says Efan.

'And me,' says Nia, but this time I don't see her looking at Griff to gauge his reaction. She stands.

313

'Can I give you a lift?' asks Efan. 'I have my car just up there, past the field. The coast path may be a bit tricky in the dark.'

Suddenly she smiles. 'I'll take your word for it, you being a professional in environmental health.' He laughs, as we all do. And I want to hold on to this feeling, right here and now, by the embers of the fire, the sound of the waves and our laughter in our ears. The feeling of being at home.

'Goodnight,' they call, and follow the fairy-lighting from the boathouse across the field to the road.

'Well, that was a good day,' Griff says.

'It was,' I agree, as Blake and Joe build a sandcastle, lit by the solar fairy-lights inside the lobster pots and fishing nets around the eating area.

'We could do feast nights here in the height of summer,' I say, picturing it.

'I thought you were only doing it this year,' Griff reminds me.

'I am,' I say, but I can't stop having ideas. 'A band playing, a couple of guitars, the barbecue. Bring your own wine and beer. Platters of seafood . . .'

'Mackerel-and-lobster nights. Mussels with chips!' Griff joins in.

'Gin-and-tonic *gelato*, prosecco!' I say.

'Space-dust flavour!' Blake joins in. 'We could offer it as a topping.'

Griff's phone pings into life.

'Who's trying to get in touch with you at this time of night?' I say.

He pulls it out of his back pocket, and it lights up his face, which is altogether more serious than it was just seconds ago.

'Griff?'

'It's Annabelle. She's back here, in Sŵn y Môr. She wants to meet and talk.'

A sudden chill makes me shiver: autumn is just around the corner.

'You go!' I swallow, hard.

'You sure?'

'Of course,' I say. 'We'll clear up here, close up. You go.'

There's a moment's hesitation and I can't look at him. As he leaves I squeeze my eyes tight shut. I have just let the man I love walk out of my life and into the arms of another woman.

39

'Joe, I'm not sure *gelato* is what I'm supposed to be feeding you for breakfast,' I say, as the morning light pours into the kitchen through the windows overlooking the pasture where the cows are grazing with their calves.

'But we have plenty of it!' he says, chocolate around his face from where he's licked the bowl. I pull off some kitchen roll and hand it to him.

'Okay. Let's get showered and down to the boathouse. Looks like it could be busy. People will be making the most of the last few days of their holiday. The weather's being very kind to them.'

It's hot. I fan myself with a place mat, then put it on the table with a pot of tea on top. 'We need to make a plan for the regatta tomorrow.' I pick up a pen and a piece of paper.

'I want to wear a hat like this,' says Joe. He's gazing at a photograph of Nonno in a straw boater, with his bike, selling *gelato* at the regatta years ago. 'And ride a bike like this one.'

'Joe, I don't have a bike.'

'Bet Griff does!'

I'm thinking about Griff again, wondering where he spent last night and if it was in Annabelle's arms. How must Nia be feeling, thinking she was finally in with a shot? If only I'd told him how Nia felt and why nothing could happen between us.

A knock at the door interrupts my thoughts.

'Beca?'

'Hey, Nia, this is a nice surprise,' I say, but really I know why she's here and I have no idea what to say to her. 'What can I do for you?'

'Can I come in for a minute?'

'Of course,' I say. 'I've just made tea.' I grab a mug from the cupboard and take it to the table.

'Hi, Nia,' says Joe.

'Go and get yourself cleaned up, Joe,' I tell him.

'And then we can make plans for the regatta?'

'Yes.'

'And you'll find me a hat to wear?'

'I will,' I promise rashly, though I have no idea where I'm going to find a boater at this late stage. How do parents do it? Fancy-dress days sprung on them, costumes for shows needed at the last minute, and, of course, there was home schooling during the Covid lockdowns. I take my hat off to them, working and doing all of that too. I only have Blake and Joe for a little longer and I'll be ready to collapse when they go.

When they go. The words whizz round my head. They're only here until their new home is ready for them. Blake has been desperate to get back to the city ever since he arrived. And Joe needs to be settled.

'So, how are you, Nia?' I say, as I pour the tea. 'Look, about last night,' I decide to plunge straight in, 'I had no idea.'

'It was me!' she says.

I haven't a clue what she's talking about.

'You?'

'Yes, me. Not Ed Wildes. I'm sorry.'

I'm still confused.

'You . . .' I start processing what she means.

'I called Environmental Health, and I'm so sorry.' She hugs the mug of tea.

'You called Environmental Health?' I say slowly. Her cheeks are pink, her eyes sparkling in the sunlight with little tears. 'Why?'

She sighs.

'I – I couldn't bear it when you came back. Griff and I, we weren't together. He has partners but they don't last.'

I think about him and Annabelle and wonder how to tell her that this one might go the distance. I glance at my phone. Still no word from him. It's getting hot but the sunshine seems muted as clouds roll in to cover the sky. It's muggy – at least, in here it is. I stand and throw open the back door to let in the breeze, as I think about what Nia has said.

'We were happy in our own way, and I could almost bear that. Then you came back and I knew there would never be a me and him again.'

I swallow. 'It's never been like that between us, I swear.'

'Maybe not for you, but for Griff it's always been you. Even Scooter can tell.'

I want to ask what Scooter has said, but don't. Right now, someone who wanted to close down my *gelateria* is sitting in front of me.

'I – I'm really not proud of this. I even got into a battle over where Scooter should go to college, or what she should do next, just to have time with him, to share what we had. I couldn't bear to let that go. Once Scooter leaves home, what will I have left to hold on to?'

'Scooter needs to make up her own mind,' I say.

'She does,' she agrees. 'And then,' she continues, 'when it looked like you were here to stay, and you were going to set up Valentino's at the boathouse, I knew I'd lost him for good. He was spending more and more time there. So . . .' her voice cracks, and the tears begin to fall, 'I rang Environmental Health and

said I'd been ill after eating one of your ice creams.'
She sobs.

I pull off some kitchen paper from the roll on the sideboard and hand it to her, just like I did for Joe, and then I put the roll on the table for any other mishaps.

She blows her nose loudly.

'And then, when I came to see you that day at the boathouse and you told me there was nothing between the two of you and promised there never would be, I realized what a mistake I'd made. But it was too late!'

'The council were shutting me down.'

'Yes.' She blows her nose again. She's a few years younger than Griff and me so in school I barely knew her. I wonder how long she'd idolized Griff before finally getting together with him. She's been waiting her whole life for him to feel the same about her as she does about him. I want to be cross, but I can't. I just feel for her. I lean forward and hug her.

Then she pulls back.

'I'm sorry, Nia,' I find myself saying.

'No, there's more.' She shreds the soggy kitchen roll in her hand and I pass her another piece. Good tip from Joe to buy it. It comes in handy for everything.

'I need to tell you something else.'

What else could there be?

She takes a deep breath. I sit back and tilt my head to one side.

'Efan.'

'The environmental-health officer?'

She nods.

'We . . . Well, when I arrived at the boathouse and he was there, helping you, I was furious with myself. I just couldn't bear what I'd done. And that's why I'd come to help, to try to make up for it. Not that I could make up for what I'd done. But I wanted to try.'

'You were a great help. And so was Efan.' I find myself smiling. 'I'm sure he wasn't supposed to join in, but it's been so busy. He was brilliant, too. He's a lovely man.'

Nia is smiling now. 'He is,' she says quietly. She glances into her mug and then gazes at me. For a moment we don't say anything. No words are needed for what she's trying to say. I can tell.

'You and Efan,' I say.

She nods. 'We got on well, helping out at the boat-house. He makes me laugh.'

'And?'

'Last night after we'd finished here . . .' she says.

'You and he?'

'I wasn't expecting it but, well, I've don't think I've ever felt so happy!' She's glowing. 'At least, not for a very long time. He's lovely.'

'And, from the sound of it, he feels the same way about you.' I let a small smile grow.

She blushes and sniffs.

'I'm so pleased for you, Nia. Really. I hope he's everything you want him to be.'

'We all need hope,' she says. 'Looks like change can be a good thing, even in a place like Sŵn y Môr.' She gives a little hiccup. 'If there's anything I can do to make it up to you . . .'

'I don't suppose you'd know where I can get hold of a straw boater, do you?'

She giggles. 'I might just have one in the dressing-up box from when Scooter was in primary school.'

'Brilliant!' I say, with relief. Now all we have to hope is that the weather stays fine for the regatta tomorrow.

40

As day turns to night, the wind whips up, thunder roars and lightning illuminates the sky and sea in a spectacular show.

I barely sleep. None of us does with the storm at its worst.

At first light, I'm out of bed and checking the cows. Everywhere is sodden with the rain but fresh. I wrap my arms around myself and breathe in deeply, just like I did when I first arrived here.

It's the day of the regatta. I'm remembering everything I need to get done before we open today. There's a sandcastle competition on the beach by the harbour, swimming races at the cove because it's more sheltered, and boating races by the yacht club. There are bands playing there later. There's a crabbing competition and another for fancy dress. Nia is going to bring

Joe's outfit to the boathouse. I've got to stock up with as much *gelato* as I can. Griff is going to barbecue mackerel and lobster once he's checked the pots. I'm going to the boathouse to set up once the boys are out of bed. But first there is somewhere I have to go.

It's early, but the town is already getting ready for the day ahead. I wave to the postman and Carys, out walking her dogs. She waves back.

'I'll be down for some of that *gelato* later,' she calls.

'Blake's got some specials for you.'

'The dogs love the plain one,' Carys says, 'but I can't wait to try whatever he's come up with today.'

I stand in front of Valentino's just as I did on the first day I came back. The lights are on and I can see movement inside. I walk towards the door and knock before I push it. It's open, despite the early hour. There's no welcoming bell. But the place has been cleaned and polished and it smells different, not like Valentino's. But this isn't the old *gelateria*. The boathouse is Valentino's now. This is Wildes.

'Ed?' I call.

He appears from the back, mop in hand.

'Hey!' he says warily. 'You're early.'

'I know, sorry, but it's a big day, for us all.' I can't see Valentino's here any more. I think of the boathouse and my kitchen, the old pine table where we created the flavours with the big wooden spoon, Nonna's carver chair, where I sit. That's where Valentino's is.

'So, what can I do for you, Beca?' he says, peeling off his yellow rubber gloves.

He's attractive, still, but I don't fancy him. I know that. There's only one man who makes me feel happy, content and excited all at the same time and he's gone back to Annabelle.

I swallow, take a deep breath, and roll my shoulders. 'I've come to apologize. I know it wasn't you who rang Environmental Health. I shouldn't have flown off the handle at you.'

For a moment, he doesn't speak. Then: 'You had every right to say what you said to me. Every right. I deserved it all. I treated you appallingly when we were young, and I don't think I've done much better this time round. Yes, I wanted Tŷ Mawr, and the boathouse. Yes, I thought I could persuade you to sell it to me with a little wining and dining. And, as usual, I hugely underestimated you. And you overestimated me, thinking I'd changed, that I wanted to put the past right. I'm so sorry. I'm such a prat at times.'

I wasn't expecting that. I open my mouth but he beats me to it: 'I mean it, Beca. I really am sorry about what happened between us twenty years ago. I behaved like a total idiot. The truth is, I really liked you. I wanted to be with you. But my parents made it hard for me, offered me all sorts to move on and set up with

Portia, the daughter of friends. In fact, we didn't really get on. We didn't last long after that summer here. I hated thinking you'd left town because of me.'

'I did.'

'I realized how much Griff hated me for that too. And I'm sorry for the gossip.'

I give a wry smile. '*I'm* sorry I covered your car with rude pictures in shaving foam.'

He smiles. 'I thought it was funny. My parents, on the other hand . . .'

We chuckle.

'We used to laugh together back then and I think we could again. I really would like to get to know you . . . for real. Not because of Tŷ Mawr or the boathouse but because we could be great together, you and me.'

He picks up my hand and holds it. I feel nothing but relief. I can let it go. I can stop being so angry. It's time for Ed Wildes to be himself, not some big shadow in my past. I'm living in the here and now, not going back to the past. And the here and now doesn't include Ed romantically. My days of being romantically involved with anyone are well and truly over.

'Ed. There isn't going to be any getting to know each other better, or a you-and-me as partners. But I would like us to be friends,' I say.

He presses his lips together, then says, 'I'm used to getting what I want, not the alternative.'

'Me too,' I say. 'We're very alike.'

'That's why we'd be great together.'

'No, Ed. It's why we should never be together, romantically or in business.'

'And, just checking, can't resist, you really don't want to sell?'

'I do not.' I shake my head firmly.

'Okay, just checking. But if you ever do . . .'

'I'll let you know.'

I glance at my watch. 'I have to go. Lots to do. Have a good day.' I make for the door and open it, this time without expecting the bell to ring. I step outside, then turn back to Ed, who is standing in the doorway.

'And you, Beca. Your *gelato* really is great. Everyone's talking about it.'

I smile widely. 'Thanks, Ed. Friends.'

'Friends,' he says, and holds out his arms. I do the same and we hug. It's over. That part of my past is where it should have stayed, in the past. The part I'm holding on to is my family's name, their *gelato*, right here again at the Sŵn y Môr regatta. As we hug, I know that we're friends. The anger has gone.

'I've really got to go,' I say, as we pull apart. 'And even though I won't be your business partner, maybe I could supply you with *gelato*!'

'I knew we could do business! Bye, Beca.'

I turn away and see Griff in his truck at the end of the road. He must be on his way to the boathouse so I hurry after him.

327

41

I see it from the top of the cliff, as I reach the end of the coast path where it looks down on the cove. My heart leaps into my mouth. '*Nooooo! No, no, no!*' I hurry down the path, long grasses brushing my sides and hands as I avoid slipping on the worn rocks.

'No!' I say, when I reach the bottom and look at the boathouse, at Griff, Blake and Joe.

'The wind's blown it over!' says Joe.

'Well, not completely over, Joe,' says Griff, looking at me. 'I would have called, but I could see you were busy,' he adds. And, for a moment, I have no idea what he's talking about. And then I remember. He must have seen me hugging Ed as I left Wildes earlier. And Ed lives over the café! Did Griff think I'd stayed the night with him?

'Oh, no, I wasn't . . .' I can't explain now. It'll have to

wait for later. And, anyway, why does it matter? He's with Annabelle.

I look back at the listing boathouse. It's no longer upright but leaning to the side, the roof sitting at a jaunty angle to the base. The bunting is flying free in the wind. The fairy-lighting has sagged and dropped on its poles. It's a mess. A disaster.

'Can we fix it?'

Griff shakes his head. 'I don't know. We'd need help.'

'I can get help,' says Blake.

'Really?'

'Yeah, the lads from the town – they hang out at the scooter park. They've invited me to go sometime. They reckoned it was better to make me their friend than their enemy after I took them on over the *gelato* tasters. They were here the day Joe went missing. Some of their dads work for a building company.'

I'm trying to take it in.

I look back at the boathouse. Could we really get it upright in time for the regatta? On the other hand, what if we leave it like that and it shifts some more, when the swimmers are at the cove, preparing for their races? We'll have to cancel those races if we can't get it upright and safe.

The seagulls are circling overhead and this time it feels like they're laughing at me. Taunting me. You thought you could do it? Ha! Think again! And the doubts wash over me in waves. There's no way we can get this sorted in time.

I look out to sea. What would Nonna and Nonno do? I know exactly what they would have done. Life wasn't easy for them, but they kept going. It's all you can do, isn't it?

I turn to Griff and the boys. 'Let's do it. Get as many people as we can to help!' I'm pulling out my phone, just as it rings.

42

I hold the phone to my ear, knowing exactly what's coming.

'Hi, Beca. It's Mo. Good news! I've got placements for the boys to go to. Back to Cardiff. The one for Blake even has a pool table and a cinema-screen TV.'

I swallow. 'Great!'

'So, I'm on my way to you. Can you get them ready for picking up?'

'Today?'

'I know it's short notice, but I'm so excited to show them their new homes. I have schools organized. The children's-home managers would like to get them settled in over the weekend. Blake's one has organized pizza night for him. Joe will love the fact there's a cat in the one we've found for him.'

'Erm, yes, of course.' My voice is tight and hoarse.

My eyes are prickling. I can't let them see me like this. I have to be positive. I turn away and blink a lot.

'It's really good news, isn't it? Just in time for school to restart. The timing couldn't have been better.'

I walk away from the boathouse to the edge of the water, just as the pod of dolphins travels by, dipping and diving, making me catch my breath. It's a fleeting trip that will stay in my memory, just like the boys. But something is scratching at the back of my mind.

'Erm, sorry, aren't they going to the same place? I think they'd prefer to stay together.'

I glance back at the little group. Blake is already testing how to straighten the corrugated listing wall, but I can tell he has one eye on me. He knows something is happening.

'Sadly, no. We couldn't keep them together. But they're both lovely placements.'

Placements, not homes. A home. It's different. I feel sick.

'So I'm on my way to you now.'

'Is there any chance we could make it Monday? Or even tomorrow, just to have one last day?'

'I'm really sorry. I can't. Like I say, Blake's new children's-home manager is keen to have the weekend to settle him in, get him mixing with the other boys his age. So I need to get them back and to their new places.'

'It's just . . . it's the regatta today.'

'Oh, what a shame. But I bet they're dying to get

back to the city. I'm sorry it took so long. Places are so tight for children of their ages. And thank you again for stepping in at such short notice. You're going to be great at fostering. And next week, we'll get started on finding you a new placement. Younger this time. More what you were hoping for.'

A new placement?

'I'll see you in a while, then.'

'Erm, okay, but mind the track to the house. We had a lot of rain last night.' I'm trying to sound as if this is just a normal conversation.

Blake looks at me. He knows. To him, it's normal. And I couldn't feel more wretched.

Joe is packed with his superhero rucksack. Blake has his black bin bag, but the hat Griff gave him is firmly on his head.

Nia, Griff and Scooter arrive at the farmhouse just as Mo does, down the now-potholed drive.

I try to remember my training. I mustn't make this hard for Blake and Joe. This mustn't be upsetting for them.

The car door opens and Mo gets out.

'Hello, boys! Lovely to see you! Right, all ready? Let's get you back to the city.'

Blake doesn't look up. Joe pushes his glasses up his nose and turns to me.

'Tell Nia I'm sorry not to be able to wear the outfit

she made for me. And, Scooter, I'm sorry I can't help with the cows. And if the coffee machine plays up . . .'

'It's fine, Joe,' I say, but it hardly sounds like my voice.

I can't remember whether I'm allowed to hug them or not. But I do. Hard. And Joe hugs me back. As does Blake, none of us saying anything. I can't trust myself.

Then Blake pulls away and gets quickly into the car. 'How long till we get there?' He's shifted into self-protection mode already.

Joe takes a little longer and I hear a sniff. I can't look down, because if I do . . . Mo gently guides him to the car and I shut my eyes tight. I hear the car door closing. I can't look.

'I'll ring you on Monday,' I hear Mo say, and all I can do is nod. My throat is totally closed. Then I hear the engine start and pull away. I raise a hand but can barely see the car, just the red tail lights, as my eyes swim with tears that can't fall before the boys have left. It feels like hell.

When I think I can, I turn and run towards the gate and down the steps to the sea. As always, it's my place of safety when I need it. I put my arms around myself and let the tears roll. The Mermaids are there, but not in the water. They're by the boathouse.

Griff is beside me.

'It's over. It's all over,' I say. 'I can't do this.'

'You can do whatever you put your mind to, Beca Valentino.'

'Clearly not. It's over. Look, the boathouse has practically collapsed and the boys are gone. It's all gone. Somehow, I never manage to hang on to the good stuff.'

Griff takes hold of my arms. 'Then fight for it, Beca. Like you did for this place, Valentino's. Fight for what you want in life!'

I stop crying.

'If you want something, you'll go after it. I know you!' he tells me.

I stare at him. He's right. Why am I standing here crying?

'Are you sure you want the boys?' he asks.

I nod.

'You don't have anything to prove to anybody.'

'I don't want to prove anything to anyone. I want to do it because I can. And not just for them, but for me too. I want to be a mum. Or whatever I'll be. It's not about giving birth, it's about cooking fish fingers for tea. About sitting around the table. I want the laughter, the arguments, the celebrations, Joe fixing things, Blake in the kitchen . . .'

'Then I'll support you all the way.' I begin to walk up the beach. 'Take the risk! Finally commit to the ones who love you.'

I turn to him, and I can't read everything written on

his face. I look at the boathouse, then back at him. But I know one thing. I don't want the boys to leave.

'Go after them, Beca! Get the boys!' he shouts after me.

And with all my might I run back up the steps, to the shouts of the Mermaids cheering me on. I run as fast as I can, knowing I'm probably too late. But I have to try.

43

I'm out of breath, and I know Mo will be long gone by now, but I run up through the field of cows anyway towards the track. My heart leaps at the sight of Lloyd Owen's tractor blocking the road, and a flock of sheep heading from one field to the next. At the end of the drive, only just on the road, I can make out the red tail lights of Mo's little yellow Panda.

'Stop, Mo!'

I yell and wave, just as the last sheep disappear into the field and Lloyd Owen starts to close the gate.

'Wait, Lloyd!' I shout, as he gets into the cab and starts his engine. I'm not going to make it.

The tractor rolls off the road, and Mo's brake lights go off as the little car starts edging forwards. Suddenly the back door opens. Blake jumps out and runs towards me, throwing himself into a hug.

44

In the kitchen, Mo has tea and chocolate *gelato*, which Joe has insisted she try after a tour of the milking parlour. Griff, Nia, and Leah from the Mermaids are there too, nervously standing by the kitchen worktop.

'Mo, I don't want to do respite, not right now.'

'I'm really sorry to hear that.'

'I want to do long-term fostering.'

'Oh.' She brightens.

'I want Joe and Blake to stay here. Long term.'

'For how long?' she asks.

'As long as they want. I'm not going anywhere and I don't want to lose them.' I look at the boys. 'If that's what they want.'

Blake's face is taut with tension.

Joe slides back onto his seat at the end of the table.

'Blake?' Mo asks.

I hold my breath.

'You can't get *gelato* like this in the city,' he says, and smiles, making me smile too.

'Well, it's a bit unusual,' says Mo, 'and these new placements were very hard to find.'

'You said yourself you're desperate for carers.'

'And it would be long term?' Mo asks.

'For ever,' I say. 'This is their home, like it's mine.'

'I'll be a guarantor,' says Griff, 'or reference. Or whatever you need.'

'And me,' says Nia.

'You can include me too, I've seen how wonderful you are with these boys,' Leah adds.

'Joe?' asks Mo.

'I knew you'd come after us,' he says to me. 'You need us here. I took the spoon!' He holds up Nonna's wooden spoon and waves it, cutting through the tension and making us laugh.

Mo finishes her *gelato*. 'I can see how happy the boys are with you,' she says. 'And if that's what you all want, I'll take it to the panel.'

45

'On three,' I hear someone call as we make our way to the boathouse.

It's a hive of activity at the cove. Everyone is there, the Mermaids, the boys from the town, Efan from the council and, I do a double-take, Ed. All working together to shore up the boathouse.

'Wait!' says Griff, running down the steps to join in, followed by Blake, Scooter and Joe. 'Looks like word got around,' he says, smiling at me.

There are holidaymakers, some of the second-home owners from the yoga class and the local fishermen who helped find Joe on the day he took Griff's boat. I stand and stare. Because that's all I can do. All of these people are here, helping to get Valentino's back on its feet for the day. All of these people were here to help when I needed them. Maybe word of mouth, call it gossip if you will, isn't such a bad thing, after all.

And looking out to sea, the dolphins are back, maybe here to stay a bit longer, like the boys, for as long as they want. It's home.

I know stormy days lie ahead, but somehow, they make the good days even better.

46

'Come on! We can't be late!' says Blake, hurrying me along the coast path.

Leah is minding the *gelato* stall. Nia has gone ahead with Joe.

At the harbour, music is playing over speakers and people with drinks are out on the grass overlooking the sea, towards the boathouse and our cove, where I sat that first day, lobbing ice cream for the seagulls.

Nia spots us first and tells Joe, who's standing beside her and swells with pride. Not for the first time today, tears prickle my eyes.

It's like I'm there, right back there when I was a child, taking part in the regatta with my family.

The fancy-dress parade is about to begin. We've made it just in time.

'And this year's theme,' says Dewi Roberts, over the

Tannoy, 'is local heroes. Let's have a round of applause for our local heroes!'

Young people dressed as bards, kings and knights parade around the small show area. I can't take my eyes off Joe. There he is, pushing a bike with a box on the front that Nia and Scooter have made, wearing a boater and a white coat, with Valentino's written on it. The *best gelato* in the west!

'He's come as Nonno!' I hug Nia. 'Thank you!'

'No,' she says, 'thank *you* for forgiving me.'

I wave a hand. 'It's—'

'No, it's not. You have to tell him you feel the same,' she says, nodding in Griff's direction.

'What?' We look at Griff, who is giving Joe the thumbs-up. 'Oh, no, I couldn't. He's obviously back with Annabelle after the other night and I don't want to upset that.'

'But—'

'I can't, Nia. I can't be the one to make him choose.'

Griff is beaming as Joe is presented with a medal and a small cup for first place. 'I won!' he shouts to me. 'I'm a local hero!!'

'You are, Joe, you absolutely are,' I tell him.

'Beca, the boys have asked if I want to go and play football. Can I?' Blake asks. Everything in my being wants to say, 'No, stay with me, stay safe. I've only just got you back.' But I say, 'Go! Be back for dinner.'

'We'll barbecue on the beach,' Griff says. 'If you'd like?'

'I would.'

Blake runs off and I couldn't be happier.

Griff and I walk back along the coast path as the sun dips in the sky. I take deep breaths, wondering if I'll ever forget this day.

'So . . .' says Griff, at the same time as I do. Despite the warmth of the sun, and everything that's happened, there's awkwardness between us, and I think it may be because of Ed.

'How's Annabelle?' I ask, with all the cheeriness I can muster: even if it's just me and the boys and I have Griff in my life as a friend, I'll take that. I never want to lose him again.

'Good,' he says. 'And Ed?'

'Good. We sorted things out.'

'Good,' he says.

'I mean . . .'

'It's okay, you don't need to explain,' he says quickly. 'You and he are back together. I'm happy for you.'

'We are not back together!' I say.

'I saw you leaving his place this morning. You don't need to cover things up. Honestly, I'm happy for you.'

'You saw me there early this morning because I went to apologize for blaming him for calling Environmental Health.'

'To apologize?'

'Yes, it wasn't him who called them. So I went to say sorry.'

'And you decided to give it another go?'

'*No!* But we realized we could be friends. That's it.'

'So when I saw you two hugging?'

'Hugging, yes, when we agreed we could be friends.'

'Good. I mean, if that's what you want.'

'I do,' I say, as we walk down the rocky part of the path, the overgrown grasses brushing our sides. We're walking in single file. Perhaps not looking at each other is helping us say what needs to be said. I hold my courage in both hands and take the risk, just like he told me to earlier today.

'And you and Annabelle?'

'She's fine. Took it well.'

'Took what well?' I pick my way over the shiny stones.

'When she asked if I wanted to get back together, and I said—'

'What did you say?'

He shakes his head. 'No. I couldn't. She wanted me to move to London.' He stops and looks out over the sea. 'I have everything I want right here.' And my stomach flips.

Suddenly I can hear laughter and turn towards the pathway over the field. There are the Mermaids, a group of them and . . . 'Is that Carys with them?'

We hurry down the path to where Carys is now sitting on a rock, out of breath but happy.

'She wants to join us!' says Leah, beaming. Which is

great but I'm not sure how Carys is going to make it into the water.

'I have a plan,' says Leah, stepping forward with a plastic chair and placing it in the water. With that, she helps Carys take off her coat and fixes a swimming cap on her head.

She and another woman help Carys over the stones to the chair, where she sits. Then Leah picks up a crabbing bucket and pours water all over Carys, to her delighted shouts. She asks to be helped up.

'She's probably had enough,' I say, as Griff and I watch.

But, no. This time, they're guiding her deeper into the water, where she finally dips her shoulders under the surface, to cheers from the other Sŵn y Môr Mermaids.

As teas are handed around after the swim, Griff lights the fire.

'I haven't done that since I was a young woman,' says Carys. 'You're never too old to remember the things you love.' She raises her tea to me and looks pointedly at Griff.

47

The sun is setting, and the cove is quiet now.

I open a bottle of wine, then walk over the sand and shingle to the firepit where Griff is cooking mackerel, silvery fish to match the silver streak from the moon across the water. When they're done, he'll put them on a board with wedges of lemon and chunks of bread.

'Where are the kids? I told them to be here.'

'They will. Don't worry,' says Griff, turning the fish and taking the glass from me. 'Enjoy the moment, what you've achieved here today.'

He lifts his glass to me and holds my gaze. I feel like no time has passed, from the last night I was in Swn y Môr twenty years ago. I feel as young and fired up as ever. Only this time I know what I want. And it's all here.

'Griff, remember what you said about fighting for what you want?'

'I do,' he says, sipping the cold white wine, holding his tongs in the other hand. His face is lit by the fire in the pit. It's been a day for big decisions.

'Tell me again,' I say slowly.

'Tell you what again?' he says cautiously.

'Tell me how you feel about me. Like the other night in the farmhouse, when you told me how you felt.'

'No. I tried that . . . I'm not putting myself through it again.' He's poking at the embers where the mackerel is crisping on the grill.

I stand and walk towards him, beside the fire, on the sea shore, where I always want to be. 'Okay, then, I will. Griff, I've loved you for ever. I've never stopped loving you. I want to be with you and love you. For ever . . .'

He looks at me.

'Home is where you leave your heart, and I left mine here a long time ago.' I hold my breath. What if he says no? I long to kiss him, on his gorgeous lips, the face I've known and loved for years. If only I'd realized it.

'Say yes!' comes a hushed whisper.

'Joe! Ssh!'

'Say yes!' says Blake's voice.

And the two of us break into a wide smile.

Our faces are close together now. I can see every bit of Griff's and know I want to wake up to it every morning.

'I think I'd better say yes,' Griff says, and finally his

lips are on mine, kissing me, and I'm kissing him back, with all my heart.

'Oh, gross!' I hear Blake say, and we break apart laughing, and suddenly we're ambushed by three young people, like overexcited puppies bundling in on top of us, hugging and whooping. We don't need words. We know. We have all this.

Finally they calm down.

'We brought *gelato*,' says Joe.

'A celebration isn't a celebration without Valentino's *gelato*,' says Blake. 'When I go to catering college, will I have to wear a chef's hat?'

We laugh.

'You will,' I say.

'And I've decided to stay here and go to art college. Then maybe do a bit of travelling. See what's out there,' says Scooter.

Joe is wearing his medal. 'I'm a local hero,' he says.

'You'll always be a hero to us, Joe,' I say, and he sidles in next to me.

Finally Griff puts down his tongs, slides his free hand into mine and leaves it there. Exactly where I want it always to be.

We have plenty of time. None of us is going anywhere.

'And what about Valentino's?' Griff asks, pointing to the boathouse.

I look back at it.

'Think we might have to rebuild it again if we're going to make and sell more *gelato* next summer.'

'Yes!' says Blake.

'In fact, I think we could supply the local restaurants and pubs round here too,' I say, my business head starting to whirr. Only this time, I'm exactly where I want to be, doing what I want to do. This time it's a family business, though, my family business, and that's what counts.

'To Team Tŷ Mawr!' says Joe, toasting us all.

'To Team Tŷ Mawr!' we reply, and that's who we are, a family. A funny, mixed-up, stuck-together-with-*gelato* family. And I wouldn't have it any other way.

ACKNOWLEDGEMENTS

First, I want to thank the *gelato* maker whose *gelato* I ate in Martina Franca in Puglia and have never forgotten! Utterly amazing! So different from ice cream!

I want to thank the two amazing, very special social workers I have come across in my time, one working right at the coal face, making families happen, and the other guiding the ship in Wales. You know who you are.

Whilst I was researching this book I also spoke to the Calon Cymru Fostering agency, who were more than helpful. Thank you. If you are interested in fostering, do get in touch with your local authority to find out more. They need you!

Thank you to the milk farmers here in Wales offering bottled milk from the farm and branching out into delicious *gelato* for inspiring me.

Acknowledgements

Thank you to all the team who worked on this book, my editor Francesca Best and the rest of the team at Transworld, and to my agent David Headley.

And finally a big thank you to West Wales, for the holidays I had here as a child, the memories and for being the place I now call home.

Read on for some delicious recipes and more information about Jo's uplifting and heart-warming books . . .

Gelato

Gelato is a key ingredient in this book! Discovering the old recipe book gives Beca a new passion and brings her 'funny, mixed-up, stuck-together-with-*gelato*' family together. Plus, it's perfect for warm days by the seaside.

Ingredients

Basic *gelato*

4 egg yolks
150g granulated sugar
350ml whole milk
250ml double cream

Mint chocolate chip flavour

1.5–2 tsp pure peppermint extract
140g dark chocolate, chopped into tiny pieces
Optional: 2–3 drops green food colouring

Rum and raisin flavour

240g rum-soaked raisins (method below)
2 tbsp rum

Method

Whether you use an ice-cream maker or not, the method for creating the *gelato* mixture is the same:

1. Whisk the egg yolks with the sugar in a stand mixer or using an electric hand whisk at maximum speed for about 5 minutes, until you have a soft fluffy cream.
2. Pour the milk in a saucepan and bring it almost to a boil. Heat for 5 minutes, making sure that it doesn't boil.
3. Transfer the egg-and-sugar fluffy cream to a saucepan. Slowly pour over the hot milk while continuously mixing.
4. Put the saucepan back on a low-medium heat and cook for another 5 minutes.
5. Turn off the heat and add cold double cream. Mix well.
6. If you are making flavoured *gelato*, add the relevant ingredients listed above to the mixture before churning.

With an ice-cream maker:

- Pour the mixture into the machine and start it. Refer to the machine instructions for the churn time.
- Once the mixture has been churning for the necessary time, the *gelato* is ready!

Without an ice-cream maker:

- Pour the mixture into a container and place it in the freezer for about 5 hours.
- Every 30 minutes you must break the frozen surface to remove the ice crystals and ensure a smooth, creamy texture. To do this, remove from the freezer and mix for about 30 seconds using a hand whisk or an electric whisk on low speed.

Rum-soaked raisins method:

- Place 240g raisins in an air-tight container and add rum. Cover and shake to evenly coat raisins in rum, let sit at room temperature at least overnight and up to 2 days.

Nonna's *ragù*

For me, *ragù* and pasta is the most comforting meal – a hug in a bowl. Here's how to make Beca's nonna's spaghetti with *ragù* that she cooks for Blake and Joe to help them settle in.

Ingredients

2 tbsp olive oil
1 carrot
1 celery stalk
1 onion
300g beef mince
300g pork mince
120ml red wine
2 tbsp tomato puree
400g tomato passata
2 bay leaves
80ml milk
Salt and pepper to taste
Parmesan to serve (optional)

Method

1. Finely chop the carrot, celery and onion.
2. In a large heavy-bottomed pot, heat the olive oil and add the chopped vegetables. Cook on low heat with a lid on, stirring every 5 minutes, until onion is transparent.
3. Increase the heat to medium and add the beef and pork mince. Break it apart using a spatula.
4. Once the meat has browned, turn the heat up to high and add the wine. Cook until the alcohol has evaporated (about 20–30 seconds).
5. Decrease the heat to medium/low and add the tomato puree, passata, salt, pepper and bay leaves.
6. With the heat as low as possible, cover and let simmer for three hours, stirring occasionally.
7. After three hours, remove the bay leaves and add the milk. Allow the milk to heat through for a couple of minutes.
8. Serve over cooked pasta. You can use any pasta shape that you like, but I would recommend tagliatelle or spaghetti.
9. Optionally, grate over a generous serving of parmesan cheese and enjoy!

Fish, chips and mushy peas

Fish and chips is a classic seaside meal that makes use of the abundance of fresh fish available in coastal towns. I love biting into the crispy batter and through to the soft, flaking fish inside – there really is nothing like it, especially when you're sitting on the sand watching the waves! Here's my recipe for how to make it at home.

Ingredients

For the fish

600ml sunflower oil
4 white fish fillets (cod, haddock or hake)
225g plain flour, plus extra for dusting
285ml cold beer or sparkling water
1 tbsp baking powder

For the chips

800g unpeeled Maris Piper or King Edward potatoes
2 tbsp olive oil
Salt and pepper to season

For the mushy peas

250g dried marrowfat peas
2 tbsp bicarbonate of soda
25g salted butter, cubed
A small bunch of mint, finely chopped
½ lemon, juiced

Method:

1. The night before making this meal, put the marrowfat peas and bicarbonate of soda in a large heatproof bowl and cover with boiling water. Leave to soak overnight.
2. Begin with the batter. Mix the flour and baking powder in a bowl. Using a fork to whisk continuously, add the beer or sparkling water to the mixture until you have a thick, smooth batter. Place the batter in the fridge to rest for 30 minutes.

3. Next, scrub the potatoes and chop them into wedges. Tip the chips into a large saucepan, pour in enough water to just cover, bring to the boil and cook until the potatoes are fork tender.

4. Once the potatoes are cooked, tip them onto a clean tea towel, pat dry, then leave to cool.

5. While the potatoes cool, heat oven to 220ºC/fan 200ºC/gas mark 7. Put a large shallow non-stick roasting tray in the oven with 1 tbsp olive oil and heat for 10 minutes.

6. Transfer the cooled chips to a bowl and toss in the remaining oil using your hands. Tip out in a single layer onto the hot roasting tin. Bake for 10 minutes, then turn them over. Bake 5 more minutes, then turn again. Bake for a final 5–8 minutes until crisp.

7. While the chips are in the oven, drain the peas and rinse them twice with cold water. Put the peas in a saucepan and cover with 650ml cold water. Bring to the boil, reduce the heat and simmer for 30 minutes until tender, stirring occasionally.

8. While the peas are cooking, heat the sunflower oil in a deep-fat fryer or deep saucepan until it reaches 170ºC.

9. Lay the fish fillets on a paper towel and pat dry.

10. Place 2 tablespoons of flour into a shallow bowl. Coat each fish fillet in the flour and brush off any excess. Dip each fillet into the batter.

11. Lower each fillet into the hot oil. Fry for approximately 8 minutes, or until the batter is crisp and golden, turning the fillets from time to time with a large, slotted spoon.

12. Once cooked, place on a paper towel and season with sea salt.

13. Mash the cooked peas and season with salt and pepper. Stir in the butter, mint and lemon.

14. Serve the fish, chips and mushy peas and enjoy!

Are you ready for a Christmas getaway? Look out for Jo Thomas' next uplifting and feel-good romance

Countdown to Christmas

Chloe can't wait for Christmas . . . to be over! Her son Ruben is staying with his dad this year and Chloe is planning to ignore the holidays altogether. Her only nod to the season is the advent calendar Ruben left her, to help count down the days till he's home again.

Then an heir hunter gets in touch, telling her there's a plot of land in Canada she may be entitled to. Surely, it's a scam? Or could it be just the escape she needs right now? They're offering to pay for her flights . . . and Ruben's latest note in the advent calendar tells her to: 'say yes!'

Suddenly, Chloe's new countdown to Christmas involves a log cabin in the middle of a snowy forest, a community that's worried for its future, a gruff lumberjack who gives her tummy butterflies and a *lot* of pancakes with maple syrup . . .

This Christmas is full of surprises!

Coming in October 2023

For more romance, family, food and fun, be sure to read Jo's other escapist and uplifting novels which are available now

One Icelandic Christmas holiday. One snowstorm. An adventure they'll never forget!

Twenty-five years ago, Freya and her three best friends created a bucket list. The future seemed bright and full of hope . . . But now they are travelling to Iceland in memory of the friend they've lost, determined to fulfil her dream of seeing the Northern Lights at Christmas.

They didn't count on an avalanche leaving them stranded! Handsome local, Pétur, comes to the rescue, showing them how the community survives the hard winter. With Christmas approaching, Freya and her friends throw themselves into the festivities, decorating and cooking for the villagers using delicious local ingredients.

But will they manage to see the Northern Lights? And can Freya's own dreams come true, this Christmas?

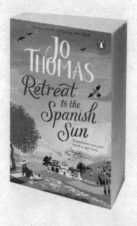

Sometimes you just need to get away . . .

Eliza has a full house! After her grown-up children moved out, she downsized to a smaller property . . . but now they're all back. Every room in the house is occupied and Eliza just needs some peace and quiet to work.

When an ad pops up saying 'house-sitters wanted', Eliza can't resist the chance to escape to a stunning finca in southern Spain for a few weeks to help her focus on achieving her dreams. But it isn't long before Eliza gets caught up in the charming local way of life.

The warmth of the late summer sunshine, delicious local food and friendly village café show Eliza that the life she's always wanted is within reach. And with the return of handsome house-owner Josep, could there be another reason for her to stay in Spain a little longer . . .?

The perfect place to raise a glass to love, hope and new beginnings . . .

When their grandfather dies, Fliss and her sisters are astonished to inherit a French château! Travelling to Normandy to visit the beautiful if faded house, they excitedly make plans over delicious crepes and local cider in the town nearby.

They soon discover the château needs major work and a huge tax bill is due . . . Unable to sell but strapped for cash, Fliss determines to spruce up the elegant old rooms and open a B&B.

But Jacques, the handsome town mayor, is opposed to her plan. When it becomes clear that the only way to save the magnificent castle is to work together, Jacques and Fliss discover that they have more in common than they think . . .